HEAD OVER
HEELFLIP

Praise for Sander Santiago

Best of the Wrong Reasons

"I absolutely adored this book, I couldn't put it down. The best friends to strangers to rekindled lovers trope is one of my favorites, and Santiago did it so well...This book will make you laugh and cry and feel so many emotions."
—*QueerBookstagram*

One Verse Multi

"*One Verse Multi* is my favourite kind of sci-fi. It was clever, it was witty, it was insightful...just a glorious time all round!...I LOVED this book from the absolute get-go. I was instantly drawn into the story, and every time I put the book down I was counting down until I could next pick it up again. It was genuinely funny without shying away from big topics and themes, and despite being fantastical felt down-to-earth and grounded...This book is a hidden gem, showcasing science fiction at its best."—*Elementary My Dear*

"Let's talk about representation! One reason I wanted to love this book more than I did is because of how cleverly Santiago works in diverse representation. Santiago himself is a queer, trans BIPOC writer, and so he writes Martin's character with a very authentic voice: Martin is a Black, gay trans man, and a significant part of the book is his self-discovery of polyamorous attraction as well. To be clear, I'm not praising *One Verse Multi* for the way it checks a lot of boxes—that's not what matters to me when it comes to representation. It's the quality that matters here."—*Kara Reviews*

By the Author

Visit us at www.boldstrokesbooks.com

HEAD OVER HEELFLIP

by

Sander Santiago

2024

Credits

Editor: Jerry L. Wheeler and Stacia Seaman
Production Design: Stacia Seaman
Cover Design by Tammy Seidick

Acknowledgments

I owe a lot of this book to my youth and the kids I was lucky enough to grow up with. The meeting place was the tiny skate park in town. I can still hear the clatter of boards connecting with metal and cement. My first kiss was at the top of a backyard halfpipe. I didn't expect this novel to feel like coming home.

Thank you to my family and to Bold Strokes Books.

Thank you.

To:
Katy
Gabriel
The people I knew when I was 12

Chapter One

Arturo

Pirate's white-blond hair was the last thing to leave the camera frame as he dropped into the bowl. It was a good, cinematic ending for the post I was pulling together. I had footage of him lifting his shirt to wipe the sweat from his face, then skating toward the edge of the bowl and disappearing. He looked like an action hero. The sixty thousand-ish people who followed his Instagram would love it. And, by proxy, our sponsors would shit themselves with joy.

"More Pirate?" Nads, our teammate, said, looking over my shoulder. "Any more of him and you might as well rename the team Pirate's Bitches."

"No matter the name, you still get paid, so suck a dick," I said, adding the usual hashtags to the video and posting it.

"Yeah, Nads. All hail Pirate! Pirate is God," said Rocky, Nads's shadow and cousin.

I held up the phone to get a picture of Rocky. He immediately assumed the position, his middle finger in the air and his shirt pulled up to reveal a skull and crossbones nipple ring. Together, Rocky and Nads had the same vibe as a Korean punk band drummer and the white guy who does his taxes, respectively. Rocky had a shaved head and was covered in stick and poke tattoos, which were almost always visible since he rarely wore a shirt. He had manic, skinny guy energy and never sat still.

Nads somehow pulled middle-aged energy despite being the same age as Rocky, which was twenty-three. He had on a tank top and jorts today, his hay-colored hair trapped under a hat, sticking out the back. The tattoos didn't help him seem any cooler. Rocky was one of the more popular teammates. Really, of the five on the team, Nads pulled the fewest views. He was lucky he was the team leader's best friend. The Major and Nads had known each other since third grade. They started the team as soon as they were old enough to compete.

I shook my head as Nads shoved Rocky into the bowl before walking his bike toward the sidewalk at the edge of the park. Our home skatepark in Denver didn't allow pegs on the equipment, so he was off to sulk in the grass. I turned my attention back to Pirate. He really was the bread and butter of the team. The Major, who was team captain, and the sponsors jumped on the chance to work with him after I took over managing his social media accounts. Pirate went from a nobody to an influencer almost overnight, which was perfect for me because social media was what I did, or at least what I wanted to do. I had big plans to turn my success with Pirate's image into a portfolio and then, hopefully, into a job. Add a win in this year's competition, and I could probably work for any company I wanted. But if you removed the camera and my bias as his best friend, Pirate was still an amazing skateboarder.

"Nads, give it a rest. If you were nice from time to time, maybe Uno would film you more," The Major shouted.

"Fuck you, Maj."

Even though they were the youngest, The Major was one of the best all-around skaters I had ever seen. They could ride anything with wheels with the same grace and seriousness that Peyton Manning played football. They were a pencil-thin, twenty-two-year-old, Black-Hispanic kid from Commerce City, who had more ambition and focus in their left foot than most people I knew had in their whole bodies. Their hair was a tower that approached a hightop, making them look taller and skinnier. Today they had on a black T-shirt that said: *How long have your nouns been pro, bro?* and black jeans. The Major was my personal hero. They made it really easy for me to be less stealth as a trans guy, not that stealth wasn't great, but there was a lot of pressure to maintain it. With them around, and having disclosed to the rest of the team, I didn't have to meet that expectation anymore.

The five of us were The Major Leaguers, a team for the Colorado Amateur Street Sports Tour. CASST started out as four guys wanting to showcase what local Rollerbladers, BMX bikers, and skateboarders could do, as well as raise some money for their community. Five years ago, they won a grant or something, and their one-town, weekend tournament became a statewide, month-long skatepark tour. Even though that sounds like a big deal, most people had never heard of it, though adding skateboarding to the Olympics did give us a boost. Now CASST was a cross between bracket-style tournaments, sponsored prizes, and city showcases.

We all competed last year but hadn't been on the same team. The Major pulled me and Pirate out of the gutter when our former team kicked us out in favor of more popular skaters a week after the last CASST ended. The Major practically begged to work with us. We spent the next few months skating together as a team and trying to formulate a strategy for the next CASST, which started today. Well, it sort of started today. It was only Wednesday. The organizers were releasing the schedule and the sponsor prize list today, but CASST didn't officially kick off until the coming Saturday.

I laughed as The Major and Nads flipped each other off across the park. I made sure to get a short clip of them both just for B-reel. The Major went back to doing whatever they had been doing on their phone for the last hour, sitting on a rail with their board under their feet. Nads rolled slowly around the edge of the park, pushing off with his foot while balancing on his pegs instead of pedaling.

He made sure to stay formally out of the park, though. There was almost always a cop around to "reinforce the rules." Their words, not mine. Skaters, bikers, and bladers were always targets, especially now that the area around the park had had a small economic boost. I spotted the parked squad car on the other side of the road. It was annoying because the park was almost empty, the kids were back in school, and it was eleven a.m. on a Wednesday. They never seemed to have anything better to do.

"All right, everyone," The Major said, waving Pirate over and nodding at me.

"Jeffx," I said.

"What's up, Maj? You calling a meeting?" Rocky shouted. He started toward us, slipping his vape into his pocket. Nads even dumped his bike just inside the park area and jogged over. We all converged on The Major at the center of the park.

Pirate hopped out of the bowl, catching his board in his hand.

Pirate was the oldest of us and somewhat old for the sport at twenty-seven. Maybe that's why the fans, mostly women, loved him. He was mature, tattooed, beautiful, and completely unreachable. To them anyway. He was gay and out, and it seemed the more out he was, the more followers he got. But the women would buy whatever our sponsor was selling. They wore the shoes and clothes even if they didn't skate or bike. There was also a growing LGBT+ section of our followers that I was trying to reach.

"Dude, are you listening?" The Major asked me, bumping my shoulder with theirs. I blinked and Pirate's face came into focus. I looked from him to the Major.

"Not a word." I laughed.

The Major held up their phone. "The schedule is out."

We surged around them trying to get a look at their phone.

"Can y'all back the fuck up?" they asked, jabbing me in the chest with their elbow. "We're going to go over things. But, fuck, I'm sweating my dick off. Let's find some AC and some lunch."

"It's Nads's turn to buy," Rocky shouted, trying to hop on to his cousin's shoulders. Nads immediately dumped him on the ground.

"Good, let's go up toward Sixteenth. I want a burrito," The Major said, gesturing for us to follow. They were on their board a moment later, rolling easily toward the center of Denver. I scanned the city, looking around at the lux apartments and new buildings facing the park. The view was different every year.

"Why's it always my turn to buy?" Nads grumbled on his way back to his bike.

I got on my board and followed him. "'Cause you never pay, cabrón. One of us is always covering your ass, but now you have the sponsor money Pirate got you, so you owe us." I pulled up the note app on my phone. I checked the lunch tally I had been keeping to see whose turn it was to buy for who. "You owe everyone at least four meals. You owe Pirate seven."

Nads didn't respond, so I dropped it. I rolled toward the entrance to the park. I pulled up the video app. Footage of us just skating around was almost as popular as our best tricks. People liked the vibe.

"Nads…Nads," Rocky sang. He was holding the back of Nads's bike and was being pulled. I heard them coming, so I slowed to catch them on my phone as they passed, trying to keep the camera steady.

"How many lunches do you owe me?" Pirate asked. I was going slow enough that he was able to walk up to me. He put a foot on the fin of my board and kicked it gently out from under me. I laughed, barely stumbling, and tossed an arm around his shoulders. He shrugged me off to retrieve my board from where it had bounced off one of the concrete planters along the sidewalk.

"I don't keep track," I said with a laugh. "Sé que me amas. I got it good like that."

He rolled his eyes, the smallest smile on his face. He kicked my board into his hand and offered it to me. The skull and wasps tattooed on the back of his hand looked like it was holding my board in its teeth. I smiled at him and took the board. He just started after the others.

The Denver skatepark was mashed into a corner of the city, right off a major road along the South Platte River. We skated there the most because it was central to all five of us, and it was also one of the bigger parks. Since it was surrounded by high-end housing and shopping, we usually skated away from it to find food. Denver, like most major cities, was patchworked with construction, so skating around was hard to do sometimes. We dodged workers with cones and ducked under scaffolding. It made for decent footage, though, watching the rest of the team skate or bike in between obstacles. I always made sure to film the No Skateboarding signs as we passed them.

Halfway to the restaurant, the five of us skating at the feet of skyscrapers and scaring businesswomen on the sidewalks, I got a notification. It was a note from Pirate. Thirty-seven tally marks. I guess I owed him way more lunches than I thought. I looked over my shoulder at him where he was coolly rolling around behind me. He grinned and winked. I laughed.

Pirate and I were slow compared to the others, so by the time we caught up, Rocky and The Major were already in the restaurant. Nads was locking his bike up out front as we rolled to a stop.

"Hey," Nads said, stopping Pirate and me at the door. He looked less annoyed but not happy.

"What's up?" Pirate asked.

"I…I'm not trying to be a dick all the time, you know. I…" The attempt at an apology was surprising, and he made it look almost painful.

"It's all good, bro," I said, patting his shoulder.

He let out a breath and crossed his arms. We watched as he shuffled his feet and didn't look us in the face. Finally, he said, "I can't really buy everyone lunch."

I laughed. He glared at me.

"That's fine, we didn't expect it," Pirate said.

Nads nodded and looked at me to see if I was going to agree with Pirate or pick up the teasing from earlier.

"I guess Pirate gets the honor of buying my lunch," I said.

A smile started to form at the edges of Nads's mouth. His smile was the transformative kind, making him look almost like a different person. He rarely did it, though.

"You wish, Ortiz," Pirate said. He went into the building, and Nads and I followed.

The restaurant was a mid-tier Mexican place The Major loved. It was the Aztec-motif kind, not the sugar skull kind of place. They were used to us by now and sat us right away, not really minding that we crammed four skateboards under the table. I always made sure to tag the restaurant when I posted while we were there. I also left great reviews for the staff, by name when I could.

"Let's *go*," Rocky yelled. He tried shaking the table, but it was bolted down.

"Dude," The Major said, glaring at him. "Indoor voice, asshole."

I eyed Pirate, who gave me the smallest look in return. Rocky usually got us kicked out of restaurants. We let him get us kicked out. Aside from The Major's light scolding, we weren't going to dump on his enthusiasm for the sake of strangers eating fajitas. I decided it was time for another photo of The Major and Nads, so I took something candid they would be mad at me for later.

"We still need a sixth," Nads said, handing out menus.

"I know, I know. I swear by Friday we'll have one," The Major said. "Now for the schedule."

The Major pressed a few buttons on their phone, then all the rest of ours pinged with a message. I opened the file. Colorado Amateur Street Sports Tour was sponsored by local businesses around the state. The next few Saturdays were booked with events. We had the kickoff event at the Denver skatepark, then the campout in Boulder, then the Blades and Bikes event in Arvada, then the finale at the Commerce City skatepark that featured bikes, blades, and boards. Some unofficial events happened around the official ones, but the biggest crowds showed up for the main tournaments. Along with the tournaments, points were available through sponsored prizes.

Each event had its own rules, but the competition had only three general rules:

1. Be at least eighteen years old.
2. Don't be a narc.
3. Don't be a bitch.

It was well put together. Everything from the branding to the actual organization was amazing. Even though people sometimes see skateboards and bikes and blades as some rebellious counterculture thing, the state loved CASST, and cities were starting to put up bids to have their skateparks host main events or they sponsored tricks, such as *land a backside 5-0 @ Louisville.* Having the cities bid for inclusion had helped triple competition participation and the grand prize over the last five years.

At the end there was a grand prize of fifteen thousand dollars, not including the funds awarded to people who won individual categories. Even split six ways, it was a lot of money. My share of fifteen thousand came out to about a month of working at my day job at Coors Field. Of course, that didn't count the fat check our sponsors would send from the publicity we brought them as a bonus for winning.

Most important for me, though, was my plan to use this year's competition as a portfolio to land a job. Getting on the media team for our sponsor, Bored Brand Skateboards, was my main goal, but I was willing to show off my credentials to anyone who would pay. I just had to build the credentials. I had done a lot with Pirate's pages as well as the team's, but if I could prove I moved people to action, then I was really worth my salt. Add in a win at the end as a ringer, and there was no way a company would turn me down. At twenty-six, I wasn't old, sure, but I was getting older, and at some point, I wanted something professional to show off. I wasn't going to become a professional skater, I knew that, but I could do media, and I could do it well.

The waiter came with food, and all my thoughts of competition or ambition disappeared. I traded my phone for my burrito. It looked so fucking delicious. I always chose deluxe, which meant it was smothered in green and red chili, queso—

"Bro," Pirate said, nudging me. "Chill. You're making orgasm noises."

"Jealous?"

His eyes went wide for a second, and his cheeks turned a slight red. It was an orgasmic burrito. I forked some and offered it to him. He shook his head and focused on his own lunch. *Great, more for me.*

"Only four major tournaments this year?" Nads asked, pulling my thoughts back to the table. He was scrolling aggressively through the list, ignoring the beautiful plate of mole in front of him. It smelled like it was made with real chocolate.

"Is that any good?" I asked him.

When he looked at me, his expression was a glare. But when he registered what I was asking, he gave me a resigned shrug and gestured for me to try it. Nads hadn't been my biggest fan, but I think he was really starting to warm up to me.

He turned back to the Major. "Maj—"

"Dude, I told you the rumors of them adding a fifth were cap," The Major said. "It would've made judging harder, and it's hard enough as it is—"

"But the money—"

I scooped some of the mole onto my own plate and dipped as I ate my burrito. It was amazing. I half heard the conversation around me, and I tried to keep scrolling through the program with the back of my hand, unwilling to put my fork down, but just managed to get queso on my phone.

"The first event is camping in the park," I said around a full mouth. "Weird that it's in Boulder this year."

The Major shook their head. "The first is Kickoff."

"Some team got most of the points at last year's Kickoff. Which one was it?" I couldn't remember.

"Doesn't matter. We weren't a team then. We are now and we're going to kick ass." Their expression was terrifyingly competitive.

"We only lost by a thousand points last year," Nads said.

"We gotta go bigger," Rocky shouted.

The Major patted Rocky on the shoulder. "You're doing too much. We also have those two this year. They scored more points together than the three bottom teams' total."

According to The Major's pointing, *those two* meant Pirate and me.

"Well, we probably need a different plan for some of the sponsored prizes," Pirate said. The whole table looked at him. "I only got that many points because of this."

He pointed to the killer tattoo on his neck. It was an owl, realistic and bold, coming at you through a snowstorm. The silly, dangerous, or strange sponsor prizes were the result of several pop culture influences, probably most recognizable from the mid-2000s. Pirate beat everyone else out for the prize: get a neck tattoo. It had been worth so much because three tattoo shops had sponsored the prize together.

"Right, I guess you can't get another one," I said. I put a hand to my own throat. I had the Mexican flag centered on my neck, not because of a prize, but because I was like that. Rocky had a skull, Nads had roses. The Major didn't have a single tattoo; they were too afraid of needles. And just because Pirate was willing to get a tattoo for the competition didn't mean we would make anyone else.

"There's other things," The Major said, touching their own bare skin in horror. "Besides, we can always do some of the fucking tricks, since you know it's a board, blade, bike thing."

I scrolled. One of the Get A Neck Tattoo sponsors was on its own this year and had put up the prize for Get A Nipple Piercing. A new skate clothing company had a prize for wearing their brand. A sporting goods store put up the prize for Kayak In A Public Fountain. And the list went on from there.

"Why are the sponsored prizes worth the most points not even about boards or bikes?" Nads asked. No one acknowledged him.

"I shoulda become mayor," Rocky said dreamily. That one was always on the list, but the competition was never held during election time, so it was impossible. The mayor of Denver sponsored it to show the city's support. They were always good sports about people coming up to them offering to do their job for the day.

"Fuck...visit a jail, sign a contract, graduate, make a spectacle at an event, and get a photo with a celebrity—who the fuck can do any of these things?" Nads continued reading in disgust.

"These are fucking impossible. I can't even pass, let alone graduate," Rocky groaned. That wasn't true. He had started college at sixteen, so he was already done with a bachelor's degree.

"I don't want anyone messing with the cops, not even for a *tour* of a jail," The Major said. "The team who won last year spent all their money paying tickets. So, no."

The Denver Police Department always put a sponsored prize as an effort to breed goodwill and to show everyone that they weren't targeting the wheeled community. Last year, the prize was Sit In A Cruiser, but the winning team forgot to ask permission.

"When was the last time a celebrity was even in Denver?" Pirate wondered.

"Fuck," Nads sighed.

"It's fine. It looks like most of the stuff on the list that actually involves wheels is the same as last year, plus some cool midrange point things I'm sure we can handle. Despite prizes and the unofficial stuff, winners are made in the tournaments, so let's focus on those. It'll be even better now because we've all had at least one real year in the competition, so we know how to do it. I'll update the spreadsheet tonight, and we'll come up with our plan," The Major said.

A phone ringing interrupted them. Nads looked at his cell and stood. "Fuck, it's Joon."

"Hi, cuz," Rocky shouted, trying to take Nads's phone. Joon was Nads's sister.

"Stop, Rock," Nads said, shoving him away. Nads stood and left the restaurant.

The Major called after him. "Nads."

"He looked stressed," I said.

"He's fine. I'll explain it to him later. So, for the skateboard tournament…" The Major continued. Their hands hovered over their plate as if they were about to perform magic on their tacos.

I tuned them out in favor of thinking about the prizes. Those prizes were half my social media plan for CASST since the fans loved them, so I wasn't about to give them up. The one that was speaking to me at the moment was Make A Spectacle At An Event. That one was sponsored by a group from the Denver Center for the Performing Arts. I could make a spectacle to a big audience if I used our platforms properly. But what could we do? There were rules about getting naked or bleeding—what else did people turn up for in droves? A funeral, I thought unhelpfully.

"What about a wedding?" I offered, the words exiting my mouth without my brain saying it was okay. For a moment even *I* was wondering where that came from. The table was quiet and staring at me. Where was I going with this? I opened my mouth and an idea came out. "I mean, weddings are the OG spectacle, so that takes care of one of the prizes. Then there was that other one from the lawyers—what was it?"

"Sign A Contract," Pirate said.

"The fuck are you two talking about?" The Major asked.

"It's a plan for the big points. Maj, think about it. There's a psychological component to any competition, right? And I think we can psych some of our competitors out by eliminating two major prizes like Make A Spectacle At An Event and Sign A Contract. They'd have to scramble to keep up."

"That's wild," Rocky said.

"Does a marriage license mean a contract?" The Major asked.

"On the other hand," Rocky said, "I love weddings."

"There are other contracts," Pirate said.

The Major laughed. "There are a billion easier things to do! Rent a car. Get a warranty on my TV. Hell, I could accept the terms for the apps on my phone that I choose to ignore!"

"That shit is boring," Rocky said.

I laughed. "Thank you, Rock. See a spectacle! Besides, marriage is also inarguably binding."

"Our cousin Sun had three hundred people at her wedding in May," Rocky said.

"I can get thirty times that many."

"I can already tell there's no talking you out of this," Pirate said.

"It could work. Thirty thousand? How?" The Major wondered, practical as ever.

"Okay, maybe not thirty, but if we did it on Saturday that's at least three thousand. It'll work!" I announced, deciding right then and there.

"Who's gonna do it?" The Major asked.

"Do what?" Nads came back to the table a little more stressed looking than before.

"Uno wants us to get married at the opening event on Saturday," Rocky said.

Nads looked around and blinked like he suddenly didn't speak the language. "Run that by me again."

I laughed. "It's for the two sponsor prizes worth ten thousand each."

"You have to be fucking joking. We can't do that."

"Why not?" Pirate said.

Nads glared at him. "It's…just…Who the fuck gets married for a competition?"

It was our turn to stare since we all knew Nads watched reality TV competition shows that explicitly involved just that. There was a tense, silent moment. Nads glared at The Major, who looked at him unblinkingly. Rocky was diligently opening and pouring chili packets into his unrolled, mangled burrito. I didn't know where he got the packets from since there was only a shaker on the table. Pirate watched Nads suspiciously.

"It's less about the wedding and more about the show," I said.

"Who's gonna do it?" The Major asked again.

"I'd do it," I said. But I didn't say it alone. I looked at Pirate, and he looked at me. *Fuck—we said that at the same time.*

"You'd marry me?" Pirate asked, his tone impossibly flat.

I almost didn't hear him over the sound of my blood in my ears. I was getting excited now. His offer was the last piece that snapped all the others into place in my mind. This could work. Also, there was a new kind of feeling too, like a jitter. What was that about?

Maybe it was Pirate. He was always there to back me up. I loved that about him. He was so cautious sometimes. I mean, he was one of the only skateboarders to wear a helmet during competition. But he was also my best friend and supported my antics, or he at least made sure I knew what I was getting into. Besides, he was so cool it was like getting the popular kids' vote. The idea of marrying him as part of this plan gave me the same feeling I used to get when a friend was allowed to sleep over at my house as a kid. It felt awesome!

"You don't have a ring, but yes," I said, tossing in a wink.

"You really think this could work?" The Major said, the hope that it would in their voice.

"We don't even have a sixth teammate!" Nads shouted.

"It's foolproof," I said.

Everyone was skeptical of that.

"Okay, I can *make* it foolproof. Maj, I guarantee you not only will this plan get us in the lead, but it'll have the other competitors so mad they'll want to quit on the spot. This isn't even the most I would do to win! I swear I want to win this."

"Fuck yes!" The Major said.

"Uno, you're stupid," Nads sighed.

"I want to be the best man...mans? Bests man," Rocky said.

"If you fuck with the opening ceremony, the competition guys are gonna get pissed," Nads said.

"Do you have to poop on everything?"

For a second, he actually looked insulted. Then he took a breath and his explanation was civil enough. "Uno. I...just want the win. Don't do anything that will get us fucking kicked out of this."

"We won't get kicked out. People are going to be foaming at the mouth. It'll be one big community boner." I laughed and took a few bites of my now-cold burrito. While the others argued, Pirate and I stared at each other. He shrugged as if saying *I could do worse*, and I laughed, trying to tell him without telling him that he couldn't do better. He smiled.

"All right, Uno. Tell us the plan," The Major said.

"Mira...here's what we're gonna do," I said with my mouth still full of food. "By Saturday, our team will have two of the biggest prizes on the list within ten minutes of the start of competition."

CHAPTER TWO

Thomas

"I'm gonna take a shower," I said. I hung my board on the hooks by the door, Uno—Arturo—following suit as he entered our apartment behind me.

"Sure," Arturo said. "You in for dinner today?"

"Yeah, I don't have plans."

He tried to tell me a few more things, but I didn't pay attention. I scooted farther into the apartment. I was about three seconds from freaking the fuck out. I went into the bathroom and was finally able to shut the door. I collapsed against it. *Fuck, fuck, fuck.* My stomach was a boiling lake inside my body, and I felt cased in cold sweat. Maybe I should throw up instead of showering. I looked at the toilet. Naw, showering was better because Arturo would definitely hear me barf. That would make him worry about me. I raced to get the shower started, overly cautious Arturo was listening. I knew he wasn't. Why would he? But in my panic, I was paranoid enough to believe I had to live the lie of showering or have my secret revealed. I was grateful for the loud crash of water against porcelain, as if the sound would block my screaming thoughts from escaping the bathroom. *I'm fucking fucked.*

"Why did you say yes, you stupid piece of shit?" I asked myself, looking at my unnerved face in the mirror. I had been playing it cool for hours since agreeing to the whole wedding idea, but there was no holding back now.

"I thought it would be funny. Maybe he'd tell me to fuck off. I wanted to get a rise out of Nads," my reflection answered. "I didn't think anyone would go along with it. I didn't think *he* meant it. Fuck me. Why him?"

Of course it was him.

"You should've just suggested Rocky," I shout-whispered at myself. My useless brain had used my traitorous mouth to bone me harder than I had ever been boned in my life. I growled at my reflection and angrily started to undress. I didn't actually want to be in the shower, but I did need a chance to think.

"Balls. Fuck. Shit," I grumbled, stepping into the hot water.

Arturo Fucking Ortiz. I turned my face into the spray and wondered if someone could drown in a shower. How was I going to do this? I had until Saturday morning to figure out if I could marry my best friend. *Well, it's more complicated than that, right?* I was also in love with him. I had been since I met him a year and a half ago.

He wasn't into me and, worst of all, he might actually be straight. I unfairly assumed he was aro/ace. I had never seen him with anyone. Well, I knew he had been with people of a few genders, but that didn't mean I knew anything about his orientation. That wasn't the point. His identities weren't the point. The point was I was fucked. *Figure it the fuck out, dipshit. You're getting married, and he's your friend. Just because you pop a boner when the guy smiles at you doesn't mean you get to con him into marrying you.*

Fuck, was that what I was doing? I really didn't want to think about it that way. I tried to get the water to be hotter, but the dial was as far as it would go. *Fuck him and his competitive ass.* He only wanted to win. That's all it was. *Well, now he's going to be your husband, and you can just go right on lying that you think of him as just a friend.* I tried to remind myself that it wasn't real, but my brain was dead set on ignoring that.

I groaned and let my head fall against the tile. Okay, sure, the solution to all of this was simple. I could just tell him. I could say, "Hey, Art, before we commit to this, you should know I actually have feelings for you, and marrying me would probably be confusing for the both of us."

I blinked and watched the water flow off the ends of my hair and down the drain. What's the worst that could happen? *You tell him, and he hates you, and you break up the team before the competition even starts. Not to mention you would lose the fucking love of your life.*

The water was shifting toward cold as it usually did in the early evening when the water pressure was low. I didn't want to freeze my balls off in a shower I hadn't even wanted to take, so I tried to focus on shower things. It wasn't easy. I poured shampoo on my loofa by accident, so I rubbed that on my head before I rinsed the loofa and started over. I washed my body with the proper soap. With my new focus on the tasks at hand, things my therapist taught me were able to surface. Richard the Therapist used to say when you get to the point of insulting yourself and reframing isn't working, try focusing on the tangible world instead. That meant shampoo, rinse, conditioner, rinse, and nothing else.

It worked well enough to give me a chance to calm down and think about things. As his best friend, I should know how he would react, shouldn't I? We had spent every day together since meeting, more or less. And when we weren't here in Denver together, we were on the phone with each other. Even though I trusted him, I couldn't trust the situation or myself. Marrying me for sport wasn't marrying me for love. Which made a good case for keeping the love out of it. I knew I couldn't, though. It would come out eventually, probably in some delusional, embarrassing way.

I closed my eyes and put my head under the spray. I tried playing out what I expected his reaction to be, but it was hopeless. I could imagine him reacting both ways. When I imagined a kind reaction, my brain immediately told me I was being fake and self-serving, that I was forcing my mental version of him to be nice to me. When I let him react badly in my head, it was so heartbreaking that if it had been real, it would have killed me. Also, I didn't think it did Arturo any favors to let him be that mean to me even in my own mind. He was never that mean to me in real life.

Besides the possibility of losing Arturo, I also couldn't afford to lose the team. They had asked me to join them because I could help them win, which meant going along with whatever the plan was. To the others, I might have been just a teammate and/or sponsor gimmick, but to me, they were, each in their own way, holding me to the surface of the planet. I guess that's a family.

Over the holidays, I'd gone home to spend time with my blood family, my sick dad and my siblings. That trip taught me that if I fucked up everything in Denver, I would be forced to go home to Georgia, and that would ruin me. In Georgia, I was obliged to live every day atoning for when I was at my worst. My blood family knew Teach, the fucked-up kid, the realest me. This team knew Pirate, who had yet to fuck up, and Arturo knew Thomas, who was "Teach in therapy." All of them and this competition were my only chance to keep living as a better version of me. Richard the Therapist would probably want me to find my best self without the others, but fuck if I knew how to do that. It had taken years and a lot of help to simply believe I was better than Georgia painted me, or than the year I spent in Tennessee with my mother. I shook my head to keep from going down that line of thought.

Are you willing to fuck all of that up for the slim chance that he would be mad, that he wouldn't give up on pathetic, weak, empty you? It's a lie to not tell him. I took a deep breath and refocused on the feeling of the cold water on my skin. *Grounding*, or so Richard the Therapist would have called it. I took a few breaths and tried to remember all the states in alphabetical order, stopping at Kentucky because that was when the spiraling feelings always ebbed.

"Okay, Thomas, pick one." I could tell him and live with the outcome, or I could not tell him and live with that outcome. Either way, I probably wouldn't get what I wanted. I wanted to be with him. And I wanted to win CASST to prove to my team I was worth their time and to actually earn the friendship they were giving me. *So, good. You haven't resolved anything.*

I cut off the water. I might not have resolved anything, but I could breathe again, the panic following the soap down the drain. I wrung out my hair, then reached around the shower curtain for my towel. My fingers met only plaster.

"Christ almighty," I grumbled. *Okay. Deep breath and be cool. Art will bring you a towel. Be cool—you have tattoos and long hair, for fuck's sake. Be cool.*

"Arturo," I shouted.

"Thomas," he shouted back. Our apartment was small and weirdly designed so the bathroom door actually faced the galley-style kitchen, through which you could see our dining room table. It had been a little weird getting used to eating dinner in sight of your own shitter.

"I forgot my towel."

"Just run, bro." Arturo giggled, but his voice was getting farther away, so I knew he was heading toward the bedrooms.

The apartment was T-shaped with a short stem and fat arms. The stem was the hall to the front door. On one arm was the bedrooms, one across from the other, doors at the far end. The bathroom opened into the stem, with the front door at the opposite end. The other arm was the kitchen that went through to the dining room and living room. I waited stupidly behind the shower curtain, wringing out my hair just to have something to do. The door opened, and a towel flew over the top of the rod and landed on my face.

"Thanks."

"No problem. Dude, you really should just leave it in here."

"I've gotten better," I grumbled, rubbing the towel on myself.

I didn't realize he hadn't left until he said, "True. But it's still often."

"Fuck off," I said, instead of saying, *Well, Arturo, I didn't make it to my room because I was trying to get away from you.*

He laughed. I knew he was standing in the doorway, probably leaning against the jamb. I took a deep breath for courage, then I wrapped the towel around my waist and pulled open the curtain. And there he was, just as I thought he'd be. My heart skipped. I always noticed his hair first, shiny and black. On anyone else it would have been an obvious mullet, but on him it was more eighties heartthrob than hillbilly. He smiled at me when I stepped out of the shower.

We'd had the towel conversation a lot. I forgot to bring a towel with me most of the time. If he wasn't home, I would run naked for my room. When he was home, I'd ask. It wasn't that I didn't want him to see me naked. I mostly didn't want to be rude. It was an arbitrary distinction, but considering the way I'd been raised, there was more shame in being rude than being naked. The towel conversation was now going to be my way of avoiding talking about getting married. I grabbed my clothes off the floor. "We could buy more towels."

"Why? So you can leave thirty of them in your room instead of one or two?"

I laughed. "I do laundry more frequently than I remember to go get a towel, so there would never be more than, say, three at a time."

"Why don't you just bring it back with you when you're dry like I do? You literally have to pass the bathroom to get to the rest of the house."

"All hail Arturo. Patrón de las toallas."

"How is it you remember *towel* in Spanish, but not *Wednesday*?"
Arturo let me slip past him. He followed me toward my room.

"You know what else I forget how to say in Spanish?"

"Qué?"

I flipped him off.

Arturo laughed. "I can't keep bringing you one, bro. As mi viejo
you're going to have to start pulling your weight around here once
we're married."

I smiled even though I didn't want to. Viejo. *His* viejo. I had learned
enough Spanish over time to know that was a term of endearment, not
just him calling me old. He was so casual about our getting married.
Looked like I wasn't going to be able to avoid it. *So, I guess it's a topic
we can talk about—joke about, even. Okay, cool.*

"Sure, buddy, right, of course. It's not like I clean or, you know, fix
all the shit that breaks," I said, trying to be casual back.

"I clean."

"Rinsing dirty plates and leaving them in the sink isn't cleaning,"
I said.

"At least I don't leave them on the couch anymore."

"Is…something burning?"

Arturo groaned and ran toward the kitchen. I laughed and shut
the door to my room. He was a good cook. And he was the best
roommate I'd ever had. My silly, lovestruck brain just kept wanting
to list the great things about him. I tried to ignore it. I dried off and
put on clothes. I stopped at the mirror on the wall to braid my hair
into one long, blond, snow queen braid and looked at the sticky notes
surrounding the mirror.

A wave of shame rolled in. The sticky notes were a product of
therapy and were supposed to help me "treat myself with compassion."
Dr. Richard Roland would have been disappointed with the way I had
been talking to myself in the bathroom. I thought about one of the first
times I had been in his office. He told me we had to work on my self-
narrative. I told him we could try, but I didn't have a lot of faith. He
suggested journaling, I told him I didn't need a running record of how
terrible I was every day. He suggested drawing. I laughed. He literally
walked across the rows of his bookshelf listing "techniques" until we
landed on the last book.

"What if I don't want to do that?" I asked after he declared it "the one."

"Shoulda thought of that before saying no to everything else," he joked. Then he said all we could do was try something. "What've we got to lose?"

Turns out the thing we were trying was fucking haikus. Well, the five-seven-five syllable form, at least. I wasn't always great at the natural element aspect or distilling life into a single moment. But it had been my practice for the last year. I looked at the wall around the mirror covered in dozens of sticky note poems. I read one.

I don't want to hate/myself or anyone, but/we make it easy.

Then another.

If I stub my toe/and no one is home to hear/can I punch the couch?

I wasn't good at it, but it was working. I could actually hear compassion in my head somedays. I turned to a haiku I had written about six months ago.

This is so stupid/and I hate that it's working/please don't tell Richard.

Reading them, writing them, counting syllables, all of it was pretty grounding. I had to take a second, find a pen, find paper, breathe, and write. It took the panic out of some moments in a way nothing else had. It also gave me a chance to hear what I was saying to myself outside my own head. My first attempts were full of words like *hate*, *apathy*, and *useless*. Over the last year of therapy, they had gotten more forgiving.

Before I went back out to face Arturo I wrote: *I can't find the words/which makes me imperfect but/I'm not a villain.*

As I walked back out to the kitchen, I revisited the line of thinking I had been working on in the bathroom. I had to trust Arturo as my friend. *Just tell him and live with the consequences.* Any conviction I was able to drum up walking down the hall disappeared as soon as he came into my line of sight. Waffling about Arturo didn't make me a bad person, but damn it, I wish I could make a decision. I knew as I arrived in the kitchen I wasn't going to tell him. And it wasn't even that I had *decided* not to tell him, but I flat out couldn't get my mouth to form the words. Arturo smiled when he noticed me. I smiled back.

"Art?" Maybe I could at least ask him what he really thought about his plan. Sometimes reality looked a little different when he wasn't trying to frame everything for social media. I was thankful he at least had enough work/life balance to never post from our apartment.

"Yeah?"

I watched him stir something simmering. He had great arms. They were thick with fine, barely there black hair. One arm was covered in ink, almost as much as my own. The other was completely untouched. He said he was saving it for a sleeve but never had enough money to get it. He also didn't have any ideas. He had round features, his cheeks turning his eyes to thin, happy lines when he smiled, and a dark, thin goatee accented his mouth. He had long eyelashes and thick eyebrows.

"What is it, dude?" he asked.

I looked at the floor and leaned against the wall. If he was ever suspicious of the way I looked at him, he never said. Nothing about the way he treated me suggested he understood how my heart raced when he walked into a room or that my skin flushed when he touched me. When I met his eye, he was staring, and he wasn't stirring even though he still held the spoon. *You gotta say something.*

"You really think this marriage plan is a good idea?"

He opened his mouth, closed it, then turned back to his cooking. "Like I said, it's more of a spectacle plan, but yeah, I do. It gets us the points we need to start off strong, and I think it'll show everyone we aren't just the misfit team. Plus, it will look great on our media."

I liked listening to him talk. His voice was warm and clear. Every conversation felt intimate and safe. He once said he was self-conscious about his voice, even when being complimented, so I didn't say often how much I liked it. I enjoyed it inside the privacy of my own body. It took a second to drag my mind back to the conversation at hand. His plan to get a job using the competition as a portfolio was a good one, despite the sinking feeling it gave me. My shitty brain wanted to ask if he saw me just as his big break into media management. My heart told my brain to fuck off, which ultimately meant I couldn't trust either.

"Yeah, but then we'll be married," I said, trying to sound neutral.

I didn't know yet how to explain all the other thoughts I had about that idea. I knew there was another source of panic, but I couldn't hear it over the indecision about telling him my feelings.

He laughed. "Claro, who cares? Maybe we can get a tax credit or something."

I hummed.

"Mira, *Pirate* and *Uno* will be the most married," he said, "but Thomas and Arturo are going to be…us."

That both warmed my heart and broke it. *No love here, shithead.*

"Sure. Okay."

"You getting cold feet, Jefferson?" he asked, dumping what was in the pan into bowls of rice. I shook my head. I watched him pull chicken breast out of the oven, slice it, and add it to top off the bowls.

"Thomas," he said, sounding serious.

"Yeah?"

"I guess…okay, so I know marriage isn't like a joke or whatever, but it's also not permanent. To me, it's a nonissue. You're my best friend and roommate, and in Denver that makes us common law married anyway."

That's not how it worked, but I didn't say anything.

"If you don't want it, we can call it off."

"I don't want to call it off." I took a breath and looked at the floor. *You really need to tell him.*

"Now, here's the most important question," he said, his cheeky smile returning. He put a bowl in my hands and stabbed in a fork. "Are you going to be an Ortiz, or do I have to be a Jefferson?"

I smiled despite myself. "Fuck you."

But that was that. I took my bowl to the table feeling like a coward. Maybe he was right. We could be married unromantically for the competition, then after it, I would tell him, and he could divorce me from there. I'd kept my feelings a secret this long, maybe I should just continue.

❖

I hadn't managed to commit to telling him during the rest of the week either. Which meant I was committed to not telling him by default and would be married by Saturday night. Arturo threw himself into the details, telling The Major to leave everything to him. So, I worked with the Major to find a sixth. It took us all week, but we managed to get our final teammate sorted out. And then it was the weekend.

The crowd at the kickoff event was enormous. The Denver skatepark was a sea of people, which was messy because it wasn't a pedestrian-friendly park. People were forced to stand on the edge of the bowls or on rails, grind boxes, or ramps. It wasn't dangerous if they behaved, but crowds rarely did. They did have the bowls roped off with caution tape, but that wouldn't matter after a few hours.

We needed a crowd for Arturo's spectacle prize. He figured the judges couldn't argue against it if he had a big enough audience. I didn't think the crowd on the ground would be more than a few thousand, but there would be news crews, and Arturo said he could get ten thousand on our live social media alone. The only issue I had with it all was that the spectacle was *me*.

Fuck me for getting me into this. I suck so bad. I'm the worst. Okay, I wasn't totally a victim because I did love the attention to some degree. I loved showing up to a place and being someone people respected. The fans were great, and many of the other teams were decent. They all knew me because I'd won the most individual points last year. Maybe I should have felt like I had nothing left to prove. That was fucking false. Now I not only had to win to keep my friends but had to keep winning to keep my fans.

I didn't know what people would do after I was married. I didn't hide being gay, but queerness was out of sight, out of mind for most people in the communities that frequented skateparks. Arturo and I were about to make it very in sight and in mind. I didn't have the best history of people reacting well to me coming out, but since I had shown up in Denver already out, maybe it would be fine.

"It's almost time," The Major said to me, bumping me with their shoulder. They were obviously excited. I nodded and tried to smile, but I didn't know what to say.

We hovered by the grandstand, taking in the crowd from the protection of the stage's shadow. The person we had found to be our last teammate was a woman named Fi York, but she said everyone called her Flip. I was standing with her, The Major, and Nads while we waited for Rocky and Uno to get back. She was slated to be our other blader with The Major, which left Uno open to be the all-around guy/skateboarder with me while Rocky and Nads focused on bike events. I mean, we would all try the other events, but The Major picked a "focus" for each of us, saying it would ensure we had more well-rounded wins as a team.

"You okay?" Flip asked me.

"Probably. You?"

She smirked and nodded. She had incredibly shiny black hair and deeply tan skin. She had a sleepy-looking face, but alert eyes that suggested she probably noticed everything.

I thought about her question. Was I okay? It was my wedding day—what could possibly be wrong? *Everything, you moronic puppy-crush-having bitch.* I forced myself to look back at the crowd filling in around the park. A DJ was blasting music, and a traffic jam of food trucks lined the other side of the street. Sponsor tents were set up in a blocked-off section of road. People were literally everywhere. For it being the CASST kickoff, there wasn't much room to skateboard or blade. Bikes had been prohibited at this event, to Nads's annoyance. I leaned my board against my leg as I waited. It would mostly be a prop tonight.

Flip was still watching me. "I'm fine."

She didn't answer, but she shifted her gaze as someone said, "Hey."

An arm came around my shoulder, and my body supernova-ed with excitement. I looked at Uno's face. He was slightly sweaty but mostly excited.

"Ready?" The Major asked.

"Yup. Rocky's over there on our live, and at least seven thousand were logged in when I left. I talked to a coordinator, and they're expecting four thousand on the ground, so can't really say over ten thousand isn't a spectacle. And this is Father Maloy."

I looked where Uno pointed. He had a mousy, balding priest with him.

"He's going to officiate. And here's this," Uno said, handing me our marriage license. "That was hard to get on such short notice, but I know a guy."

"Perfect," The Major said, throwing their arms around Uno and me. "This is going to be fucking amazing. Thousands of points in less than five minutes."

I reached out to shake the priest's hand. I wondered if he knew it was me and Uno who were getting married. Would he be cool marrying two men?

"I've never done anything like this," the priest said. He was smiling, which was a good sign. He put his hand in mine. "I'm Father Bart Maloy."

"Me either. I'm Thomas…Pirate."

He unfolded a scarf thing that was black except for the mini Progress Pride flags sewn on the ends. He happily hooked it around his neck and asked, "How soon until it's time?"

Secretly I thought about how lucky it would have been if the priest hadn't been an ally. I was still scared shitless about marrying my huge secret crush. And if the priest was a homophobe, we wouldn't be able to pull it off. But also, it was really cool to see those colors on a person of God.

"Do you know when this starts?" he asked me.

"Oh, um…" I realized I had been staring at Maloy's scarf thing. I blinked and looked around. *You need to fucking get it together.* I hadn't slept well all week, and it was making me feel everything in a psychedelic, bad-trip way. The competition emcee, a guy called Waste, spoke up before anyone could answer the priest's question.

"Good morning, Denver!" Waste screamed. The crowd screamed back. There were a few minutes of hype and crowd call and response. Then he started going over the competition rules. We were waiting for the team announcements. When he called our name, we were going to rush the stage and do the thing.

Do the thing. I looked at Uno. He looked so excited and obviously proud of himself. It was both awesome and shitty. He was excited to start the competition and to stuff thousands of points down everyone's throats immediately. He wasn't excited to marry me. The fact that his arm was around my shoulder didn't account for anything. He turned suddenly, and we were eye to eye, our faces only an inch or two apart. I stared at his mouth. It was smiling.

"Like I said," he said as if reading my thoughts, "Arturo and Thomas are still just us, okay?"

I nodded and turned back to the stage.

"Right. Let's run down the roster," Waste said, reaching for a clipboard being handed to him.

We all started shuffling closer to the stairs with Father Maloy sandwiched between Uno and Nads. The Major and Flip fell in behind me. We were practically single file, and Uno's arm was no longer over my shoulder, but I could still feel the warmth and weight of it.

When they called our name, The Major Leaguers, instead of screaming so they could find us in the crowd, we climbed the stage. The bouncers didn't do a whole lot to stop us, and Waste just narrated the whole thing into the mic, baffled. I had been instructed to get to the center of the stage with Uno, and people would get the picture once they saw the priest. The noise around us was impossible to decipher.

Uno took my hands when he faced me, and then he looked at Maloy, who was saying stuff, but I wasn't capable of listening. I just watched Uno. When Waste finally got the hint, he held the mic up to Maloy and everyone heard him say, "For as long as you both shall live?"

And they heard Uno say, "I do."

Maloy's voice was loud and echoed as he said, "And do you, Thomas 'Pirate' Jefferson, take this man in happy matrimony? To have and to—"

I considered passing out. The only thing really keeping me on my feet was Uno holding my hands. When Maloy stopped talking, the mic came in front of my face. I stared at it and must have said "I do" because Maloy nodded and moved on. Waste was freaking out now, and the crowd was a mix of absolute excitement and raucous disdain.

"By the power vested in me, I now pronounce you maritally joined. You may kiss your husband."

I froze. We never talked about the kiss part. So, when his mouth, Arturo's mouth, *Arturo "Uno" Ortiz*'s mouth crushed against mine, I ignited into a fireball of elation and terror. Time sped up and slowed down all at once. I had kissed him so often in my daydreams that reciprocating felt almost second nature. I tuned in to the soft feel of his mouth, the hard grip of his fingers around mine. He kissed me—*was kissing me*. Then time snapped back into place and he stepped away. I now knew what his mouth felt like, what he tasted like. And worse than that, I absolutely wanted more.

I was completely fucked.

I stood by, dazed, as Uno finished up the show by having Flip and The Major sign as witnesses, and then he signed and I signed, then he handed the paper to Waste. He also pointed to Rocky and showed that we had eight thousand people watching our live social media. Waste let him have the mic, and he explained what it all meant. Waste was joined by some of the CASST officials, one of whom was on the phone. They told us we had to wait to see if the sponsors for those prizes agreed that we had pulled it off. That's who they were on the phone with.

Uno and The Major answered questions while the rest of us waited. By the jeering and cheering coming from the crowd, I knew everyone was experiencing the same bubble of suspense. All of this only mattered if we had the points. Out in the audience, the other teams and their fans wanted us to fail as much as our own fans wanted us to succeed.

A sustained mix of cheering and booing came from the crowd until everyone saw the organizers hang up their phones. Then it was scarily silent. The organizer asked for the mic, and Waste handed it over. They said both sponsors had declared the points were legit. The chorus of noise all around me was explosive, as bright and dense as the sound from a firework show finale. I was crushed into a group hug, and somewhere I was aware of cameras going off.

"Wait," Waste said after letting the cheering go on for a few seconds.

We waited.

"The CASST organizers had also issued the first penalty of the competition." Waste handed The Major the piece of paper that represented the deduction of points. Waste said for the crowd, "Don't rush any more stages."

The Major shrugged at the number and handed the ticket to Uno. The crowd took The Major's lead and laughed it off. The Major offered Waste their hand, and Waste shook it.

We were stuck on the stage for a while. Waste asked The Major and Uno more questions about our plans for the rest of the competition and if we were worried about retaliation. I tried to fall back into the shadows, standing only slightly behind Father Maloy. I couldn't get too far back because of sound equipment and backdrops. Father Maloy, God bless him, was standing in the way of the stairs. I could have knocked him down if I wanted, but that would have been rude.

"Congratulations," he said happily when he noticed I was near him.

"Um, thanks."

The whole ordeal probably lasted ten minutes from getting on the stage to being escorted off, but it felt like hours. When it was finally fucking over, I followed everyone back down into the crowd. The rest of the team was still wildly excited and were hugging each other and me when I was within arm's reach. I was as excited, I think, but I was also one hundred percent overwhelmed by feelings and sounds and sensations. I was a little desperate for any substance that had a numbing effect, even a little one. *Novocain or tranquilizer dart or*— Luckily, I didn't have to resort to anything too drastic when a fan I recognized but couldn't quite remember the name of offered to buy me a drink. I accepted.

CHAPTER THREE

Arturo

"Look, I know we didn't ask, but you don't really pay us to ask." I laughed, trying to unlock the door, carry Thomas, and talk on the phone at the same time.

Thomas was absolutely drunk. Our spectacle was a hit. Well, it was a hit with the fans. They thought it was awesome. We actually gained ten thousand followers because of it. The other teams spent their night trying to dispute the points. They shut up after Flip added to our lead by knocking out three of the top blade prize opportunities. She had managed to get a small crowd to move out of a bowl so she and some of the other women competitors could show off their skills. I had never seen anyone skate like she did. Flip was almost more amazing than The Major.

"Uno," said the director or CEO or liaison or whatever his title was.

To me, he was just the guy from DropCloth Clothes. DropCloth was a subsidiary of Bored Skateboards, and our role in their business was mostly merchandising. Even though we were paid to wear their clothes, we weren't becoming millionaires off them. This guy liked to push his authority with us anyway. Considering my plan and a few recent meetings that hinted at some bigger deals from Bored Skateboards, though, I figured I should play nice.

"Boss," I said. That's what I called all of them. I held the phone as best I could with drunk Thomas draped over my shoulders. He was awake but had insisted on being carried. "We have this under control."

"You also have a contract."

"Yeah, and I'm pretty sure it says you pay us to wear your gear and get attention. The only way I know how to get attention is to do dramatic, stupid shit and win the competition," I said. I finally got the key in the door and let us into the apartment.

"Yeah, but if you'd given us a heads-up, we could've added press and got in front of the fallout."

"Right. And your press would've tipped off the competition, then all the other teams would've tried to pull the same shit or beat us to it. Now they can't."

"Arturo, I don't want to have to have a discussion with Bored—"

"That's actually a good idea. Look, call back in the morning, and I'll fill you and Bored in on the rest of my plans for the comp. But I'm warning you now, I don't fucking know everything I'm gonna do."

"Fine, but our media team thinks you should get rings."

"What?"

"It tests better with subscribers."

I laughed. "Whatever, bro."

"I mean it. They're gonna put together some sort of Uno/Pirate ring deal for the box."

"Good night." I hung up.

The box was Sk8Box, a new product they wanted us to start endorsing. It was a subscription box service with swag and skate equipment in it. The annoying thing was most of the people working on it were new to the skateboarding scene, so they were kind of needy. DropCloth and Bored Skateboards were throwing a lot of money at teams because of the special collectors boxes for CASST which, despite being a Colorado contest, was getting national attention. I wanted to be a part of all of it from a media standpoint, but they only saw me as a skater. Hopefully that was temporary with everything I put together today to start my portfolio.

I tossed my keys and the phone on the kitchen counter as I passed and headed for Thomas's room. It wasn't until we were inside that I realized how long the day had really been.

"Dios mío."

"What'd they want?" Thomas asked, his breath a warm breeze on my neck.

"Too much."

He hummed. When we got to his room, I squatted so his feet met the floor and he slid off my back. I held on to make sure he wouldn't fall over and slam his head into his nightstand. I didn't want to be a widower.

Bro, you're married, my brain said. *Only for show*, I reminded myself.

"What'd they really want?" he mumbled, swaying.

I laughed. "They want us to get rings."

He heaved his shoulders once and tried to scrape his hair off his face. It had been in a bun on the top of his head most of the day, but the more shots he took, the more it had fallen all over the place. Now it was just a bright cascade around his face. I helped him out by combing it back with my fingers. It was soft and faintly smelled like his citrusy shampoo. He closed his eyes.

"Scale of one to ten, how likely are you to piss the bed?" I asked.

He grinned and blinked his eyes open. "Seven."

"Can you manage the bathroom?"

He nodded, and I followed him back down the hall. He went into the bathroom. I waited outside the door, not that it was shut, until he came back.

"I want to sleep," he complained, drying his hands on his shirt, soap still on them.

"Let's go." I laughed.

He blinked at me. "You're coming with me?"

That question was a surprise mostly because of how gentle he sounded. Was that the right word? Gentle? Quiet? It felt like two or three questions all at once.

"I'm going to help you."

He nodded and swayed back down the hall. He flopped on his bed and kicked his shoes off.

"You gotta lie the other way."

He grumbled and flopped around until he was in the bed properly. He seemed asleep before I even backed out of the room.

I crawled into my own bed, thinking I'd be asleep as fast as Thomas. But my eyes wouldn't close. I felt like I could fly. *What a great fucking day!* We were ahead in the competition by strides. And even though the sponsors were pissing and moaning about it, their checks would be fat because of the stunt we'd pulled.

Something didn't sound quite right about the word "stunt." It didn't feel like a stunt. *You got married today.* Even though it was for the competition, something about it was starting to feel...feel what? I let it play out again in my head. It had been hard to get someone to officiate. I didn't want to lose the points on a technicality and knew I needed someone real. Most people treated marriage like marriage, saying it was serious. I knew it was supposed to be, despite all the divorces.

And maybe that's the difference. It wasn't as much of a...*joke* as I thought it would be. Looking up at my ceiling, I realized I was as serious about being married in this case as I had ever expected. I always figured I'd marry a good friend because I hadn't ever really fallen *in love.* I tried to explain that to my parents once, and they said I was just confused because I had transitioned. They couldn't sort out my sexuality on those grounds, so they thought I must not be able to either. I honestly hadn't *tried* to sort it out since my feelings were always kind of shallow. What I felt for Thomas was the most I'd ever felt for anyone. So maybe that's what made the wedding feel as real as I had ever expected it to. Or maybe I was just thinking too hard about it because it hadn't even been eight whole hours since it had happened.

I thought of Thomas and the mild alarm on his face when I took his hands in front of Maloy. Then I heard him say "I do" again in my head, and I thought about kissing him. To my surprise, my pulse raced at the memory. So I thought about it again. And my heart skipped again. That was new. It's not like Thomas was my first kiss, but it was definitely the first one that made my heart do that. Was...did I want something physical with him? I had sex with a girl in high school. And while we had kissed and fucked and whatever, my heart had never jumped. And after her, I'd made out with a few guys. There were also some gender-unknown individuals in a few nightclubs and one person I had tried to date for three months before she decided it was "passionless." Even with all of that, no racing pulse.

It was probably just the excitement of the day. I closed my eyes. But the kiss played on a loop behind my eyelids. I got married. And the whole world knew. A bolt of fear struck my spine like a bullet. I sat up terrified. *My mom is probably freaking out.*

I snuck back down the hall and got my phone. There were thirty missed calls, mostly from family. I had been ignoring my phone most of the night except to post and to take the call from DropCloth. It was way too late now to call anyone back, and most of the texts were people telling me to call them anyway. I opened the chat with my sisters.

Amilia: *Arturo Sebastian Ortiz you better be fucking joking.*

Ariana: *You're so dramatic. Mama won't stop crying—don't worry, she's happy—and abuelito keeps saying es de la acera de enfrente cuz Papi told him that's what he should say.*

Amilia: *If you got married without the family, I'm going to kick your ass.*

Ariana: *y a un gringo...*

I sighed and took the phone to bed. Listening to the thirteen voicemails from my mother did help me fall asleep.

I spent the week working at the baseball stadium. I had agreed to the extra shifts months ago so I could get the time off I needed for competition events. No one at the stadium said anything about CASST or my marriage even though I knew some of them followed the team. It was weird to have the news all over my social but to go about my work like it was any other day.

I was also wildly busy with the team media and my plans. I did have that meeting with Bored Skateboards and DropCloth, and I made sure to push my numbers under their noses. They seemed impressed and were easily distracted by what they wanted from us, no surprise there. I also got verbally murdered by my parents and sisters for getting married. Telling them about The Plan softened them up a little. We were a career-minded family, after all, and my dad wanted to run my portfolio by a professional friend of his, so that was a win. I didn't tell them kissing Thomas made my heart race. I tried to avoid thinking about that too much. But the memory did distract me from an introduction thread about Flip I was making and from properly fitting a gasket on a hose at the field. It was one of the busiest, weirdest weeks of my life.

Then it was time to be Uno again. This weekend of CASST was the campout. The point of the event was to camp with other teams at a skatepark and compete in an unofficial event Friday night for the fans, then the tournament all day Saturday. The skatepark stayed open later than usual and food trucks came. Fans weren't permitted to sleep overnight at the park, but that didn't stop some from milling around all night. It was sort of a free-for-all, but there were enough cops to keep any real shit from happening. Then the judges and Waste arrived Saturday morning.

By Friday afternoon, I was pumped for the event. Plus, I missed my friends. I had a low tolerance for not being able to hang out with people. I had grown up in a huge family and a community that had been close. Even though it had been my idea to move to Colorado, I spent the first few months betting on when I would crack from the loneliness. Then I met Thomas. I missed Thomas most. Maybe more than usual? He also had to work and had gone to bed early most nights. I was kind of used to it. He was an insomniac, which meant some days after long sleepless stretches, he would do nothing but sleep. All that really amounted to was that we hadn't seen each other much since the first night of the competition. *Since the wedding.*

Even though I was excited to hang out with him over the weekend, he was in a pissy mood as we waited to be picked up. We had been waiting out on the sidewalk for about twenty minutes, and I had asked him questions even though he was wearing his earbuds. He mostly grunted. He did look more exhausted than usual despite the sleep he'd managed. I was just about to try a topic I knew he couldn't resist— baseball, of all things—when we heard the SUV. Nads was honking at drivers who were turning onto our street slower than he wanted, so we heard him before we saw him. He stopped in front of us, and Rocky opened the door from the inside.

"Oye!" I said, tossing my backpack into the SUV before I crawled in after it.

"*Uno!*" Rocky shouted, dabbing me up.

"Hurry up, we're going to miss the good tent spots and end up in a parking lot," Nads growled.

From the back seat I put out a hand to take Thomas's bag. I wasn't ready to make the switch to nicknames. It took me so long to pick out Arturo, yet most of the state knew me as Uno. I chose Uno too, I guess. Thomas handed me his bag and then plopped into the seat next to me. The door was barely closed before Nads was rocketing back into traffic. I high-fived Flip. Rocky rubbed my head in greeting. They were taking up the middle bench-style seat of the massive SUV, so Thomas and I were shoved in the back. I tossed our gear behind me into the trunk on top of everyone else's.

The others greeted Thomas too, but he just waved and said nothing. He crossed his arms and didn't take his earbuds out. It didn't seem like he was planning to say anything ever again. I didn't realize I was staring at him until he turned and looked at me. I couldn't see his eyes through his shades, but I smiled at him.

"Here. This came in the team mail," The Major said, tossing a box back to me and Thomas.

"What is it?" I asked. It had my name on it, and the address was for the team post office box.

"Open it, loser," The Major said.

I laughed and did. Inside were two small jewelry boxes. "What the fuck is this?"

"Rings," Thomas said softly, taking one.

"I…how…did they just *pick some* for us?" I was floored. I honestly had forgotten the sponsor said to get some.

"Sk8Box called and told me to do it. They sent me to a site and said they'd pay. So I did. Here. There should be some team stickers in there, too." Thomas opened one of the two smaller boxes he'd taken out while Rocky snagged the bigger box and was rifling through the stickers.

The box Thomas opened first apparently had my ring in it because he offered it to me. I held out my hand, not the ring hand, but the other one, palm up. Nads went over a curb on a turn, and the ring bounced to the floor. We both went for it, but Thomas got to it first. He took my hand in his to steady it, then put the ring into my palm. Then his hands were gone. He opened the other box and put a thick, silver band on the appropriate finger. I put my ring on. I didn't look away from his hands until I realized my ring fit perfectly.

"How'd you know the size?" I asked him as quietly as I could.

"I guessed," he said, equally quiet.

Then his head fell back, and he crossed his arms again. I took that to mean the conversation was over. I looked down at the ring. It was thick and matte black with the smallest band of gold around it, but off center in a cool way. From the right angle, it looked almost like a tattoo. I didn't have any tattoos on my left side, so it was kind of surprising to look at. The ring was exactly what I would have picked for myself.

I put my head back and closed my eyes too. It wasn't that I didn't want to talk to the others, but the exact fit of the ring in both size and taste was overwhelming. It brought back all the thoughts and feelings I had over kissing Thomas.

I hardly noticed the drive but was shaken to attention when we arrived because Nads practically parked on a barrier. He screamed at us to get out and was first to start throwing equipment out of the SUV. The Major shouted at Nads, trying to get him to be less of an asshole, and Rocky and Flip wandered off somewhere, probably sizing up the other teams so we could get a read on the competition. Rocky had also taken all the stickers.

The event planners were smarter this year and had assigned the registered teams designated camping spots marked off by chalk and spray paint. We had even been directed to our spot by some lackey CASST had hired for the job. At least teams wouldn't have to fight about it, and the only people who ended up in the parking lot were fans who wanted to hang out all night.

This park, unlike Denver, was off on its own. It was part of a greater park complex with sports fields and playgrounds. It was also green and forested in a way Denver wasn't. Our designated campsite was on a glorified median on the edge of the parking lot. I couldn't complain; it was easy to get to and easy to keep the SUV near in case we needed something, like power to charge our phones. Some of the teams had to hike onto the baseball fields.

Pirate and I worked together on the tents. *Because it has to be Pirate and Uno now.* He was surprisingly efficient. Then again, his family was from the country. I had seen most of them on video chat when he visited home last winter while his dad was sick. Their Southern accents were hilariously thick, and I gave Pirate shit every time I heard his. He gave me enough shit for mine. My family was from Mexico and had immigrated to the US when I was a baby. My dad's parents were still in Mexico City. My mom's parents lived with them in Arizona. When I first moved—

"Hey, if it isn't Mr. Illegal Citizen himself," some dick from another team said, shoving me as he walked past us on his way toward the skatepark.

I could have laughed at his timing. It's not like I hid being born outside the United States. The Mexican flag was tattooed on my neck, after all. The pole I had been holding slipped out of my hand, and the tent collapsed. Pirate and I made eye contact before I turned toward the guy who made the comment.

"Fuck you," I said, moving to shove him back. Pirate caught my arm before I could. The other guy's buddies stepped in closer, ready to back him up.

"Marry some fag to become a citizen?" The asshole laughed. "Pretty desperate, Ortiz."

"Someone had to make an honest man of me. Your mom wasn't willing to commit," I said with a shrug, going to retrieve the tent pole he had made me drop.

"The fuck did you just say?" the guy said, stepping closer and bumping me again.

Pirate stepped between us. Pirate was about two inches shorter than me and about a foot shorter than the guy fucking with me. The guy looked familiar, but I couldn't place his name. He was some generic brand of dirty white guy. And Pirate looked ready to shred him. The guy postured, looking down his nose at Pirate, but Pirate didn't back down. He also didn't say a word.

"Hey, back the fuck off," The Major said. Nads followed slowly behind them.

"I ain't afraid of some fairies and their fucking gardener," the guy said. His teammates started to look a little stressed. They tried pulling him back by his arms, but he didn't budge.

"They're the least of your problems," a Boulder cop said, stepping closer.

The guy stared at the cop for a hard second, almost as if he were wondering if he could take her on too. Then he said, "Fuck it."

He stomped off, continuing in the direction they had been headed. His buddies trailed behind him, looking at the ground, and had the decency to be embarrassed.

"Thanks Officer…Sanchez," I said, reading her badge. I had expected the cops to be around, but I was surprised one had stepped in. I backed off. Pirate and The Major eyed her warily, but she didn't have the same vibe as some of the usual cops we encountered.

"You should report that," she said, nodding, not seeming to notice our apprehension toward her. Or she ignored it. "I read the rules for this. They could get disqualified."

"I'm pretty used to citizen jokes, recent politics being what they are. At least he didn't say anything about the wall," I said.

"That shit gets old fast, I get it." She smiled at me and walked off. All threats gone, Pirate went back to setting up tents and The Major back to managing Nads.

"Should we report it?" Pirate asked.

"I don't know," I said, shoving the pole into place a little harder than necessary. The tent fabric rustled threateningly.

"I'm sorry," he said, putting his hand on my shoulder. The silver band caught the failing sunlight and looked almost gold.

He was my best friend, in my corner, wedding ring or not, and even though we had been forced to wear them, it did feel uniting. It felt like I *expected* wearing a ring with a spouse *to* feel. I looked at him and nodded. "I'm sorry too. All of that was pretty fucked up."

He blinked at me, and I could tell he was trying to think of something to say. I smiled at him. He frowned harder and leaned in toward me. He adjusted the pole in my hand and went back to the other side to raise the tent. If he could drop the issue, so could I.

"We got challenged," Rocky announced, running up to us some time later. He hopped over the gear pile and crashed into The Major.

My blood thrummed with excitement. Tonight was listed on the schedule as a meet and greet, but for the last few years, it had been CASST tradition to play Skate via direct challenge. So now it was an unofficial event. Skate was like Horse in basketball. One person would go head-to-head with a person from a different team and perform a trick. The competitor had to do the same trick. You got two tries before you got a letter, and the first one to spell Skate lost. Since it had a lot of participation and a lot of fans, rules were put in place to keep people safe, and one team was designated to coordinate.

"Who challenged us?" The Major asked.

Flip walked up and shrugged. "Everyone."

We stared at her.

"It's going to be a long night," The Major said.

Everyone meant that one of us would have to face one person from each team, so that was nine challenges total. You could only challenge a team once just to keep the event from going all night, but if every team used their full challenges, that was still forty-something rounds.

"Who's coordinating?" Pirate asked.

Rocky was basically running laps around us with excitement. "The Animals. Dusty's gonna host."

The Animals were a good team. I liked them. They were a crew of middle-aged guys who got into skating later in life and did CASST for the fun of it. They were near the bottom almost every year but were some of the best people I had ever met. Their blade guy, Roger, got me my job at the stadium.

"Okay," The Major said. "This can only help us."

"Unless they all kick our asses. Some of those people made it to Olympic tryouts," Nads said.

"Who cares? Even if they all beat us, that's only three thousand points. We're up by three times that. All the other teams are going to start pulling in some major points. We have to be strong as we lose ground. We keep going and stay focused. Now it's marathon time," The Major said, putting a hand on Nads's shoulder.

"I..." Pirate started. We waited. "I think we're going to be targets for issues."

"What do you mean?" I asked. We all stepped in closer, trying to close out some of the rest of the world.

"Those guys that came after Uno...I don't think it's going to stop there."

"There's always a shithead or two," The Major said.

"What guys?" Rocky asked. I let The Major explain. When they were finished, Rocky said, "We can take fucks like that."

"The officials will be so pissed if we fight anyone," Nads said.

"That's not the point," Pirate said. "I'm just saying there's bound to be more of that shit, could be any of us. I mean, they might have started with Uno, but they managed to insult me and The Major too. I just want people to be aware."

"I told you this was a bad idea," Nads said. "If there are enough issues, they'll kick us out of the comp, and I need to win this."

"We'll win. It's fine, let them target us. This team has some of the best, and we'll keep proving that," The Major said, talking almost exclusively to Nads.

The team agreed, even though Nads didn't look convinced. I watched Pirate. He didn't look satisfied either.

I decided to check on them, starting with the person I knew the least. "Nads."

He had started to walk back toward the SUV but stopped. I walked toward him.

"What?"

What did I want to know from him? "You've been talking a lot about needing a win. Is everything okay?"

He blinked. Then he squinted. After about three seconds, his expression relaxed. "Yeah, man, it's been a fucked-up year. I love this, and I want to have a good season."

I smiled at him and patted his shoulder. "I get that. I swear I'm not trying to stress you out. This will lead to overall good. I promise."

He looked like he was considering it. Finally, he said, "Whatever, Uno. Just focus, okay?"

He walked away before I could ask what he meant. I didn't think too hard about it. I just went to check on Pirate. He was standing back by the tent, watching the crowd.

"You okay?" I asked, reaching for him.

He shrugged away and grumbled. "I'm gonna go find food."

I felt a pang of hurt that he was walking away from me, but then he turned and sighed.

"Sorry, I...Do you want anything?" he asked.

I nodded. "Get me whatever you're getting."

"I'll go with you," Flip said.

He didn't tell her no.

CHAPTER FOUR

Thomas

I marched toward the food trucks gathered on the far end of the baseball fields. The crowd ignored me for the most part, or maybe they decided it wasn't worth it to try to talk to me when they saw my expression. Flip fell into step beside me. She was taller than me by a little, her long legs making her movements languid. I hadn't noticed her actual height before because every time I talked with her, she had been wearing blades or had on massive platform shoes. Today she wore sneakers, overalls, and a lot of plastic jewelry that clattered as we walked.

"Why did you follow me?" I said, feeling both irritated and relieved.

"I'm not following you. I told you I was coming," she said. "You make it sound like I need permission."

"Why did you come?"

"Food, silly," she said. I squinted at her. She laughed. "Fine, you looked like you could use a friend."

"I have friends."

"Sure you do, but your best friend is now your husband, and no one else might notice, but I do," she said.

I stopped walking. "Notice what?"

She made a silly face and mocked, "Nothing. You're totally not obvious."

I crossed my arms. *Fuck me.* Okay, it's fine, she said no one else could tell. Even if someone else knew, Uno was clueless. He should have been the first to notice. Was I really that obvious, though? Maybe it was because she was new or because she was a girl, as sexist as that was. Maybe it's just those eyes that seemed to see everything. *Fuck her, what does she know anyway?*

"Okay, you're not *that* obvious. I noticed, but I notice most things. If it matters, I shipped you guys from the start. The pining is, *mmm,* chef's kiss," she said. Her words broke my panic slightly.

"Shipped…the start?"

"Yeah," she sang. She walked past me and kept going toward the food trucks. "I saw you guys skate together last year. The way you talk to each other or look at each other. It's obvious you really care about each other. But I hoped it was more. You're cute together. And it's comforting to know there are more queer people in the industry."

"Uno isn't…what do you mean the way we look at each other… last year?"

She laughed. "My guy, you're doing too much."

Christ on a Christmas plate, I'm losing touch. "I don't have any idea what you're saying."

"Fine, I can code switch into grandpa," she said. She closed her eyes and took a breath. When she opened them, she said, "Chill, bro. You're, like, spazzing out."

"No one says that."

She giggled.

"Flip, just tell me what you're talking about."

She sighed. "Fine. I can tell you're in love with him."

I tried to keep my face neutral. I didn't think I could lie to her, but I could avoid the question. "It's not like that. We did this for CASST. Uno's going to make it all part of his portfolio or whatever."

See, I get that he's not into me. Even more reason not to say anything. I wanted Uno to have everything he ever wanted. But I hated his plan sometimes. *I'm a friend and practically a media client, nothing more.* She had said the way we look at each other, not just the way I look at him, and my heart doesn't forget stuff like that. Flip coming at it from her angle was making it hard to keep my head and heart from full-on rioting inside me.

"Sure, the marriage was for CASST, but like I said, you have looked at him like that since last year. Listen, I'm not here to air your business. You just wanted to know why I thought you needed a friend.

And you don't have to explain anything. I'm not trying to pry. I'm offering you the opportunity to talk about it. I can just listen."

I muttered and kept walking. "I don't have anything to say."

She nodded and fell back into step next to me.

"I don't think he thought this through as much as he believes he did," I found myself saying.

"What do you mean?"

I read the signs of the food trucks. "His sexual identity isn't something he talks about. And he takes a lot of shit for being from Mexico. Especially with all the stupid stuff happening in politics. Now that he's married to me, people are already giving him a harder time. Burritos."

"I'm in," she said.

She was quiet the fifteen or so minutes we were in line at the burrito truck. The vendor was excited enough to see us and asked for our picture. She said she was a longtime fan, and we were half the reason she was glad to win the lottery they had set up for the food vendors. She wished we had brought everyone from the team, though. Flip said she would let the others know they were missed, and we posed for the vendor's picture. She was so grateful, she gave us six burritos on the house. She even remembered that Rocky was a vegetarian. I would have to make sure Uno tagged her truck so she could get more business.

"I think what you might be trying to say is Uno gets a lot of shit for being from Mexico, and now he's going to get more shit because people are going to think he's gay too," Flip said after we started back.

"Yeah." That was it exactly.

"I mean, he might not have the LGBIA thing figured out, but as a trans person, don't you think he would be able to handle some of that?"

I was trying to carry four hot burritos in my arms, or at least that was my excuse for not answering her. Flip had the other two. She was curling them like weights as we walked. I don't know how they weren't burning her hands like they were mine. Even through the foil! I finally said, "I'm sure he can, more or less, but it's also different. I mean just in numbers alone. So few people know he's trans, but now tens of thousands know he's married to a man."

She shrugged. "They also know why you got married. Maybe they'll be objective."

"Maybe. I really doubt it, though."

"Is this something you can talk to him about?"

"Probably, but he isn't the cautious type."

She nodded. "Do you want my advice?"

"Sure."

"Talk to him anyway. He cares about you and what you think. If he knows his behavior scares you, he might be willing to be more cautious. And I would trust he knows how to handle the haters."

"It's not just the haters," I said, not sure how to follow up on that. "It's...he's only being *perceived* as gay because of me."

She nodded. "Oh, I see. You're worried about him turning on you for 'making' him gay."

I didn't answer. I adjusted the burritos in my arms.

"I don't have advice for that except to say if he was worried about that, you'd probably know by now. You two have been close friends and *roommates* for a long time. You've been out the whole time too. If he had a problem with being *gay* by association, I think you would've seen it sooner. You really don't know his preferences?"

I shook my head.

"Interesting."

"Why's that interesting?"

She laughed. "I could say a lot, but I also know it's not fair to speculate on people's identities. Not that I don't want to, but, you know..."

I smiled. I liked knowing she felt that way. It made me feel like I could trust her. Maybe I should ask her some of my other questions, get her opinion on whether or not she thought I was an absolute douchebag for marrying the guy I had feelings for, but not telling him about the feelings. Or maybe she would confirm I was a dick for enjoying the feeling of being married to him anyway. *It's only been a week.* There hadn't been much difference, but the new weight of the ring was hard to ignore, and despite my worry, I liked knowing people could see it.

Flip hesitated. "We're almost back to the tents. You want to talk more about this?"

"Maybe later. I guess it's nice just knowing someone else knows."

She smiled and kept walking. I followed. It *was* nice knowing someone else knew. But it also added to the fucked-upness of it since the one person who should know was still in the dark.

❖

Eating burritos at a skatepark with my friends was the most normal I had felt in days. I sat on the ground at Uno's feet. He sat on his board. His thigh bumped against me every now and then. When he was done eating, he put his arm over my shoulder in the same casual way he always had. I tried not to make eye contact with Flip even though I could feel her eyes on us. *Trust him*, she'd said. *Fuck. Do you trust him?* An easy five syllables.

Arturo was literally the least judgmental person I knew. It's not like I hadn't told him some fucked-up shit about myself. He knew some of the darker crevices in my past. Then again, there were still tons he didn't know about. I had never told him about what my mother had done and her conversion therapy era. Or about my first boyfriend outing me to the baseball team. Those seemed like way more relevant traumas than my self-harm. Would knowing any of that help him understand how dangerous it could be to present as a gay couple?

"You okay?"

I turned. Uno was leaning down to be eye level with me, his thighs flopping open a little to make room for his belly. His voice was soft so only I could hear him. I wanted to thread my arm under his leg and hold him. I wanted to pull one of his hands toward me and slide my fingers in between his. My eyes betrayed me and looked at his mouth. *Crap*. I could literally feel the cold sweat break out on my body from just being that close to his mouth again. An inch or less, and our lips would connect.

"What?" I asked.

He smiled, and I had to force myself to look at his eyes. "Are you okay?"

I shrugged. "A lot on my mind, actually."

"Wanna talk?"

I almost accepted. Only, I knew it was almost time to start the challenges. "Later?"

His annoyingly handsome smile replaced the worry on his face. We really did only have about five more minutes of goofing off, then we heard the cowbell. From where we were sitting in our designated tent area, we could see the crowd start to flow into the skatepark. We went too.

Moose from The Animals explained the rules with a bullhorn as we gathered. Each challenging team would pick a skater from an opposing team. With ten teams at the event, it meant that the most challenges any team could make or accept was a total of nine with one redemption challenge to rechallenge someone they lost to if they wanted to use it.

Moose was hot, like Idris Elba with locs. I did more looking at him than paying attention. Not like I didn't know the rules anyway. Dusty, a lanky nerdish man, stood by with the scorecard. A letter could only be awarded if Dusty or Moose agreed to it. The other four members of The Animals were on the sidelines available to challenge. The organizers trusted The Animals because they were genuinely fair and believed in rules. That and maybe because they were almost ten years older than the next oldest competitor. Which, after I thought about it, was probably me.

"I'm gonna draw for first up," Moose announced as Dusty held out a hat full of slips with the team names on them. Moose stuck his hand in and drew out a slip. "First up is…The Hard Sox."

The Hard Sox was a weird, preppy team made up of mostly frat guys who spent their time on long boards. They were the type of guys you would expect to invent a new drinking game based on something worthless like prime number scores in basketball. One of the guys rolled forward on a street board and told Moose who he was challenging.

"All right, the challenged team: The Major Leaguers—Pirate," Moose said through the bullhorn.

I high-fived my teammates and rolled out to meet Moose and Hard Sox Guy at the center of the park. This skatepark was long, narrow, and mostly full of fans. The contest coordinators had roped off an area for tomorrow already, so me and the other guy stepped under the caution tape. I put on my helmet. I looked at Moose, waiting.

Moose got the signal from Dusty and rattled the cowbell to start the match. Hard Sox Guy named a combo of ground tricks. I didn't watch him do it. I watched the crowd. We weren't the most popular team, but we were gaining. I felt a little bit more pressure than usual since more people knew my name. We had made such a dramatic statement with the marriage and the other early points. We'd probably look like posers if we started to fail. *Good, I know I have to win for the team so they'll want to keep me around, but now I have to win to protect our honor? Neat.* The crowd cheered as Hard Sox Guy landed the trick.

When he was done, Hard Sox Guy rolled back to the caution tape, and it was my turn to replicate what he had done. I did it, of course, and did my best to wave at the crowd as I rolled back to Moose. Uno called it *fan service.* Then I got to choose the next trick. I looked at The Major. They flashed me a peace sign, meaning two, then they crossed their arms and tucked their hands into their armpits. *Just a kickflip?* At the end of the last competition, The Major had gotten it in their head that some of the people fucked up the simplest tricks more frequently, especially under pressure. Slightly stoned one night, I helped them make up hand signals for some basic tricks and simple combos. I honestly hadn't been sure if they were serious. I guess they were.

I named the trick and executed. Hard Sox Guy looked at me at first with cocky surprise, then with stunned irritation when he didn't land the kickflip. The Major was right this time. Hard Sox Guy's next trick was a longer combo that included the rail. I watched him this time to make sure I knew what the trick looked like. Only slightly impressed, I looked at Uno knowing he would share my thought. I found him in the crowd, and he looked at me from around his phone. He smiled and half shrugged.

"Your turn," Moose said quietly as the other guy worked his way back. I nodded and headed for the rail.

I loved the feel of a board under my shoes and the concrete and iron smell of a park. I could feel the slight vibration that matched the smooth whisper of my wheels on the perfectly crafted park surface. A good board and a good park made me feel invincible. That was the only reason I was able to risk the bodily harm that came with skateboarding, because on the board you were a celestial being, and landing the tricks made you a god. Even if you ate shit on an attempt, you were still pretty cool.

Which was good news for me, because as soon as my board hit the rail, it cracked apart. My face was almost a casualty. Fortunately, my reflexes were fast enough to catch myself before I connected with the metal. It wasn't enough to keep me on my feet, though, and I landed on a wrist and an ass cheek. The sound of the board snapping was lost to the cheer of the crowd. I looked back to see one piece skid off toward the bowl. I stood and waved as I went to get the piece of the broken deck. The other half had spun out into the crowd. A skater for a new team gave me a friendly hard time before handing it over. Our conversation broke up, though, when everyone started to cheer louder. I looked around. Uno was crossing the park with his board in hand. I started toward him.

"I'm surprised this is the first one this year," he teased.

"That you've seen." I laughed.

Uno usually snapped decks, he was sort of a hulk like that. Lucky for us, there were bonus points for broken decks. I dumped the broken pieces into his arms and took the board he handed me. I had been expecting it to be one of the new boards that Bored Skateboards gifted us. We had a stash of them. But Uno had handed me *his* board.

"You sure?"

He smiled. "Why wouldn't I be?"

Fuck if I know, bro. Don't act like this is skating as usual 'cause it ain't. We're married now, and any nice thing you do is gonna fucking make me love your big, oblivious, blind self even more. I took the board. "Thanks."

He grinned and looked at me in a way I'd never seen. It was an intense mix of curiosity, awe, and something else. I loved the way he looked at me most of the time, with his smile and his attentive eyes. And maybe I would have liked that look, a lot, except for everyone else watching us. I couldn't stand being held in that kind of gaze, so I started to walk away.

"Ask me if I remember the combo," I said over my shoulder.

He shouted after me, "You have letters to spare."

I rolled off on Uno's board, the trucks a little looser than I liked. The tail was also chipped, which would make it harder to do some tricks. But it felt right and totally reassuring. I scanned the crowd, hoping to see if I could spot the team that had harassed us earlier. I found them sneering and looking full of themselves.

"Dude, I can see now why you wear a helmet," Hard Sox Guy snorted.

"Hey, if you were as pretty as me, you would too," I said, then I completed his combo better than he had. I beat him with only an *S*.

The next team up challenged Flip, then Uno, and so on until we had been challenged by the nine other teams in the first nine rounds of the night. Moose had started out drawing randomly, but when he saw how it was playing out, he just called all the other teams out to challenge us. Thankfully, we had managed to win seven rounds. Nads lost by three letters. That made him pout, but he liked skateboarding least, so I didn't know why it bothered him that much. Uno lost one and won one. Despite being allowed the opportunity to use our revenge challenge, we didn't. The Major and Uno wanted us to engage with the crowd and do our due diligence for the sponsors. That made Nads even more angry. He stomped off somewhere, saying he was going on a walk.

Some of the other teams went on to challenge each other, and we mixed in among the fans to shoot the shit and network. I signed the pieces of my smashed deck and gave them away at the request of some young fans. There were also a handful of influencers, so we did some things with them to try and gain new followers. I mostly hung around as Uno answered questions and attempted dances. He made me join him on a few, and I had fun despite myself.

The skatepark, like most others, usually closed at dusk, but the event coordinators had convinced the city to leave the lights on until midnight. Around eleven, there was a slow stampede back toward the tents so people wouldn't have to set up in the dark or with just the streetlights. Most teams arranged some kind of party at their tents. Those usually got busted before they really got started, so we weren't going to bother. Uno would make sure we weren't considered losers, though, and would upload tent videos and other ludicrous antics we had throughout the night after lights out.

"Want to head back?" I asked Uno around eleven fifteen. He was observing the crowd and doing whatever calculations in his head that would add viewers. He would tell you I was the reason we had a successful social media presence, but it was really all him and his plans.

"Sure, let's go find the others so we can eat."

I had been kind of hoping for a minute to talk to him, but I was hungry. I nodded. I had been goofing off on his board, so I popped it into my hand and gave it to him. He took it and tossed an arm over my shoulders.

Uno and I found the others already on their way to the tent and fell in with them. The SUV was the first stop for everyone after the food ordering was delegated to Uno. Nads opened the doors and turned on the vehicle so the rest of us could use its built-in chargers to recharge our phones. He also started to shove even more stuff out. My backpack of clothes was first. I caught it as Nads flung it through the door.

"Fuck, Nads, can you chill, bro?" The Major said.

"Can you just let me do one thing without riding my ass?"

I laughed as they argued and went toward my tent. I noticed Flip standing by it looking like she had never seen a tent before.

"You're supposed to go in it. People generally stare from the *inside* out. What is that?" I noticed Flip remove something from the tent before she faced me. She was trying to hide it behind her back, but it was too big. I asked again, "What is that?"

"It's nothing. Just something I found." She tried to hide it even more as I came closer.

"Flip?"

Her face changed. Whatever it was, she really didn't want me to see it.

"Flip." I wasn't asking this time. It was a deck. It looked new. New decks were awesome most of the time, but Flip's face made it clear something was awful about this one.

"Pirate, I—"

I walked over and practically snatched the deck from her. It was so new it didn't even have grip tape. Someone had twisted wire through the bolt holes so it would hang like a picture. On the top someone had written in Sharpie: *Mr. Green Card and Mr. Fairy. Honeymoon Suite.*

"Pirate?" The Major said.

"God damn it," Uno sighed.

"Motherfuckers," Rocky added.

"Pirate, are you okay?" Flip asked.

I wasn't. "I need a minute."

Everyone was suddenly so close. Even though they were friends, I couldn't handle being surrounded at that moment. My shame and rage and fear were so molten, I was going to explode if I didn't leave. I shoved the board at Uno and headed for the SUV. It was the only place around that had solid doors and wasn't made of cloth walls. I shoved Nads out and pulled the doors closed.

Fuck.

CHAPTER FIVE

Arturo

I came close to losing my fingers as Pirate slammed the SUV door shut.

"Shit. Is he okay?" Rocky asked, looking genuinely alarmed.

"Maybe I should talk to him," The Major said.

"Naw, hold off. Give him a minute," I said, looking back at the board in my arms.

It was fair for them to be rattled by the sight of Pirate breaking down. No one on the team save me had seen it. He didn't lose his composure often, at least not this way. Even when he was enraged, you almost couldn't see it on his face. The look of fear we had all seen was profound. Then again, things like this didn't happen often. Mr. Green Card and Mr. Fairy. Fucking assholes. Part of me wanted to believe it was those same jerks from earlier in the day. They would have even more cause to hate us since Rocky beat their skater without getting a single letter. But I wasn't a detective, so it could just as easily not have been them. Either way, everyone sucked ass.

The Major said, "We really need to report this."

"I know. Maybe...well, let me figure it out? I'll make sure it gets handled," I said.

"Great, so even more of them can hate us," Nads said. "First for the points and now for being narcs?"

"It's a literal hate crime," Flip pointed out.

Nads just rolled his eyes. "I mean, they didn't damage anything—"

"Nads," Flip warned, her voice low.

"Fine, Flip, I get it. But we have a lot riding on this competition—of which rule two is not to be a narc."

"Harassment is against the rules too, the fine print rules," Rocky said. "They just want you to go to the organizers instead of the police first."

"I said I'll figure it out. Give me a chance to think about it," I almost snapped.

"Just think before you do anything," Nads added. I stared at him. I couldn't be sure what my face looked like, but Nads deflated and said, "I *am* sorry it happened."

The others added that they were sorry too, their outrage distilling into empathy. I told them thanks and asked for time. They all backed off, and I gave Rocky my phone so he could finish ordering the food. I tucked the board into the tent with my stuff, careful to hide it so Pirate wouldn't have to see it again. Thirty minutes later the food came, so I took my order and what I had ordered for Pirate into the SUV.

"Hey. I brought dinner. Mira, take this," I said, trying to get through the door and hand him the food at the same time. He was lying across the back seat with earbuds in. He sat up and took the boxes. I pulled the door closed. The muted silence was comforting, a relief.

"What is it?" he asked tiredly, making room for me to sit with him.

"Glizzies," I announced. He paused, opening a box and staring at me. I laughed. "That's what the kids are calling hot dogs, or so I heard."

"Stop listening to the kids," he said. I could hear the laugh in his voice.

"Fair enough. You wanna talk about what happened out there?" I asked.

He responded by shoving food in his mouth. I started eating my own meal. We were silent for a few minutes eating designer hot dogs from one of the only restaurants left open that wasn't pizza. I decided to push him a little. He would sometimes get around to saying what was on his mind, but other times it would fester until he freaked out for real. He already seemed on the brink. I started. "So, looks like I have a new deck."

He scoffed and started in on the fries at a dangerously fast pace.

"It even has my name on it."

"That's not funny," he snapped.

"It's a little funny."

"Uno…"

"Uno? Yeesh, is it that bad?"

He sighed, then put his food down on the seat in front of us. He wiped his mouth before he turned to talk to me. "Arturo, maybe this was a bad idea."

"The hot dogs?"

He glared.

"Okay, okay, but I don't think so." I put my food aside too.

"You don't think anything you do is a bad idea."

"That's because I rarely have bad ideas. They're risky, sure, but they always pay off."

He rolled his eyes. "Paying off isn't the same as good. Either way, is this really worth the points?"

"I don't think I know what you're talking about," I said. Of course it was worth the points.

"I don't know how to explain it better."

"So explain it badly, but explain the whole thing. I feel like you're telling me the answer is three without telling me what the question is."

He groaned. "We are getting hate-crimed, and you still think everything's okay?"

"To me it is."

"How? Maybe you don't know how bad it can get to be harassed because of your sexuality. I'm not saying you have to come out or something, but as far as anyone could tell, your sexuality is a mystery at best, and people, including the ones who put that sign on our tent, probably thought you were straight. Since you married me, people are going to think you're gay. Fuck. I'll own not having thought of that before. But since you're the other half of this, I'm asking if you thought this through." He took a breath and looked at me.

I blinked. "I definitely hadn't thought about any of that stuff."

"See? Look, we can get an annulment and then people can stop lumping you in with me, and I doubt they'll revoke the points."

Oooohhhh! I heard it that time.

"Thomas," I said. I moved closer. He was talking animatedly, and I had to wonder if he even heard me say his name. I caught one of his hands. He froze but didn't pull away. "Thomas. I don't care if people think I'm gay. Listen, you're right. I'm not one hundred percent sure what my sexuality is."

"I told you I wasn't saying that so you'd out your—"

I interrupted in Spanish as if talking to myself. "Que muchacho! No nací ayer."

He smiled. "Fine."

"Like I was saying, I don't know what it is. And I don't care what people think most of the time. There's nothing wrong if people think I'm gay because there's nothing wrong with being gay. And there's even less wrong with people thinking I'm gay because of you. Any time anyone associates me with you, I'm grateful. You're my best friend, and you're amazing. I'm not going to change my mind about you based on what someone else decides I am because of it."

He rolled his eyes, but I could see the hint of a smile. I replayed his whole argument in my head and thought of something else. "Also, no one except you has really accused me of being gay."

"What?"

"They called *you* Mr. Fairy. I have been called green card and illegal but not anything gay."

He blinked and looked somewhere in the distance of his own thoughts.

"I mean unless they intended you to be Mr. Green Card and I have it backward." I could see him thinking about it. This afternoon when they had insulted me, it was for being Mexican. And the sign implied that only he was gay. "Actually, now that I think about it, *you* might actually be getting hate-crimed because of *me*."

The realization of what I was saying hit him, and his eyes went wide with alarm. That expression was replaced immediately by embarrassment. His cheeks went red. He groaned and collapsed against the back of the seat, hiding his face in the crook of his arm. "God damn it."

I couldn't help myself. I started laughing.

And he did too. "Fuck me. Maybe I'm so gay I can't even tell hate crimes apart."

"It's a lot to deal with."

He squinted at me and seriously asked, "Isn't it sort of a microaggression for a white guy to turn racism—"

"Nationalism, technically."

"Into something about them?"

"Naw. Well, sometimes. I think in this case it's just trauma."

"That sounds worse."

I could see him gearing up to grovel. He wasn't much of an apologizer, but he was very willing to persecute himself on someone else's behalf. I spoke quickly to try and prevent his self-deprecation. "No. Escúchame, I know you know what it's like to be targeted for an identity, and when you saw it happening to someone else, you wanted to help. I also get not being able to talk about it in any other language than the sexuality identity—"

"Okay, I get it."

"Then you add in the stress of also being a target—"

"I got it," he said, shoving me. "Stop defending me."

He sighed and started to chew on the nails of his free hand, chipping the black nail polish more. I could tell a million thoughts were racing behind his nervous gesture. Some of those I would never know, and some he would maybe tell me in time. There was one more thing I needed him to know.

"I don't know all of what you've been through, but no matter how hard this gets, I'm not going anywhere. Even if we weren't married, you're stuck with me."

He smiled and his eyes softened.

"Also, we can't afford a divorce unless we win the competition."

He laughed. It was a deep, throaty sound and kind of unexpected from him. His laugh seemed like it was meant for someone bigger.

"Even then, I'd do it if you wanted to. I appreciate you being worried about my actions causing me issues, but I'm more worried about them hurting you. At your word, I'll start backtracking."

He thought about it, now chewing on his lip ring. "Naw, I'm good. I think it was just a surprise I wasn't ready for. I knew we'd get shit from other people in the competition, but I didn't think it'd be like this."

"Okay. Fair. Now, the question becomes what do you want to do about it?"

He looked at me. "Do?"

"Yeah, we can report it. I think we should report it."

He squinted. "What? No big Arturo-style plan for the public?"

I looked out the window behind his head. This part of Boulder was mostly park and trees. It looked dark and mysterious outside the windows. "*I'd* do it that way if it was just me. But since it's a *you and me* thing, I want to know what you want."

He put his head back on the rest and closed his eyes. "I hate that we even have to deal with this. But I don't want anyone else to have to put up with it or for whoever did this to think they can get away with it. So yeah, public is fine."

"Cool, 'cause I was thinking—"

"Naw, rule applies even if we aren't at home."

The rule was, no discussion of Arturo's social media agenda after eleven p.m. I laughed. It was a fair rule since his rule was that he couldn't bring up what HGTV gets wrong on their fixer-upper shows, and my boi had a lot of opinions on that.

"Right, sorry."

He smiled at me. "Thanks for this."

I shrugged. "Well, you know what they say. Behind every great man is a greater, depressed hermit who makes sure he thinks about his actions."

"It's a full-time job."

I laughed. His smile faded as I watched him look out the back window. His resting expressions were always so sad. He looked like a painting of someone in mourning. When he looked back at me, very little of his expression changed. It was only a subtle shift from eternally forlorn to temporarily not alone. But it was everything.

I hadn't noticed a feeling in the actual moment our bodies made contact, but I got a jolt now every time I remembered the kiss. I wished it hadn't gone by so fast. I wondered if I would feel it in real time if I kissed him again.

That was a surprising thought. Did I want to kiss him again? I looked at his mouth. He shifted, his hand still resting in mine. Thinking he meant to pull it away, I stopped him, holding tight enough to make it clear I wanted his hand. Then I looked back at his face. I didn't understand his expression. I knew consent was meant to be a verbal yes, a positive tone. I wondered if I asked him, would he say yes?

"Arturo," he said in a very small voice.

He didn't move and didn't say more. It felt like all the air in the car was moving, leaving, as if the air knew privacy or intimacy could only be obtained in a vacuum. I had heard from most people that I'd know it when I felt it, even though no one could explain what it was or what it felt like. Was this it? I watched him breathe in slow motion, his lips parting. I was an instincts guy, the calculations in my brain usually operating so deep that I often didn't know I was going to do something until I did it. But here in the moment, my skin touching his, his eyes slightly surprised, slightly unknowable, I believed for the first time I felt aware of what I was going to do.

"Can—"

But I didn't get to do anything. The dome light came on, and Thomas and I both groaned at the brightness. To my surprise, Thomas didn't jump back from me, though he was almost sitting with my arms around him. We were very close together. His hand even stayed in mine. It was The Major.

"You guys okay?"

"Yeah, Jeffx, we'll be out soon."

"Good, 'cause we want our shit."

They closed the door before we could say anything.

"God, I don't want to go out there," Thomas sighed. He pulled his hand out of mine, climbed over to the next row of seats, and started gathering his dinner trash.

"Do you need more time?" I followed his lead.

"No, I'm just embarrassed now."

I thought about what to say for a minute. "Everyone was just worried. This team is already worlds better than our last."

Thomas didn't say anything. He just opened the door and went out. *Geez, was I really about to kiss him? Where is my head at tonight?* I couldn't deny that I wanted to. *But why? Am I into Thomas?*

I followed him. We helped everyone get the rest of their shit set up as best we could with our phone flashlights and the streetlights. Then without much discussion, everyone went into their tents for the night. Thomas settled in to sleep, and I putzed around on my phone for a while before I committed to doing some work. Then I sat with my laptop open, fingers poised over the keys. I could look up whatever was happening in my brain with Thomas, or I could work on the bigotry issue. I had no ideas for either option.

"You okay?" Thomas asked, making me jump.

"Yeesh, yeah, I'm just stuck." I decided right then to go with working on the bigotry thing. I couldn't tell Thomas about my half-baked understanding of the thoughts I was having about him.

"Stuck…" He was illuminated by the backlight of the computer. His hair was down, flowing and pooling on the tent mats. Alarmingly, the shirt he had on was mine. Our laundry got mixed up a lot. *Of course, that's all.* He couldn't possibly have wanted it *because* it had been mine. I wondered briefly what it was like to be that shirt.

Shit, now I'm really losing it.

"Arturo."

"Oh right, um…" It was taking longer than usual for my brain to change subjects. "I'm just trying to think of the best way to go about this. Like, I want to make a statement without making a statement."

"Like picket signs or a march?"

"Naw, that's too big. I want it to be more personal."

"Too big for you? Interesting."

"Something that seems rebellious. We do have a reputation to maintain."

"Riot."

"Thomas."

"Okay, okay, um…"

"I guess I could look up civil disobedience."

"Small and personal."

"Yeah, but also profound."

"Like kneeling during the national anthem?"

That was a match that ignited a plan in my mind. It came almost fully formed. "That's brilliant."

"Whatever you say, bro, but they don't play the national anthem at our shit."

"I don't need them to." In my excitement, I reached over and kissed his head in a strictly bro fashion.

He grumbled about his hair and rolled over. "You good now? Can you stop staring like that weirdo from that paranormal movie camping edition? You also owe me ten minutes of broken rule time. Get ready to listen about foundation carrying capacity."

"Yeah, sure." I poised my hands over the keys again, but the laptop blinked and warned it was about to die. "Shit, I need the extension cord."

I tried to stand and leave the tent, but my legs twisted in the blanket. I tipped sideways and landed on Thomas's legs.

"Fuck, dude," he said, kicking me.

I laughed. "Sorry, I'm stuck."

"How," he said. I could hear him trying not to laugh. There was a small scuffle before I got free. "Now leave me alone," he said.

"Shut the fuck up, you guys," Nads shouted from the neighboring tent. We ignored him. I had to practically wrestle our one allotted extension cord away from Rocky, who was watching a movie on his phone. When I came back in the tent, Thomas was watching me, so I waved the cable at him. He rolled his eyes and rolled over again to sleep. I got to work.

❖

I woke up to the sensation of something touching me. My fight-or-flight response was usually freeze, so I froze. I held still, trying to figure out what could have possibly gotten in our tent and captured me. It wasn't heavy, and it had a cool familiarity. My heart started to race. It was a snake. It was a snake that was going to eat me hand first. It was wrapping around me and sensed me wake up and was just holding really still.

I took a breath and cracked one eye. Gripping my wrist was a black shape with white tentacles. My heart spiked painfully, and I prepared to scream and run, but then my brain caught up. It was a hand. In his sleep, Thomas had found my wrist and was holding it. I let out a few long breaths. I smiled, and again a feeling, different from fear but no less thrilling, rose in my guts.

I watched Thomas's face for some sign he was awake. He wasn't. His eyes were closed tight, and his earbuds were still in. My guy could sleep like the dead. I, on the other hand, was wide awake and ready to go with my first alarm. I also knew he slept with a stuffed turtle named Gomez and had one of the best comforters I had ever felt.

I looked for my phone, trying not to move my hand. I didn't want his to fall away. I liked it. Maybe he thought I was the turtle. I got my phone and took a photo of where his hand met mine. *Wait, why did you do that, Arturo?* Um, good question.

Was it part of the wanting to kiss him thing? I looked at his face then at his mouth. My pulse immediately reacted. Yeah, I did want that. Por qué ahora? Why so suddenly? I looked at our hands again. The blue canvas of the tent made it feel like dawn, though I knew it had to be much later. It gave his skin a dramatic, gothic tint, like an old vampire movie. I looked at my phone. I thumbed open a browser.

What do you ask the internet? What does it mean when—when what? When you get a weird stomach feeling thinking about your best friend's mouth? I typed that as best I could one-handed and looked at the first few results.

Most of the top results were sites about dealing with your first crush. Not that I could really name a crush I had in the past. *Is this really the first?* I was low-key obsessed with this one girl in high school. Was that a crush? She used to draw dolphins on everything. I thought about her and felt nothing now. I thought maybe I only liked her because she was who I would have wanted to be if I'd been a girl. She had been cool and weird and indestructible. Was that this, then? Was my new emotional reaction to Thomas related to the kind of man he was? Did I simply want to be him? I changed the search so my question started with LGBT.

There were some foundation sites that I scrolled past. Then there was a link that I was about to follow when my phone exploded with sound. The alarm was going off. I shouted and tossed the phone because it scared the shit out of me. I also jerked away from Thomas. He startled a little and looked at me. My phone landed on the other side of him, still alarming.

"What the fuck, bro?" he grumbled, flapping a hand around to try and get my phone. I practically leapt for it as if my phone was going to disclose my search history in a single touch. I ultimately landed on top of him.

"Fuck, Art. What're you doing?"

"Sorry, I—"

"Good, you're awake," Nads said from outside the tent. "Time to pack up."

We watched Nads's shadow unhook one of our tent poles, and the whole thing collapsed on one side.

"Morning," I said to Thomas, trying to sound casual as we fumbled under the fabric of the half-collapsed tent.

"Morning," he answered, annoyed. He still reached my phone before I did, handing it to me without opening his eyes.

CHAPTER SIX

Thomas

"So, I have a plan," Uno said around a mouth full of whatever he was having for breakfast. I opened one eye and tried to see him. Mostly it was taking all my energy to not fall back asleep.

"What? You gonna divorce Pirate and marry Rocks?" Nads said.

"I do," Rocky answered to annoy his cousin.

"Saving that one for the Olympic tryouts. No, I mean about this." Uno produced the deck with the slurs on it.

"A plan for that?" Nads groaned, "Come on."

"Shut the fuck up, bro, this is important," The Major said.

"God, I know, but can't we just report it quietly like normal people?"

"I want to hear the plan," Flip said diplomatically.

Uno looked at me for backup.

"It's a good plan," I said.

I didn't know the plan. I didn't need to know the plan. Uno could want to hang a banner from the moon, and I'd figure out how to get to space. I yawned and leaned forward in my camp chair, resting my arms on my knees just to get some relief from supporting my own body. *Fucking hell, bro, good thing you can keep your mouth shut with that romantic-ass shit.*

"Bueno, so here's what I was thinking," Uno said. "I have five email drafts on my phone. The first is a formal email to the CASST organizers about the deck and the harassment from earlier yesterday.

The second is for Officer Sanchez. I wanted to see if she could ID the people who did this. The third is to a T-shirt company—"

"T-shirts for what?" Nads interrupted.

We all glared at him.

"He's literally explaining that, damn," Rocky said.

Uno went on. "If y'all agree, I'll release the story to our team social media and to mine and Pirate's personal. You can share from there if you want. The message will explain what happened, that we expected more from our skate community, we're hurt, but we want good to come from it. My shirt will have *Mr. Green Card* crossed out, and the back'll list naturalization help orgs our followers can donate to under the slogan *#skateequal* but with a number eight in *skate*. Pirate's will have *Mr. Fairy* crossed out and will have LGBT orgs. Maj, I have two options for you, one that has a mix of orgs on the back or, since those assholes insulted you too, I have one that has trans-specific orgs. The rest'll have the crossed-out hate shirts, or you can say no. That's the plan."

"I love it," Flip said.

"How is that a plan? What are you trying to accomplish? What about the sponsors?" Nads asked.

"What about the other two emails?" The Major said.

"Bored Skateboards is one of the other emails," Uno said mostly to Nads.

Uno crossed to me and sat on the grass by my legs. He sat close enough that his arm grazed my calf, and I was overwhelmed by his smell. It was probably just bulk Old Spice, but to me, it was him. He smiled at me.

"What the fuck, Uno? You gotta stop! The sponsors are gonna drop us, and we're going to be forced to go back to scraping together money. It's not like *you* can pay us," Nads practically shouted.

Uno sighed. "They won't drop us. Nothing in this plan violates our contract. Besides, our social media influence alone is worth their money, no matter what we do. They have just as much to lose as we do. My email to them is going to explain what we are trying to do with this—"

"*You're* just doing this so they'll give you a fucking job. Don't act like we don't know what all this is really for. You don't care about the rest of us so long as it works out for you." Nads abandoned the coffee he was drinking, setting it on the grass in favor of pacing. The Major and Rocky looked at each other as if wondering who should interrupt.

I curled around myself and buried my face in my arms. *All this* included me. Each reminder Uno didn't share my feelings was like a burn on raw flesh.

"You're being kinda intense, cuz," Rocky said.

"I'm being intense?" Nads said, rounding on him.

"It's fine, I get it," Uno said. He put a hand up, and Nads looked at him. "I'm not hiding the fact that I want to use this as a portfolio, but everything I've done is for as many relevant and genuine reasons as it is for media. I want to support people like me, people like all of us in this community."

"Fuck community! Damn it. Fine, can you guarantee they won't drop us?" Nads pushed.

"I couldn't do that even if we said nothing."

"Can't you at least talk to them before you do anything?"

Uno thought about it. "If I start asking them for permission now, I'll probably have to keep asking. I'd rather maintain what control we have."

"Fuck!" Nads kicked his board, and it rolled under the SUV. Nads was almost hoarse with annoyance while Uno's voice was calm, bordering on cheerful. I didn't know Nads as well as I probably should have after the last year-ish, so it was hard to place his intensity. He was starting to rub me the wrong way. I turned to look at Uno. His voice conveyed an easiness I didn't see in his eyes.

"Look, bro," The Major said, "I don't know who shit in your soup today, but you need to lighten up. This is a big deal. We have to stand up for our community and ourselves. But since we all have to be united in it, let's vote." They stood and tried to calm him down.

"Fuck your vote. We all know it's going Uno's way, but I swear if we lose one sponsor dollar, I'm kicking his ass. I just don't get why everyone has to participate. Why does it have to be so public?"

The Major stood. "Nads, it's public because people shouldn't have to put up with this shit privately or silently. It's public so this community that we fucking love and live in has an opportunity to understand how it's hurting people. We are skaters and bikers and bladers, and it shouldn't matter what else we are when we're here."

"Besides," Rocky said, "if they're doing it to us, then they're doing it to someone else. Them's the truths."

Nads could stand up to me or Uno, but he stood no chance against The Major and Rocky. You could see his own realization about it on his face as he listened to them talk. He sighed, his only audible surrender, and went to fish his board out from under the car.

That settled the matter enough for everyone else, and they started asking questions. Uno answered them as they came. It was calm until Uno went into more detail about the shirts, and the team turned into a stampede of opinions. Well, everyone except Nads and me. I watched Uno, awed. He was one of the most efficient people I knew. His confidence was almost unshakable. He turned to me, probably sensing me staring at him. I looked at the ground.

"You still with me on this one?" he asked softly in that way he had that made me feel like the only person in the world. He even leaned in slightly.

"Who the fuck else?"

He smiled. *Fuck me, he's too close.* A panic rose in my chest. I had been stupid last night. I tricked myself into thinking we were…what? Mutually attracted to each other? Was I so touch starved that I really believed he was enjoying holding my hand in the SUV? *I mean, stupid fucking question because yes, you are that touch starved.* But God, the way he looked at me.

There was a hint of something in his eyes that morning, though. He looked at my mouth a lot. Maybe he was doing that so he could understand what I was saying. It was loud, and he probably couldn't hear me. There was a growing dull roar as the other teams started to rouse and the fans started to show up.

"Pirate," he said, his hand coming up as if to touch me.

I stood. I didn't know if I could keep from confessing if he touched me. I refused to be rejected before noon. "I'm gonna go hunt down an energy drink. You want one?"

I was hoping he would take that as a clear sign I didn't want him to come along.

"Sure," he said, his smile never fading.

"I'll go with you." Flip stood.

I shrugged like I didn't care. I did, of course. I popped my board into my hand, and she followed, grabbing one of the spares out of the SUV.

Nads was leaning against the SUV smoking Rocky's vape. As we passed, Nads said, "I really am sorry, Pirate."

I stopped to look at him. He did look sorry in almost equal measure to the anger he was still exuding.

"Are you okay?" I asked, not knowing anything else to say.

He stared for a second, then deflated. "Fine."

Flip and I nodded and kept walking.

"He's in a place," Flip said, looking over her shoulder at him.

I wanted to say more about Nads having the privilege of being cis, white, and straight or at the least passing in all three, that his freakout about what Uno was trying to do didn't really inspire me to empathize with him. Instead, I got on my board.

I expected her to keep talking, especially when we moved out of earshot of the others. She didn't; we just skated. We found a gas station and went in. I filled my arms with energy drinks, and Flip grabbed an orange juice and some honey buns.

"Those aren't all for today, are they?" she asked as I started to pay. My monthly energy drink budget was always near the triple digits.

"Probably. The others'll drink one. Well, not Rocky."

"Not me, either. That stuff makes me feel like I'm gonna burst."

"I'm kinda useless without 'em."

She shrugged. I also grabbed a new pair of shades. That made Flip laugh. I looked at her. Most days Uno was my only friend. The Major, Nads, and Rocky were teammates, which was close, but also different since I was still winning them over. Flip had literally volunteered for the role. I bought a second pair of glasses and gave them to Flip.

"So," she said on our way out. She preened a little in her new shades.

"So?"

"Why'd you snub Uno this morning?"

I cracked a can and stared at her while I took a long, loud sip. Finally, I said, "Who says I snubbed him?"

We were apparently walking back since she made no effort to get on her board.

"I'm saying it. Super shady." She stabbed the orange juice box with the straw and looked at me. She had the presence of a lawyer when she wanted to know something.

I sighed and told her about the vibe in the SUV last night, leaving out some of the conversation. I wouldn't out Uno no matter how much I wanted advice on it, especially if he still had a lot of questions himself. He might not be straight, and that was as terrifying as it was elating. I only told her about my own careless, shameless want flooding the space with pheromones or hormones or whatever it was.

"Dude," she practically cheered. "He wants you back, you big shit."

I groaned. "Or I imagined it all."

"Did he hold your hand?"

"He was comforting me."

"Straight dudes don't comfort their gay friends like that."

"Even if he's not straight, that doesn't make him into me."

"Pirate, you're killing me."

"Why?"

"First, you said he was *too* straight to want to be with you. Now, even if he isn't straight, which it seems like he might not be, you still don't think he'd want you?"

"Yeah."

"But what if he does?"

"That'd almost be worse."

"How?" she screamed, sloshing orange juice on the pavement as she threw her hands in the air.

"Why now?"

"Ugh. God, come get this man."

"Fuck. If he's just now figuring out his sexuality, then I would be some test. I could be a lot of things, but not that. Being some experiment would kill me." I couldn't tell her I was already feeling like Uno was using me. I knew he wasn't, but the sting of his plan and the constant reminders made me feel like dropping into a bowl face first. Maybe I wasn't ready for her to try and reassure me. So, while this wasn't a lie—I did worry about being a test or an experiment—it was only a tiny fraction of my worries overall.

She relented. "Yeah, that does sound tough."

I bowed slightly as a way of thanking her for seeing it my way. She sipped her orange juice and watched me.

"Why are you looking at me like that?"

"I think maybe this isn't all the way about Uno's reaction to *you*."

"I don't know what that means."

She squinted. "Yes, you do."

We locked gazes. It was a stare-off, and we stood eye to eye for a solid minute. When one of us finally blinked—me, of course—we started walking again. The silence returned. *Maybe this isn't all the way about Uno's reaction to you.* Fuck that. She was trying to say my concern was really about my reaction to me. What the fuck *would* I do if he really had feelings for me? What would I do if any man really had feelings for me? I didn't have an answer.

"I don't think it would hurt to tell him," she said.

I groaned. "Can we please stop talking about him? This conversation wouldn't pass the Bechdel test."

She laughed. "First of all, that's between two women. I'm the only woman on the team."

"See, perfect! Tell me about that."

She rolled her eyes and obliged, telling me about how it felt to have joined us and how it felt to participate in the competition.

Back at camp, the teams were already gathering around the roped-off section of the park. Waste and the judges had arrived and were setting up in the grass. I found Uno leaning against a fence on the edge of the park talking to someone. He was handsome with half-black, half-blond hair, and he was wearing a grandpa sweater. I steeled myself and walked over. It wasn't jealousy, at least not the romantic kind. I was self-doubting enough to believe even my friendship with Uno was hanging in the balance constantly. I would not be surprised if one day he walked up with someone and said, "Hey, Pirate, here's my best friend," bringing me down a peg or two. I would be decimated but not surprised.

"There's your better half," the handsome dude said with a wink.

Uno turned and smiled at me. "Pirate, this is Matty. He works at the T-shirt shop."

"The shirts are done already?" I asked. "You sent that email like an hour ago."

"I maybe sent it last night in the hopes that it would all work out."

Matty raked his hair back with his fingers, his hand lingering on his neck. "They were simple enough. I did it in like forty minutes. It's not every day you get an emergency email from local celebrities."

Uno rolled his eyes. "Ay Dios, please."

Matty laughed.

"We have to go," Uno said, waving.

Matty and I locked eyes for a moment. I had a morbid curiosity about him. He looked at me with an interest that matched my own. I understood. Matty had rushed the order because he had feelings for Uno, who was completely oblivious. I had the sudden urge to shake Matty's hand as comrades in unrequited love. Instead, we waved at each other, and I followed Uno back to the others. I was pretty sure Matty had sized me up in much the same way.

"Here," I said, trying to hand Uno an energy drink.

"Here yourself." He smiled and took the can, putting a shirt in its place.

"That was really fast," I said again.

"Matty's the best."

Yeesh, I'm sure he is...so great...so fucking perfect for you. Great. "Have you known him long?"

Uno thought about it. "No. He made our team shirts last year. His shop also has a line of merch for you specifically that's been okayed by the sponsor. I think they're even going to put some in a Sk8Box. I'm hoping DropCloth won't shit too many bricks knowing we used Matty's store for the shirts. I couldn't wait. Besides, they can make the rest for the fans."

"Don't tell Nads. He's already gonna murder you about the sponsors."

"What's his problem anyway? I know he doesn't like me, but this seems worse."

"I don't know, man," I said with a sigh.

"Well, I have it under control. Bored read my email already."

"I don't think you know what under control means." I was teasing but was surprised anyway when he just laughed. I didn't want to talk about the sponsors or Nads. "I have merch?"

Uno smirked. "You know you can access your own Insta any time you want."

I never wanted. I considered the shirt in my hands. It was black with white letters. *Mr. Fairy* was crossed out and *#sk8equal* was printed under it. I looked at the organizations on the back. One was a very minor sponsor affiliate who split the profits on their products between themselves and nonprofit organizations. The other seven were various, mostly local LGBTQIA+ groups.

"Is it okay?" he asked.

I lowered the shirt. He was standing right in front of me, his brown-red lips right in my line of sight. I had to swallow before I could answer. "It's great. You sure you can handle the fallout from this?"

"Fallout? Fallout! What's with that? Between you and the sponsor and Nads, all I hear about is fallout."

"Chill, bro, shit. I'm, you know, worried." I pulled off the shirt I was wearing and put on Uno's campaign shirt.

His expression softened. "Right, Pirate, lo siento. Pero I got this. I'm a professional."

I rolled my eyes. He laughed. The problem with the absolute optimism Uno lived by was that when doing the math for one of his plans, he always set the consequence factor to zero. He wasn't ever worried about it because he simply didn't think it would happen.

The first official tournament of CASST was a last-man-standing skate-off. The first elimination round was a fast-paced obstacle course, and with sixty skaters to get through, it was important that it went smoothly. The first elimination left the top thirty, the second—with an added obstacle—narrowed it down to the top sixteen, and from there, it was a regular person-versus-person tournament where the tricks were generated by the competition organizers.

The team had put on their new shirts, even Nads. Rocky had to remove the sleeves first. We joined the crowd. I worked hard to ignore the buzz around us, the word "shirt" coming up more than usual. The others didn't seem to notice everyone else reacting.

"Y'all, let's do this," Rocky said, jumping on mine and Uno's shoulders. We shoved him away with a laugh.

"You ready?" Uno asked me.

"Always. Look, I don't want you to feel bad. Remember when *I* win, our team wins."

"Huh, if I remember right, someone took thirty-ninth last year," he said smugly, adjusting the gloves he liked to wear. They were more for show than protection. "How far away is that from first?"

"If I recall, someone else took fortieth," I said, feeling a genuine burst of competitiveness. I put my helmet on my head but didn't buckle it.

"No sé, pero ya veremos."

"I like your optimism, but competing for second and third is a little silly. I guess I'll save you a seat when I take first," Flip added, coming up between us.

I shook my head.

Waste called roll and announced the first set of skaters. There were ten in each heat, so we were looking at six rounds for the first elimination. No one from The Major Leaguers was called first. We watched from the sidelines, getting a vicarious feel for the course as the first ten skaters worked through it. The most successful seemed to get out of the middle of the crowd earliest, either by pulling ahead looking for speed points or falling behind looking for trick points. One person missed a rail and ate shit, snapping a board using mostly his face. He was probably out for the rest of the event.

"Don't worry," The Major said. We applauded the guy as he walked away with the paramedics. "Every team in that round has barely half our points."

Uno was the first up from our team, joining the third round of skaters. He rolled into the line. To advance you had to do three of the four tricks and use two of three obstacles before time ran out.

"Oh shit," The Major said, pointing.

The rest of us looked up. The guy who had harassed us yesterday was in line to the left of Uno. Being himself, Uno joked with the skater to his right, not obviously ignoring Bigot Guy, but also not giving him any attention. Bigot Guy, however, couldn't pull his eyes away from Uno.

"That guy looks like he wants to kill him," Flip said.

I was grinding my teeth. At the whistle, they were off. Uno pulled ahead, which meant he had his pick of obstacles. He chose the 5-0 on the rail, but out of nowhere, Bigot Guy fell in behind Uno and clipped his fin with his foot. If you didn't know skateboarding, you'd just see the two skaters competing for space on the rail and colliding. If you did know skateboarding, you'd know Bigot Guy was aiming to take Uno down. Uno's 5-0 was ruined, and the other guy raced on ahead, not actually performing a trick. Uno needed to land the rest of the tricks to place. Uno laughed it off and skated well enough to qualify.

"That was fun," he said, trotting back to us.

"That guy—" The Major and I said at the same time.

He shook his head. "It's all good. I placed, so fuck it."

The Major flapped their hands in helpless annoyance and went to line up for their own match.

"Uno," I said, not willing to let it drop.

He looked at me, his eyes betraying a small amount of trepidation. "I know, okay? I know it was on purpose. Pero, what's it matter now?"

"You both placed," I said as a warning. "And he has teammates."

He nodded. "Claro, so do I. We probably won't be in the same heat again."

I stared at him through narrow eyes. He smiled, not his show smile, but that same comforting smile he usually gave me when we were alone.

"Can you fucks focus?" Nads said, coming out of nowhere.

I nodded and turned to watch The Major skate. By the end of the first placement round, our whole team was in the top thirty. There was a thirty-minute break. I went to get another energy drink. Uno went to work the crowd. I had just found my backpack in the SUV when someone called my name. I turned and saw three of the guys from the environmental activist team. They strolled over, looking like burlap sacks in their hemp outfits and smelling of sunscreen that was also probably hemp.

"What's up?" I asked, trying not to sound weary.

"Wow, man, we wanted to say we got mad respect for your cause," the blond one said.

I nodded and tried to look grateful.

"Seriously," added one of the others, a guy wearing a bucket hat. "We thought y'all were full of shit before, but now we fuck with ya."

"Excuse me?"

"Yeah man, we knew Uno was down for anything to get the W, but you seemed like you had more going on, ya know." That was blondie again.

"What, this doesn't count as doing anything for the win?" I asked, pointing to the neck tattoo. The three guys laughed.

"I guess...but marriage to a straight guy, bro?" the third one I named Freckles said.

I felt a prickle of annoyance. "What about it?"

They shrugged. Freckles continued, "Man, it didn't check out, but we get it now."

"What the fuck are you talking about?"

"Bro, I know we don't have a reputation of being the smartest, but we figured it out eventually. This campaign is pretty cool. I like the juxtaposition of gay rights—"

"LGBT, man," Bucket Hat said, hitting him.

"Right, LGBT rights and immigration. Two of the biggest issues in the country today. Legit." Blondie actually bowed in respect.

They respected the awareness campaign that Uno had designed. And up until I had married Uno, they had respected me. They respected me again after they came to their own conclusion that the marriage intentionally led to the campaign. It was the most logical fuckery I had heard in a while. Uno hadn't put anything about the marriage in the social media posts about the campaign, but it really wasn't that hard to see how a person could make the leap that the environmentalists had.

"Well, we workshopped trying to squeeze in global warming, but we couldn't get a polar bear in time," I said. I didn't want to talk to these guys anymore. I recognized my tone shift to impolite even if they didn't.

"Legit, bro, but hey, we got you covered, you know." Freckles held up his board. Their team had decks made from recycled materials.

I said, "What're you guys called again?"

"Team G House Gas," they said together, forming drunk-looking Gs with their hands.

"No, I know that, I mean your names..." I didn't add that I usually relied on Uno for names.

"I'm Benny, that's Chive, and Lil' Steve." Blondie-Benny said, introducing Chive-Bucket Hat and Lil' Steve-Freckles respectively.

"Thanks, guys. We should probably get back over there."

They laughed and walked away. I pretended to follow, but let the distance between us grow.

Great. *Fuck my feelings, I guess.* It was one thing for people to think we got married just for the points—*which you did, loser, and for no other reason.* But now the marriage was a part of the *campaign.* Fuck! Did those guys even realize we were actually being harassed? *Good, now if I confess, that will be all part of some epic social message and not because I love him.* I walked back to the competition feeling completely out of sync with reality. *All a part of some/epic social message not/because I love him:* right number of syllables, shitty poem.

Chapter Seven

Arturo

I looked around for Pirate. Ever since waking with his hand on my wrist, I felt like I was constantly looking for him. I should have been focusing on the competition and monitoring the reaction to the campaign on social media. Thankfully I was good at delegating, and Rocky was good at listening. After about twenty minutes of glancing around, I spotted Pirate walking back from the car, his expression a void.

Weird. Shouldn't he be happy? He was in the top thirty—fuck, we *all* were in the top thirty. I wondered what happened. I started toward him but didn't get very far before a set of fans stopped me. I spoke to them and kept an eye on Pirate. He fell in with Flip. Waste called the next heat, and I went to stand with my team. I stepped in behind Pirate, but he acted as if he didn't even know I was there. That was weird too. I was used to him turning to talk to me, seeing me.

"Hey," I said, putting a hand on his shoulder.

He jumped.

"Shit, siento," I said.

"I was just trying to focus." And he said no more.

I could feel Flip's eyes on me, but I didn't look at her. This competition season was turning out to be the source of more new feelings than I had ever had in my life. We watched Nads eat shit during his heat, taking him out of the competition. Rocky made it through. Then it was my turn again. As I skated over, I noticed I was with that dick who had tried to knock me off a rail.

I looked over my shoulder. Pirate's expression was tense. I hadn't expected to have to skate with that guy again. I closed my eyes and took a deep breath. Thinking about Pirate or the asshole skater wouldn't help me win. *Focus*. I tried to put another skater between us. She didn't seem to notice the tension. The asshole, on the other hand, stared straight at me. I kept my eyes forward. The bell rang, and I let the group pull in front of me. I didn't want to have a run-in with that guy again, so even if I took a hit on time, I could complete enough tricks to place. I banged out two, no issue. Then I landed an invert and heard my cheer from the crowd. "If you know, you Uno," they chanted. I coasted to wave at the onlookers along the fence. Which meant I wasn't paying attention to the other skaters.

I was off my board and on my ass so fast I didn't even know it until that guy was towering over me. I had even less time than that to register the flash that was Pirate coming between us. Pirate shoved the guy back. The guy looked like he was going to shove Pirate but instead elbowed him across the mouth. Everything seemed to freeze. I had once seen Pirate walk away from taking a rail to the teeth with dry eyes. All he said was he had two older brothers. So it was also no surprise that Pirate remained on his feet and wiped the blood off his mouth. His smile was a sneer of rage.

"What the fuck is your problem?" Pirate asked in a low voice. Flip helped me to my feet. The others fell in behind Pirate, shielding me from the guy.

"Hey man, I was just skating," the guy said, putting his hands up. "I don't know why you pushed me."

"Just skating? Like hell," Pirate said. "We watched you come after him."

"Don't worry, princess, your beaner's gonna be fin—"

The rest of the guy's words were lost under Pirate's fist. The guy stumbled back, probably both not expecting the punch nor expecting Pirate to be able to throw one as hard as he could. I had seen his brothers; they were massive.

"Fuck," The Major and I said together. We pulled Pirate back just as the guy's teammates, an organizer, and Waste walked up. They had been watching the whole time but had only just made it through the crowd to intervene.

"Enough! Pirate and Mickey, you're both disqualified from this event," the organizer shouted.

"What the fuck! I didn't do anything," Mickey shouted back. "*He* punched *me*."

"Keep talking, and it'll be the rest of the competition. Or worse, the rest of your team," Waste said.

Mickey turned on us and pointed a finger. Pirate stared as if daring him. Mickey snatched his board from his buddy and stalked off. Half the crowd cheered. The other half booed. Pirate didn't say anything, he turned and started walking the other way. Flip even tried to hand him his board. He didn't take it. Fuck. It happened so fast, I could not register a single emotion. Everything I felt came and went, not sticking because I was so surprised.

"The Major, get your team under control. This is a warning." The organizer handed The Major a points deduction card. Everyone groaned, and Nads started to argue with the official.

My shock was ebbing, so I turned and walked away. The only thing I felt by the time I caught up to Pirate was guilt. I snagged his arm to try and get him to stop moving. I could hear the commotion behind us, but it felt like we were a million miles away. My hand closing on his skin made me feel like no one else could see us, like when that hobbit put on the ring.

"Pirate."

"Uno," Pirate said, shaking me off. But he stopped walking and turned. His eyes were so turbulent that I couldn't think of any words. He continued. "Just go skate. Win."

"Thomas, I—"

"He called me princess. If you're gonna insult me, you could at least call me the highest title. Queen is a queer reference anyway," Thomas scoffed. It was a joke, but there was more there that he didn't say.

"That was fucking wild, dude," I said, ignoring the queen comment.

He grinned a little. "It was stupid."

"This is CASST. I'm surprised there's only been one punch thrown so far."

"It's only the first group event," he said, smiling all the way. "Don't get any ideas. I can't punch everyone for you."

"I don't expect you to punch anyone for me. I'm sorry that happened." I couldn't figure out what else to say. Should I tell him he was right about people coming for us? Well, it was too late to do things differently. But what could I say to Thomas about it?

Instead of saying anything, I took his hand and inspected it. It was red where it wasn't tattooed. Some of it was blood. Most of it was from the raw impact. Once his hand was in mine, though, I didn't want to let it go, so I didn't. I pulled him slightly closer and looked at his face. It was red, and his lips had a slight bloody tint.

"Is it your teeth or just your lip?" I asked. I had to swallow. I was now trying to find a place to put all the energy my body had stored from the conflict. Standing with Thomas, so close, made that fuel quicken, racing all over my body.

"Lip. I think he snagged my ring," Thomas said, tonguing the metal loop. He made a scrunched face. "I think it's bent."

I wanted to touch him, run my finger over his lips as if to check for myself. He sensed me coming, though, and stepped back. His hand caught mine midair and pushed it back toward me.

"Are they gonna kick us out?" Thomas asked. He closed off physically, wrapping his arms around himself, his eyes going to his feet.

"No, they threatened the other team with it, but I can't believe they actually would kick anyone out, which is probably part of why that guy thinks he can get away with all this. Are you going to—"

"I'm fine. Go skate, man. I'm gonna go nap in the car."

I watched him walk away.

I can't punch everyone for you.

The farther he got from me, the more the world returned. I gained awareness of the crowds, and the noise was like waking. The feeling I got when he was around was starting to feel mystic or fae or encantado. I went back to the park.

"How ya doing, buddy?" Rocky asked as I joined him on the edge of the course.

"I'm fine," I said. I didn't know how I was feeling. "How's everyone else?"

"Nads talked the officials out of docking our points. He cited your campaign and the email you had sent. Once the officials realized Mickey was the same guy from the deck, they backed down."

"Nads did that?"

Rocky looked at me like I had said the strangest thing. "Nads isn't a bad guy. He's annoying and competitive, sure, so maybe he did it all to keep the lead. Who knows. Either way, he did it because he cares about this."

I hoped Nads cared. I hoped that about everyone, but it was interesting that the news would come from Rocky, who for the first time seemed like he was in a somber mood.

When I didn't say anything else, he tossed an arm over my shoulder. "It sucks that people keep fucking with you and Pirate, bro. But I guess with Pirate around, you don't really need anyone else to watch your back. That guy's like a super soldier. He was so fast! But either way we got you, too."

I looked at Rocky. He was taller than me by a few inches. He smiled down at me. This team really was different from our last.

"Thanks, man."

"Sure, and let me know if you want to talk or something."

He didn't wait for me to say anything. He crossed to Flip, who was going to skate next.

❖

By the time we got to the top four, it was five p.m. and everyone was flagging. After a break for food, the last three rounds would start at eight. To my surprise and pretty much everyone else's, The Major and I were still in the running. If we beat the other two skaters, we wouldn't have to compete against each other for first or second, and even if we both lost, we'd still get points. The Major was explaining and calculating as we arrived back at the SUV. I didn't know if anyone else had noticed, but no one from Mickey's team placed. They hadn't even stuck around, leaving after their last guy was dropped.

Pirate was sitting in the open side door, talking on his phone. He was smiling, so he was talking to either his sister or one of his many nieces. His expression fell when he saw us. He told whoever it was that he had to go.

"Well?" he asked as he stood.

"We're in, boi!" The Major shouted, lifting Pirate off the ground in a hug.

"Fuck, yeah!" Pirate said as The Major spun him around. The lower left of his face was turning the slightest purple. Back on the ground, Pirate turned to the rest of us. "Look, I'm sorry I got kicked out. I just reacted."

"Don't worry, P, we get it," The Major said.

"You just got to him first, bro," Rocky said, winding up his fists and pretending to step up to Nads. Flip didn't say anything. She flopped in the grass near the car.

"Don't be so fucking careless next time," Nads said. I thought about what Rocky said about Nads standing up for us, but I didn't say anything.

The Major thumped Nads in the chest. "Can you be cool for even two seconds?"

Then The Major turned to the rest of us. "We're in this together, okay? Yes, try to keep it within the fucking rules, but we aren't going to let anyone shit on us, either."

"Amen." Rocky laughed.

"Well said. I figured you could use some dinner."

We all jumped a little and turned. The person who spoke to us had a deep voice, was fem presenting, and seemed unfamiliar. Well, not *totally* unfamiliar. I squinted at them. *Do I know her?* No one else reacted; they only stared. She was wearing a DropCloth hoodie dress and black boots. She could have been anyone, but I thought I knew the voice.

"Who are you?" I asked.

The woman laughed and held up bags of Styrofoam containers. "You, Uno, probably wouldn't know my name if I told you since you insist on calling me Boss."

"Oh shit," I said, placing the way she said my name, "it's a sponsor."

"Which one?" The Major asked, standing and trying to look professional all of a sudden. "I mean, hello."

"The main one," the woman said, her hands full. "I represent Bored Skateboards."

"Rachel Weise," I clarified, landing on the name.

"Thank you, Ms. Weise, we didn't expect—"

Weise came into our little circle and handed a bag to Flip on her right and a second to Rocky on her left. "I know, I wasn't expected. We're having a meeting. And don't call me Ms.; Rachel is fine."

"I didn't bring my *meeting* fork," Rocky said, casually looking in the bag.

That threw Weise off enough that she turned in a circle, not sure where to place herself.

"Wanna sit down?" Pirate said, pointing to a board so Weise wouldn't have to sit on the ground. All of the camp chairs were already packed into the SUV, thanks to Nads. Pirate took the bag from Rocky, and he and Flip made sure people got some food. He handed me a box with a small smile.

"You aren't dropping us, are ya?" Nads asked. His usual gruffness was gone. He sounded like a kid who was on the verge of getting detention.

"No," Weise said, sitting stiffly on the offered board. The silver chains on her leather wristbands jingled. "I'm here to make a proposal."

We all waited. She seemed surprised we were going to hear her out. I couldn't blame her. I spent a lot of time on the phone with the sponsors trying to end the calls. I bet she expected everyone else to be as impatient as I was.

She cleared her throat. "There's obviously been a huge reaction to the campaign you launched this morning. And the wedding, of course. Fake marriages sell, I guess."

Weise looked at me, and I offered my best look of innocence. Her expression clearly said the campaign wasn't in the plan we discussed. She wasn't wrong, I hadn't known it was going to happen until last night. I didn't react, so she moved on.

"We like the energy it's getting, but it's taking on a life of its own too fast. The recent altercation is amplifying that."

"That's fair," Rocky said. "Uno and I have talked about it. It's a mixed reaction on our platforms. Some are on our side, some are not, and some are just confused. It's hard to keep the situation at the top of their feeds. The confusion eased after Uno pinned the main campaign messages. They are working and getting a lot of traffic. Uno and I are both answering messages now."

"And we're matching the minimums I outlined in the email. It also doesn't help that the team account is younger than our personal ones, but since we all shared from the main account post, we're still getting decent click-throughs," I said.

"Right," Weise said, looking surprised again. Rocky's media management skills were on par with mine, even without my degrees. Weise shook her head and continued. "Well, our proposal should help. Bored Skateboards thinks we need to either back down or focus the conversation in a way that gives us more control. Despite never being consulted, your sponsor supports this. We picked your team and you as skaters to support for a reason. Bored Skateboards is limited in its reactivity, but DropCloth and Sk8Box can be more visible immediately."

"We aren't backing down," I said. The Major made a sound of affirmation.

"I figured," Weise said, pulling papers out of her satchel. "That's why I propose this."

She handed The Major the packet of pages. "I want you all, and specifically those two, to do a series of interest pieces for a magazine—"

"Which one? *Time*? *Esquire*? *Playboy*?" Rocky interrupted. Nads shoved him and told him to shut up.

"For *Contend*."

"The queer magazine?" Nads said.

Weise nodded. "For LGBTQIA+ sports and athletics. *Contend* is often picked up by other platforms since it's a no-charge digital magazine, and they have a growing audience base as well as a dedicated set of subscribers. Plus, their content aligns with the story."

"It's not just a story, it's our lives," Pirate said. I looked at him. The tone in his comment wasn't rude or contentious. He said it as a way to remind someone representing a company that they were working with real people. He heard the money in her proposal.

Weise nodded. "Sure, but you're also the ones who went public with everything, and if this is going to continue, you might as well make sure the story others repeat and share is the one you want them to. And, yes, make a few more dollars in the process."

Pirate rolled his eyes and looked at the grass.

"Pirate, this magazine cares about how it represents the people it features and won't tarnish their reputation by telling a bad or…hurtful story," Weise said. I was surprised she would think to say that to Pirate.

"If we don't do the human interest story?" I asked.

"Then nothing new gets posted about this, it ends with the end of the day minus whatever the fans say about it, you go back to dressing like you pulled your clothes out of the trunks of your cars, and the competition goes on."

"Fuck. That's easy enough," Nads said. He obviously wanted the whole thing to end. He seemed relieved until he looked around and saw no one else agreed. "You can't be serious."

"What does the magazine need from us?" Flip asked.

"Well, they proposed a three-issue story. Part one will introduce everyone. Part two will introduce the details of the campaign and the competition. The last part will wrap it up, more or less. The reporter will stay with you all the rest of the competition to observe and do his thing."

"God damn it. Why can't this be over?" Nads said.

"You're the one most concerned with money," I said to him. "This lady is offering a chance at more. At the minimum, we get paid for getting more followers."

Rocky added from his other side, "Dude, we got a thousand new followers today alone."

"Fuck a duck," Nads groaned. "Do whatever you want."

"When would the reporter show up?" The Major asked.

"You have an interview scheduled on Tuesday at your house," Weise said directly to Pirate and me.

I looked around the circle, getting nods of confirmation from everyone. Pirate stared at me so intensely, he would have sliced me in half if he had laser vision. I knew he was looking for reassurance. I smiled and thought *If you're with me, I'm with you.* Finally, he nodded.

"Let's do it," I said.

Weise looked pleased and stood. "Great. I'll email you. Also, Pirate…"

Pirate looked up at her.

"Don't punch anyone else. The audience likes it, but it makes the shareholders nervous, and they sign the checks."

Pirate didn't say anything. He inspected his red, slightly swollen knuckles.

"Flip, if I could have a word with you. Since you're new to the team, there are some things I want to go over."

"Okay," she said, rising.

They walked off.

❖

The night ended with The Major in third and me in fourth. It was a pretty happy victory; points were points, and we were still in the lead. But Nads's bad mood and Pirate's absence from the final leg of the event made for a quiet drive home. Pirate and I didn't even sit together. Flip was already in the back seat with him when I got in the SUV. I shouldn't have been surprised by my jealousy. I was a piñata of new emotions. Not that jealousy itself was new. I did have two sisters, after all, and I was the youngest. But I had never been jealous of someone for simply getting to talk to someone else. Someone I wanted to myself.

They dropped us off without much fanfare, and Pirate let us into the house.

"You okay?" I asked him.

He nodded. "Tired is all."

"I..." But I didn't know how that sentence ended. I mostly wanted to keep him in front of me, in my line of sight. But he didn't stay. He said good night and went to his room.

CHAPTER EIGHT

Thomas

I knew I wouldn't be able to sleep, so I didn't even try. I hadn't slept Saturday night after the event and had slogged through Sunday. I pretended to go to bed but I paced my room until I heard Arturo go to bed, and I iced my hand in the kitchen. Then I just lay there on my bed staring out the window. Someone had painted over it with something semi-opaque and iridescent so the neighbors couldn't see in. It made the light that did shine through look like glitter.

I was terrified by the idea of having a piece in a magazine written about us. First of all, it would be about *me*, and second, it would be in a magazine. *Anyone could get access to that*. At least with social media, I could pretend it didn't exist since I never personally checked it. But a magazine! Even a digital one was different, maybe more permanent. What if it came out that the Eco Guys, and my worst thoughts, were right? What if I really was just part of his campaign and his plan for a career?

I knew I was his friend, I knew the marriage was for CASST, and I knew the campaign was for justice or some shit. That was how it happened chronologically. But that didn't stop my trauma brain from running away with the idea that I was part of some show to make Uno and Pirate famous. Just like I had been part of my mom's mission to prove to her church how devout and worthy she was.

I took a deep breath and went to my desk. I pulled out a note and wrote. Another of Richard the Therapist's rules was *If you're thinking of your mother, write a poem about you.*

I wrote:

You are who you are
Not what she tried to make you
Give it back to them
They once sold cocaine
labeling it medicine
people get stuff wrong

I wrote a handful more, trying to work the line *the Eco Guys were at least cute* into something. I scrapped that one. It did make me feel better. I stood and put the new stickies on the wall with the others. There were so many.

I could tell it was morning because I was getting hungry. I went to the kitchen. If the stove clock was right, a fifty-fifty shot, it was six thirty a.m. I took a box of cereal along with all the fixin's into the living room. Light from the sun rising was starting to pour into the window, tinting the shabby room yellow.

Oh shit. What a fucking dungeon. It was like I was seeing our living room for the first time. It looked like we lived in a prison. We had nothing on the walls, shit was still in boxes, and it was about half as furnished as it should have been. The HGTV voice in my head scolded me. It would be a cold day in hell before I let anyone into this fucking apartment with it looking the way it did. I took the box of cereal with me and left.

When I got back at ten, Arturo still wasn't up. It wasn't like him to sleep in, but this weekend had been a lot. I had also heard him moving around his room much later than usual. I tried to set everything down quietly. I had bought a few hundred dollars' worth of decorations, some furnishings, and a couch cover. It was all from fairly cheap places, so there was way more stuff than I had intended. I had rented one of the city's park and go cars and had gotten all the stuff up the stairs to the door in two trips, even with an aching hand.

I almost got it all into the apartment without making a sound, but of course, I was betrayed by floating shelves. As I turned to pull the ottoman through the door, a bag I had over my shoulder snagged one of the five-foot planks. The first shelf tipped into the second, and that toppled a side table with all the hardware I had bought on it. I practically jumped out of my skin in the cacophony of banging that followed. The last sound was the tittering of a hundred screws rolling around on the hardwood.

"Fuck." I slumped and let go of the door, which banged shut, scaring me again. "Shit."

"At least we don't have downstairs neighbors. What the fuck are you doing?" Arturo asked.

I looked down the hall and immediately forgot what words were. He was leaning in his doorway, wearing only black sweatpants. Hello, wet dream. *Dude, this is your fucking friend.* Still, he was beautiful. His black hair was tousled and surrounded his sleepy face. His skin was warm, deep, coppery brown. He had a wolf tattoo on one pec. I stared. What else could I do?

"Thomas?"

"I'm…um…chillin'." I shrugged, helpless to find words and look at him at the same time. I had seen him shirtless a hundred times. But this was the first time seeing him shirtless and knowing what his hand felt like holding mine, what his lips felt like.

He rubbed his eyes and came down the hall. The smile on his face let me know that he was game for whatever I was planning. He said, "Right. I hear you chillin'. What's all this stuff, though?"

"Stuff?" I said, finding my composure. I looked at the stuff and was reminded that our house looked like we had moved in yesterday. I gestured at the apartment feeling my anxiety-fueled enthusiasm ramp back up. "Look around, Art. It's like two frat guys live here."

He looked around. "That bad?"

"If we were even one percent worse, our couch would be made of dairy crates."

He laughed. "Okay, okay. Well, I have to work today, but I can help you with whatever when I get home."

I nodded. "I can probably do it myself."

I moved to pick up the fallen shelf. His hand caught my wrist. I looked at him. He was an arm's length away but felt too close. His black eyes caught the light with an amused gleam.

"Thomas, I want to help, so save me something. Bien?"

"Okay, sure," I said, hoping he'd understand there was no guarantee.

"Do you want breakfast?" He let me go.

I didn't answer.

"Fine, you're getting eggs."

I smiled to myself and started emptying the bags.

❖

Arturo almost got a hammer to the face when he came in after his shift. Rather than doing anything else to get my attention, he came up behind me. He pinched my side and I screamed. I lowered the hammer when I realized it was him. He was snorting with laughter.

"You got lucky," I said, pulling my earbuds out.

He shrugged it off. "It looks great in here. Where the fuck did you get all this stuff?"

He was admiring the black floating shelves I'd put up across the room. They'd been a steal at the thrift store. That had taken most of the morning since the shelves were about thirty separate pieces with no instructions. I had unpacked some of the knickknacky shit we both had, and I tossed some of our old skate gear up there in a way that looked cool. There were some other things: the end table, the striped couch cover, a poster.

"It's a start," I demurred. I turned back to the curtain rod bracers I was trying to hang. Someone had hung the last ones with nails, and I was trying to yank those out to put in my screws. "How was work?"

Arturo sat on the floor and started threading the curtain rings on the rod, adding the heavy teal material as he went. He told me about work in a few brief sentences, then he went back to asking me about the stuff I had planned for the apartment.

"I want to put that wallpaper up for an accent. Then hang the pictures that you see around."

"What kind of wallpaper? Flowers?"

"If it was?"

"Well, I've only ever seen two kinds of wallpaper—flowers and stripes."

"Why wouldn't it be stripes?"

He laughed. "I don't know. You seem more flowers than stripes to me."

I *was* more flowers than stripes, our new couch cover notwithstanding, but I didn't say anything.

"I guess I've seen duckies in a bathroom once."

That made us both laugh.

I said, "Well, it's not duckies. It's a pinstripe-style skull and crossbones."

"I can help with that."

I was about to step down from the ladder to get my drill, but he stood and tried to hand me the assembled curtain rod.

"You don't have to. I realize this is *my* anxiety project."

"Do you not want me to help?" he asked.

I looked at him. He wasn't prone to self-consciousness. I knew if I told him to stay, I was admitting to something. So maybe that's what he was feeling too? Maybe he was saying something? He held my gaze.

"Do you know anything about hanging wallpaper?" I asked.

He smiled. "No, but I'm ready. And I think I can put up with you micromanaging me through it."

"Hand me that drill," I said with a sigh.

I wasn't ashamed of my work history, but it wasn't glamorous or interesting compared to skateboarding, so people didn't really get to know that side of me. My brother's business partner got me my first job with his son-in-law's construction company. Then I helped my brother with his land appraisal business and my sister with her real estate business. So I had a lot of feelings about home design. Arturo asked a lot of questions about it and genuinely listened to the answers. He was helpful, followed my instructions, and made it look easy since he was so intuitive and careful. When we finished the wallpaper, he offered to make dinner.

"No, I'll make dinner. You made breakfast." I liked getting to cook for him. He enjoyed cooking more than I did, but if it was for him, I would at least attempt to make something edible.

He grinned and nodded. "Thanks. I've heard of newlyweds nesting, but this is way nicer than I expected."

"Go fuck yourself, Art." I sighed hoping my face wasn't red even though I could feel the heat on my cheeks.

He pointed to the pictures I had leaning against the walls and said, "You want me to hang these?"

"Can you? Properly, I mean?"

"Yeah, sure. They have glue on the back, like envelopes, right? Mejor empieza a lamer."

I ignored him and went on the hunt for all the ingredients for spaghetti.

"Seriously though, bro, is all this for the reporter, or were you watching HGTV all night?" he called.

"The reporter."

"Are you worried? What're you worried about?" he asked.

"I don't know how to explain it."

"If it matters, I'm pretty worried too."

I stepped back to look at him in the hall, hammer in hand. He was working on more abandoned nails. When he turned, he grinned at me over his shoulder. "I mean, yeah. Or maybe I'm nervous. Worried sounds old. I'm excited to do it, but I kinda want to barf too."

"If you're excited, what's the problem?"

"Well, what if they ask me a question I don't know the answer to?"

He leaned in the doorway with his arms crossed. I turned off the water for the pot I was filling and gave him my attention. "What kind of question?" I said.

"What if they ask me what your favorite color is? Or your favorite sport?"

I laughed and maybe even blushed. "First of all, they won't ask you about me, and second of all, you don't know my favorite color?"

He smiled at me. "Naw, I do. It's no color or all colors, you choose a different one every time someone asks. And your favorite sport is baseball. But that doesn't mean I have all the answers. People don't know what they don't know, you know? Besides, why wouldn't they ask me about you?"

"They'll probably ask you about yourself."

"Well, you're a part of me, right? Oh! Mira, I don't know what your second grade teacher was called."

"Neither do I." I blinked, not able to come up with her name. I would probably have been able to remember if he hadn't said I was a part of him. What in the actual fuck does that mean? A part of him.

He laughed. "Great. So now they're for sure going to ask that and neither of us know."

"You're ridiculous. They aren't going to ask about second grade."

He continued speculating on questions as he turned back to the wall and started measuring out the space for the pictures. I watched him for a minute more, then went back to my cooking. It had worked, the sly bastard. His teasing really did help me feel less worried. They were only going to ask about me, and while that was scary, I knew all the answers. We sat on our couch to eat. We usually sat at the table, but I had covered it in random crap. It was only spaghetti, but somehow it was fucking amazing.

"Mira," Art said after a few minutes. He put two pills on the coffee table near me.

"What're those?"

"It's allergy medicine, but the drowsy kind."

I met his eyes. He was going to drug me to sleep. It was kind of fucked up that allergy medicine knocked me out in a way no sleeping pill ever had.

"If I take that, I'll sleep through to next week," I said.

He laughed. "No, you won't. I'll wake you."

"What about the rest of the shit I have to do?"

"You already told me what you were doing. I can finish it."

I stared at the pills. His hand fell on my knee. *God, has he always been this touchy?* I had to work really hard to act casual about the contact.

"I want you to take care of yourself. And since you don't on your own, I'm going to at least do what I can. You don't have to take them, of course. There's no judgment at all. But if you haven't slept since yesterday, you should."

I groaned and downed the pills with a mouth full of noodles. He would never know how much his caring about me mattered. I had told Richard the Therapist once about occasionally using allergy medicine as a sleep aid. He definitely didn't condone it. He did almost agree later, though, that my new coping skills were better than getting shitfaced every night on stolen booze like I used to do in high school.

"Hey," Arturo said, shaking my leg slightly. I blinked and looked at him. He smiled. "You looked pretty far away just now."

"I was. Thanks, though. I know people need sleep. I've seen the slasher movies."

"Okay. I'm here if you do want to talk. Anyway, don't worry about the rest of the apartment. I have it covered. How hard could it be? It's just a nail or two, right?"

I didn't bother saying anything because I knew he was trying to annoy me. I must have made a face, though, because he giggled. We ate and I did dishes while he cleared the trash from the living room. I yawned.

"Good, now go to bed," Arturo said, taking the sponge from me.

"It's only nine thirty."

He smiled. "Yup. Plenty of time to get the eight to twenty hours of sleep you usually need."

I didn't fight him. I was asleep before I even realized it. I woke to the sound of my phone ringing. It felt like I had just lain down. By the light in the room, I knew I had slept all night. I sat up and looked at the time on my phone. It was ten. I had one missed call from my brother. I crawled out of bed and went to the living room, anxious that the house was a mess.

"Fuck."

I was amazed. Arturo was cleaning. He really had finished my vision for the room. I had wanted to put the entertainment center up against the wallpaper so the big skull looked like it was staring at you over the TV, but that also meant rotating the coffee table and couch. He had done all of that and hung the rest of the pictures.

"You did it," I said.

He jumped, dropping the DustBuster. "Fuck."

I laughed.

"Morning." He grinned, picking up the vacuum and turning it off. "How'd you sleep?"

That wasn't sleep, that was a long blink. "Great, but don't get all smug about it."

"I didn't say anything. What do you want to do this morning? I'm pretty much done."

"Do? What do you mean *do*? I have like five hours to finish cleaning everything else before the reporter comes."

"What's everything else?"

"My room, the bathroom, the kitchen."

"The bathroom and the kitchen I get, but why your room?"

"I don't know why, but I have to. They could go in there."

"Why would they?"

"Why *wouldn't* they?"

He laughed. "Fine. I'm gonna watch TV and chill. There's food."

I went into the kitchen and got the corner store breakfast burritos he left me. He finished vacuuming then sat on the couch. I watched him scroll for a movie while I ate, then I got up to start on the kitchen. A few minutes later I heard a show come on. Then I heard the word *skate*. I looked out into the living room. From its new place you could see the TV perfectly from the kitchen. He was watching an anime.

"Is that about skateboarding?"

"Come sit down and find out." He patted the couch next to him.

I sighed. I wasn't going to do that. I had to make sure we wouldn't be judged for our house by a reporter, but the show kept playing. I caught myself more than once doing that thing that dads do where they watch the show standing in another room or a doorway to make it look like they aren't watching.

"Nothing about the tricks in this show make sense," I said after the first episode came and went.

"That's because you're watching from the kitchen instead of the couch."

"That sentence doesn't make sense."

"Thomas, come and fucking sit down."

I did. There was another episode and then another. At some point, an energy drink and a bowl of popcorn arrived. It was entertaining, actually.

"That trick is impossible," I cried when the character pulled it off.

"I bet you could do it," Arturo said coolly.

I stared at him. "Art, it's impossible."

"Try it."

"No."

"Chicken."

"Don't start."

"Noob."

"Fine, get up." I growled and went to get a board.

In order to do any trick in our apartment, I needed to use the kitchen and the living room. Arturo was in the living room leaning against the back of the couch.

"This is stupid," I said.

"Your mom," he said.

"There's not enough room."

Arturo laughed. "Either try it here or we can go outside, but you aren't getting out of this, Jefferson."

I sighed and lined up with him at the far end of the hall. The first attempt resulted in me kick-turning and rolling back at him.

"You have to go faster," he said, putting his hands up to stop me. He pushed me back away from him.

"Why? That's the whole thing!" I shouted.

"Faster," he demanded.

I sighed and did it. It was as simple as move away, turn (which was scarily tight in the kitchen), then roll back toward him. Even though it was simple, it was also apparently dangerous. My wheel caught a rogue screw Arturo and I had both somehow missed in our respective cleanings. I rocketed off the board and slammed my shoulder into Arturo, sending us both over the couch and onto the floor on the other side. A split second after we landed, popcorn rained down on us.

I started laughing first. Then Arturo. He had landed almost completely on top of me. I could feel his deep laugh through my whole body. As if it were the most natural thing to do in that moment, as if it were something we had done a million times instead of just once, I kissed him. It was like stepping into the ocean on the hottest day of the year. For a nanosecond—a quantumsecond—we froze, lips together. Then he kissed me back. Elation raced through my nerves, short circuiting every higher thought system. *Fuck yes.*

Arturo kissed hard, pressing down on me with his hips. His lips were smooth, and the pressure of them against mine was perfect. I wanted to drink him in. His mouth communicated so perfectly. He was saying *Open for me, let me in,* so I did. His tongue found mine. One hand caressed my arm and wrist, following a path to where my hand was above my head. He laced our fingers together. I was completely surrounded, held down by him. He wasn't light and there was force behind his movements that communicated safety and want.

Want. That one word was enough to turn my whole dreamy happiness into a nightmare. *I forced myself on him. Fuck.* He couldn't possibly have wanted me to kiss him. It was a reaction. It was politeness? Pity? Either way, it was a problem. I pulled away as best I could and took a breath.

"Thomas?"

"Fuck I…I don't…" I said.

I only knew that I had to get away so he wouldn't be able to look at me. The only feeling I had left was shame. I scrambled off the floor and went into the bathroom since it was the nearest place with a door. I could feel him following, but I didn't stop. I shut the door and slumped to the floor. My chest burned as my heartbeat surged and my breath weakened.

God damn it, you piece of shit. He's your friend. What the fuck were you thinking? Do you realize you'll lose everything if you lose him? You can't keep your fucking hands to yourself for one—

"Thomas," Arturo said through the door. He knocked gently. I didn't answer. "Thomas, fuck, I'm sorry."

What is he sorry for?

"I…I know I shouldn't have kissed you without your permission. It's pretty shitty to say I couldn't help it, pero I don't know any other way to explain."

Did he think he kissed me? I kissed him. What was he talking about? *My permission? Help it?* My confusion released a pressure valve on my spiraling emotions. I stood and opened the door. "What the fuck are you talking about?"

He had been leaning against the door when I jerked it open. He almost fell in on me but jumped back. I stared at him. He took a step back from me. "I'm apologizing."

"For what?"

"For kissing you without—"

"No, see, you didn't."

"What?"

"*You* didn't kiss me. I kissed you. I need to apologize to you."

He blinked. "What are you talking about?"

"Arturo, I kissed you."

"No."

"Yes."

"Okay, fine then…it doesn't matter."

"Doesn't it? I didn't have your consent."

"Yes, you did."

"So, I should…wait what?" I stared at him, entirely thrown off.

He grinned. "You had it…my consent to kiss me. Fuck, Thomas, you have it now."

"It doesn't work like that," I said slowly. One part of my brain was still in fight mode. There was still a problem that needed solving. The rest of my brain, however, heard him. *He consents? This must be a stress dream. I'm still asleep, hopped up on allergy meds and anxious about the interview.*

"I know consent doesn't work that way, but I was literally thinking in that moment, that you could kiss me if you wanted. Then…wow."

I stared into his earnest face. *If I'm dreaming, I should be able to do calculus…what's the third derivative of nine X to the sixth power…* Well, I didn't know the answer. I didn't even know if you could do the third derivative of anything. I blinked and focused on his face.

"Run that by me again?" I asked.

He stepped toward me and put his hands on my shoulders. "I'm saying you *have* consent. Kiss me whenever. Fuck. I don't know how to explain what that felt like."

I couldn't explain a whole lot of things, starting with reality. I was about to say something, probably something stupid, when the doorbell rang.

"Oh, fuck, the reporter," I hissed.

He laughed, then shouted, "Hold on, coming."

He looked at me, sliding his hands slowly down my arms. The tips of his fingers grazed my palm, down my fingertips, then there was no contact between us. His expression, intense and solid, was enough, though. I believed him completely.

"We good?" he said.

I met his eyes. "You really wanted to?"

His smile was the brightest I had ever seen. "Still do."

But he didn't. Instead, he went to the door. It didn't matter. Something inside me snapped. Not in like a serial killer way, but in a glowstick way. His wanting to be kissed shed light on the way I'd been feeling for days. Nights ago, being together in the SUV was probably as potent as it had been because it was fucking mutual. It wasn't him saying he wanted to date me or that he loved me, but it was one truth about us.

"You have popcorn in your hair," he said, breaking my thoughts just as he was about to open the door.

"Bastard," I sighed, pulling the bun loose. I wasn't ready for him to let the reporter in. "Wait."

He stopped.

"I…you…have my consent too," I said it before I could rethink it.

He looked up, surprised. *Yeesh, Art, don't look so alarmed. It's not a bad idea for you because you aren't in love with me. I, on the other hand, really enjoy fucking myself over. Yes, Teach, give the one guy who could curb-stomp your heart unfettered access to your mouth.* Yeah, it was probably a bad idea. I smiled at him anyway.

It still felt like the biggest leap of faith to cross to him. If he meant it the same way I did, then what I was about to do was the safest thing in the world. If he didn't, though…well. When I reached him, I fell against his mouth. I let it be just our lips, a kiss that said *Okay, here's me hearing you,* and he matched the energy.

Then he stepped back and opened the door.

Chapter Nine

Arturo

"Hello," I said.

The reporter was standing with his back to our door, looking down the hall as if he was expecting someone. At my hello, he turned. His expression was one of excitement, and the first thing he did even before speaking was hold out his hand. He was wearing a Denver Broncos ball cap, a blue button-down, and dark jeans.

"Hello, I'm Chandler Nation. He, him. You're probably Uno."

I nodded. He was simultaneously friendly and intimidating, like a college professor. Maybe it was because he was a reporter. He was shorter than me by a few inches, and a few shades browner. I shook his hand. My mouth still tingled from kissing Thomas. His lip ring and stubble had left traces of his presence on my skin. I wondered for a second if Chandler could see it.

"Can I come in?" he asked.

"Oh, shit right, yeah. This is our house. That's Pirate. You can call me Arturo," I said, stepping out of the way. "Oh—he, him too."

Thomas held out his hand to the reporter, long hair cascading in waves around his face. He raked it to one side as he shook the reporter's hand. "Call me Thomas, he, him."

"Interesting. So, are those less like nicknames and more like stage names?" Chandler asked.

Thomas and I looked at each other.

Chandler laughed. "Yeah, I get that a lot. Listen, how about we talk about how this works, then we can start the interview."

"Okay, come this way to the living room," Thomas said. He led Chandler. I followed. Thomas kept talking. "Do you want a drink? You can put your bag on the table. Do you want to sit on the couch? Shit."

I looked past them. There was popcorn all over the living room, a skateboard under the table, and anime paused on the TV.

"Well, the internet said you two are a good time," Chandler said with a laugh.

"I'm sorry, it doesn't usually look like this. We were…there's a… is it too late to cancel?" Thomas sighed.

"Grab the vacuum, I'll get the board and start some coffee," I said, patting Thomas on the shoulder. He nodded and went to the hall closet.

"You wanna sit while we figure this out?" I said, pointing Chandler to the table. He nodded and kicked the board out to me as he sat. I grabbed it and the empty popcorn bowl. I also turned off the TV.

"So, coffee," I said. "We have some leftover pumpkin spice from the holidays a year ago or cheap shit from Costco. Either way it's gonna suck 'cause it's from our coffeemaker."

He nodded as if I had said the most interesting thing in the world. "Dealer's choice."

I put in the Costco stuff. Thomas vacuumed while I made the coffee. I grabbed mugs, sugar, and oat milk on the way back to the table. I set the mugs out in a row and poured the coffee before sliding Chandler his.

"Here, good luck," I said, toasting him with my mug. I put the last one out for Thomas at a place on the table across from Chandler, but next to me.

"You know, this place is pretty cool. I expected dairy crates and naked walls," Chandler said.

"It wasn't far off two days ago. This was all Thomas," I said.

"It kind of defeats the purpose of decorating to pretend like we have class if you tell everyone that that's what we did," Thomas said, joining us at the table. He raked his hair again and grabbed the handle of his coffee mug as if it was his last hope. I could see the Pirate mask slip into place a little. He wasn't sure who he should be.

I finger-gunned in his direction. "Yeah, that makes sense."

"I'll leave it out of my article," Chandler said, humoring us. "Here's how it's going to work."

Chandler said he would ask us questions designed to get to know us. He wanted us to treat it like a conversation. Even though he had a few questions planned, he was ultimately striving for some organic interaction in all three stories. The first would catch people up on who we were. The second was about the competition and the campaign, and a third about how it all turned out.

"That means I'm going to be at the next few events. I know a photographer is coming too, but I'm not in charge of him."

"Bien! Vámonos," I said.

Chandler shook his head. He pulled out his phone and pressed some buttons. I assumed he was recording.

"Right, so…stage names?" he said to the phone, then looked at us.

I looked at Thomas. He shrugged, which I took to mean I should say whatever I wanted. I smiled. Then I looked back at Chandler. "We were Thomas and Arturo to each other before we were Pirate and Uno. Our team last year asked us to come up with nicknames. We met, then joined that team. But yeah, for me, I feel like I can relax from that public image a little by letting go of the street name at least while we're home."

"And you?" he asked Thomas.

"Same, I guess. I've never really been Thomas, though, except to Art. My family back home calls me—"

"Teach, I know," Chandler interrupted.

Thomas looked scared for a second. "You looked me up?"

"Didn't have to. Your brother is dating my nephew," Chandler said with a laugh.

Thomas blinked. "Lucas! You're the uncle?"

"Yes," Chandler said.

Thomas actually looked relieved. "Why didn't you open with that? Jesus, man!"

"It was in the email, but considering the way you introduced yourself, I figured I'd tell you." Chandler's expression somehow shifted, and it felt suddenly like we had all known each other before.

"I didn't read the whole email," Thomas admitted.

Chandler said, "Shit, I owe your brother twenty bucks now."

Thomas laughed, and that seemed to be enough to remove the Pirate mask altogether. In fact, I was treated to something rare. Thomas was rarely Teach, the Southern family guy, even with me. His accent was detectable on some words, but he hardly talked about home. I knew it was kind of sacred to him, or hallowed maybe, like the family plot in a cemetery. He talked to his second-oldest brother nearly every day. It made me sad knowing how hard it was for him to be his whole self sometimes.

He smiled at me. I made sure he got my best smile back. I said, "That's a crazy coincidence."

Chandler shook his head. "Naw, I practically begged for the job when I found out it was him. I might be a journalist, but I'm also a sports fan. There are no coincidences, only good omens and rituals. It was a good omen that it was Teach Jefferson from Painted Waters, Georgia."

"I feel that way about him too," I said. They each looked at me with very different expressions. Thomas looked suspicious, and Chandler looked amused.

"Care to say more?" Chandler pressed.

"Look at everything that's happened since I met him. My boss literally gave me this apartment the day Thomas showed up. My roommate ad was on Craigslist for thirty minutes before I bumped into him at the ATM around the corner from our house. Now we're national heroes."

"I wouldn't say that," Thomas said, looking like he was ready to hide under the table.

Chandler tapped a pen against his coffee mug. I don't know where he got a pen from or what he needed it for since there was no paper.

"That's very interesting. So, you would say you're friends."

"Obviously," I answered.

"And now you're legally married?"

I fiddled with my ring. "Sí."

Chandler nodded. "Let's talk about the Un-Mister Campaign."

Our followers had dubbed the campaign the Un-Mister Campaign since all the shirts had Mr. Something written on them and crossed out. I explained what happened at the campout and what had happened since. Thomas added his reaction here and there. Chandler asked a few questions about the mechanics of the campaign and wanted some numbers, like how many more followers we had gotten since it started and how much money we had raised.

The coffee went fast, so we offered him some other food or soda, but he declined.

"Let's talk backlash. Some of the Crew, as I learned Pirate's fans call themselves, are upset that he married someone not as openly identified as a 'man attracted to men'—to paraphrase them."

Thomas looked at me. "Are they?"

I rolled my eyes. "The Crew gets offended if you put your shirt back on. But yeah, I've had a few DMs that were a little less than friendly."

"Do you have any comments to offer on your sexuality?" Chandler asked me.

"What does that have to do with skateboarding?" Thomas said.

"It's *most* relevant to the question and the comments fans are making. And, in all fairness, you two are the ones who made it public twice, so it's not irrelevant," Chandler said, unfazed.

"Twice?" Thomas asked.

"You got married, then the campaign," Chandler answered.

"Oh."

Thomas's expression got distant as he thought about it. I guessed it was a good point. Don't put it out there if you don't want to talk about it, right? I had to think for a minute if I wanted to answer, if I even knew the answer. Chandler focused back in on Thomas, though.

"Thomas, to speak to some questions that have come up that are marginally more general, do you think marrying for sport is a mockery of everything the LGBT plus communities did to make marriage an option?"

Thomas shrugged. "I think marriage mocks itself no matter who's involved. I haven't married anyone except Arturo, but I've seen plenty of queer couples get married and divorced just as fast as straight ones. It's a crapshoot sometimes. My oldest brother and father are both divorced, and my second brother and sister are still married. You know all that. But my point is it's a little hard to say what the intention of marriage even is."

"Love?"

"As for the people who did the work," Thomas said, ignoring the comment about love, "no, I don't think it mocks what they did. I'd marry a man anyway. I guess he wouldn't really have to be gay. He could be bi or pan or neither, but he's still a guy. Hell, they could be masc NB—either way, that part doesn't change for me. Those who put in the work gave *us* the option, and that is ours to do with what we want.

So, if this is a mockery, then those who never marry would be mocking it too. To me, it's up to the individuals if they want to do it, and even more so as to why."

Chandler nodded. Then he turned his intense eyes on me. "Do you agree?"

"Oh." I hesitated. Chandler gave off only trustworthy vibes, so I felt like I could tell him. For the first time in my life as a public figure, I wondered how the fans would react to what I had to say.

"As far as openly identifying, I guess Thomas and I both do that in the way that feels most genuine to ourselves. I'm trans. And I'm happy with how open I've been about that. As far as sexuality, I'll admit transitioning hasn't made it easy to figure out. Sometimes I don't know if I like someone or just want to *be* like them, you know? The big problem for me as a transman and I think the bigger issue in the question is that people take my ability to pass as straightness. It's not.

"As far as marriage and the work, it comes down to a question of legacy. People worry about how our reactions today reflect on the past and worry if we're erasing something. Well, I've been a part of a legacy in a different way for a lot longer than I have been out as trans or married to a man. The story kind of tracks the same, though. As a Mexican who's naturalized, I have to honor those who paved the way and make a good name for our people. Pero, y qué? I have my own history to make, just like Thomas does. We get to be a part of the narrative too. I don't believe history should control a person's narrative just because it happened. Inform it, maybe, but not control it. No *one* person should be generalized by the history of a community any more than anything else should generalize them."

"If you guys get any more honest, I might need a fourth article," Chandler said. He pretended to write on the table, the pen cap still safely in place. "Okay, well Thomas said he always expected to marry a man. But what about you, Arturo? What's it like for you to be married to a man?"

"Actually, I never contemplated the gender of my spouse," I said, drumming the table softly. "Also, I experience sexual and romantic attraction differently from how I think others do, I guess. So, on the rare occasion I thought of marriage, I figured it would be to some really good friend, for the benefits or something. So, I guess like Thomas, I *did* marry who I expected to."

I couldn't stop myself from looking at Thomas. I wanted to see his reaction since this was news to him, especially the sexuality part. My chest constricted, and my hand remembered the feeling of his fingers laced with mine. His brown eyes were steady and his expression was perfectly guarded, even from me. I had no way of knowing what he was thinking. But under his gaze, I felt as if every place we had ever touched was glowing and visible.

"What you both are saying is that, even though you married for the competition, this is going pretty much how you expected marriage to go?" Chandler said, breaking my focus on Thomas. We both nodded, turning back to him. He laughed. "That's wild. I didn't see that coming. Well, another fan favorite question is, are you staying married?"

I hadn't been prepared for that question. I hesitated.

"Who knows? If we didn't, it would probably be after the comp since we'd need to win the prize money for a divorce anyway," Thomas answered coolly.

I hadn't expected that answer. And I was surprised to find an echo of my own words in it. I was joking in the van about divorce. I hadn't honestly considered it until Chandler asked. And Thomas's dismissal of it made it seem like he wasn't thinking of it either.

Chandler seemed to take it as a hint to move on. "Speaking of winning and competition, have you been surprised by the reaction of some of your competition mates? This campaign is a response to a recent hate crime, yes, but were you surprised?"

I looked at Thomas. I hadn't really thought about it. "I'm not, but I'm not really sure why."

"I'm not. I even warned the team that we might be targets. The campaign and our lives are too important to keep quiet, though. But no, I expected it. Arturo might be willing to give people, as a whole, the benefit of the doubt. I don't, naturally. This isn't the first time either of us has been harassed in this city, even though Denver is generally thought of as liberal and friendly. If the last few years have taught me anything, it's that there are people in every community who are going to hate some aspect of you. This country's never really been kind to the Mexicans who move here—"

"Even if they're naturalized like my family," I added. Thomas was spot-on so far.

He nodded and smiled. "And the LGBT plus community is no

different, from an intersectionality perspective. As far as the skaters and bikers, they're from all over and have just as varied beliefs as the general population. I try to keep it in perspective, because in the grand scheme of things, the harassment was from six guys out of the sixty in the competition."

"I'm thinking it was more like one or two. Some of the guys on that team were pretty pissed at our harasser," I said.

Chandler looked at Thomas. "That's the benefit of the doubt you were talking about?"

Thomas laughed.

Chandler sighed. "As a Black, trans sports journalist, y'all are preaching to the choir. Let's get on a different train for a while and talk skateboarding."

"Okay," we said together.

"I learned today that there's a skateboarding anime," Chandler said with such seriousness that it could only be teasing. I snorted a laugh and Thomas groaned, putting his head down on the table.

The rest of the interview was much less personal. Well, that's not quite right. It was personal, but I didn't feel like I was confessing anything. Chandler never went back to sexuality questions. I felt nervous about Thomas hearing about my sexuality, though. Well, if the kissing that afternoon stood for anything, I was less confused at being "not straight." But that alone didn't define sexuality. And it couldn't be enough for a "real" relationship, right? At the end of the night, I knew more about who I was but less about what I wanted. Win some lose some, I guess.

CHAPTER TEN

Arturo

The only event of CASST that wasn't really about skates, boards, or bikes was Dog Days of Denver. It was a compromise with the city where CASST got to hold their competition and ignore some of the No Skateboarding signs while the city got an economic boost. Dog Days was like a city tour. The teams had to go business to business. We collected points for visiting and tagging proof of a visit to social media, and we got more points if we tried a product. It really was good for businesses because it was the event with the most fan turnout except for the Crowning on the last day.

Chandler met us outside our place and we gave him a board. He was skeptical, but he managed it perfectly. Then we went to meet the rest of the team at the business closest to mine and Pirate's apartment.

"What up," The Major said as we rolled up.

"Hey Jeffx, this is Chandler the Reporter. He's gonna be hanging out." I pointed between them. They shook hands.

"Yeah, Uno, we all got the email. Let's get this going. Hi," Nads said tersely. He propped his bike against the wall and went into the building.

"To the fro-yo," Rocky shouted. He followed Nads into Cold Cup, a by-weight frozen yogurt spot.

"So, you're the acclaimed leader," Chandler said to the Major, ignoring Nads.

"I don't know who acclaimed me, but they were probably lying," The Major said.

I looked around for Flip and Pirate. They were talking quietly behind us. That left me a little on my own. I was about to follow Rocky and Nads into the store when The Major and Chandler looked at me.

"What was the question?" I asked.

"The Major said you saved their life?" Chandler said.

I laughed. "Yeah, from a pack of street chihuahuas. I sacrificed three corn dogs for them."

The Major took over the story from there. They tried to keep me engaged, but my thoughts were drawn back to Pirate, watching him with Flip. They seemed close. It hadn't taken much time, had it? I wasn't jealous. Right?

"Did you take the pic?" Nads said, shoving me. Rocky trotted out with a tub overflowing with frozen yogurt.

I felt only a little guilty for my distraction. "Shit, no, I didn't. Come on, let's get one."

"Maybe you should focus since you're exploiting all of this for a job." Nads shoved past me to get back on his bike.

Nads for once was right. This wasn't just a good time out with the buds, it was work. There was a lot of money in it for us if we won, and while we had maintained a steady lead, it was narrowing as the other teams busted ass to catch us. Besides, I couldn't slack off now. A lull in progress halfway through the competition wouldn't look good for my portfolio.

I called everyone to come be in the picture. They gathered in front of the Cold Cup door logo, and Rocky dragged one of the employees into the shot. I snapped the photo and uploaded it with the necessary hashtags for points.

"Let's get a move on," Nads called, already on his bike and slowly moving away.

"Let's hang out for a minute," I said.

"Why?" Flip asked.

"The point of this event is to bring awareness to Denver businesses. None of the fans are here, and if we leave now, they won't come to this place. If we hang out for a minute, this place will get its due, and our fans can catch up with us."

"The point of this is the points," Nads insisted. He was weaving in and out of the cars parked along the street.

"Can you just summon fans out of thin air like that?" Chandler asked.

I grinned. "Whenever the Crew finds out Pirate is around, they show up. The other fans—the Majorettes, the Rocky Brigade, and the Wild Cards will show up, sure, but none so fast as the Crew."

"Nads and Flip don't have fan bases?" Chandler asked in a tone that made it clear he wasn't trying to be insulting.

"I don't want fucking fans," Nads snapped.

"He has fans because everyone loves a good mystery. Nads won't talk to anyone, and that makes people want to talk to him more," Rocky said.

Flip shrugged. "It's my first year really in the game. But I have time. I'm only nineteen." We all looked at her. She laughed. "Yeah, I know. How did I find myself on a senior citizens team? Well, y'all were the only ones who had room."

Just then people started to come around the corner looking for us. The team talked up the Cold Cup enough to appease me, so we started to the next business after only a few more minutes. The fans were chatty, so it was easy to get into the spirit of the event. Chandler and I walked with the fans while the others skated or biked, showing off tricks as we moved deeper into the city.

❖

Seven businesses later, I was watching through a window as Pirate got his hair done. A salon had been brave enough to put their names on the event list even though most of the competitors were men. The owner and her assistant took one look at Pirate's beautiful hair and begged him to let them style it. He gave them two rules: no cutting and no color. I grinned as they wrapped small bunches of white hair around big curling irons. Rocky was with him, and so were twenty or so women members of the Crew.

"This has been a wild event," Chandler said, coming to stand by me. He was watching the crowd. Without knowing what it was, all the people probably looked like the Strip in Vegas combined with a very niche street fair. People performed and shopped and milled. It was loud and there was no conflict for once.

I laughed. "Yeah, even though I know it's just a capitalistic gimmick, it's one of the more fun events."

Chandler shook his head at my comment. "Hey, I wanted to ask you something. Do you want me to leave the sexuality conversation out of my article? I know you don't hide being trans, but I didn't know if you were ready for people to know about your sexuality."

I stiffened and looked around. The crowd, in its immenseness, was ignoring us. I looked at Chandler. He gave me a patient smile.

"Would you do that?"

"I work for an LGBTQIA plus magazine. If we weren't kind about people's coming-out stories, who would be?"

"I hadn't really thought about all this as coming out. Pirate tried to warn me, but I wasn't really thinking about it."

"It can be like that."

I looked back in the window. Thomas was smiling. Somehow, he fit in perfectly even though the salon looked like a cotton candy store while he looked like a goth boarder.

"I guess I don't mind it being in the magazine. Good luck trying to explain it, though. I'm happy I married Pirate, you know. And I guess a natural progression of that would be to then consider my own sexuality. But since I haven't given it much thought until now, it's confusing. I don't care if people know, I don't know how to explain it better than I have to you."

"It's confusing for more people than you think, even if they feel like they can label it. For some of us, the label is the closest approximation, even if there are aspects that don't quite feel right. Don't let the mainstream fool you into thinking everything is perfect once you land on the label. You'll find something close eventually. Demi, aro, ace—some new one the next generation is smart enough to come up with."

I looked back at Chandler. "I've looked into those, pero no sé."

Chandler nodded. "Well, I promise to be as just as I can in the article. At the very least, you seem like you're in good company. The orientations of your team run the full spectrum, not that I believe in spectrums."

"I guess they do." I thought for a moment. "We've never really talked about it specifically. It's sort of funny, but I think we just got a vibe, and were drawn to each other without outing ourselves."

"That's really nice."

I nodded. We both watched Pirate and Rocky through the window. Rocky looked almost like he was directing the stylist about what to do with Pirate's hair. He pointed and handed them pins while Pirate rolled his eyes.

"Look, I have another question. I'm nosy by nature, and I think the fact that it wasn't my first question shows that I'm growing as a person. Buuuut is there something actually going on between you and Pirate?"

My gaze snapped to him so fast it hurt a little. Even without me saying something, he gave me a triumphant smirk.

"There's nothing formally," I said. It wasn't a lie. And I guess I was starting to have the same question myself. "I'm not sure."

"Cute." I waited, but that was all Chandler had to say about it.

"What, um…makes you ask?"

Chandler pulled a notepad from his pocket. He flipped to a page in the book, then tore it out and handed it to me. He started to back away. He said, "I think I have a few more questions to ask…over there."

I looked at the page. He had written out a portion of mine and Thomas's conversation he must have heard through the door. I had been shouting.

A: What are you saying?
B: I'm saying you have consent. Kiss me whenever. Fuck,
I don't know how to explain what that felt like.
Question: Involved? Love?

It was the last line that really threw me. *Love?*

I let out a deep breath and put the piece of paper in my pocket. Good questions. I didn't know. I wasn't used to not knowing this much. I was sure about most things most of the time. And I was sure about Pirate; I just couldn't tell what I was sure about anymore.

"Uno," some fans said behind me. "Can we get a pic?"

I smiled and looked at them. "Hell, yeah."

It was another thirty minutes before Thomas and Rocky came out of the salon. I had been distracted by the fans, teaching some of them to ollie and kickflip. They all saw Pirate coming before I did.

"Oh wow, he's fucking gorgeous," one said, looking over my shoulder.

I turned. Thomas came toward me through the crowd. His hair was curled in big ringlets falling down his back, the top was pulled up in a curly bun with threads of braids. He looked like a star ready for a royal ball.

"Hey." He grinned at me. "Ready to move on?"

I laughed. "Bro, how'd they do this?"

I put my hand out, wanting to stroke one of the curls by his face. I paused, knowing better than to touch without asking.

"It's mostly hairspray," he said. He stepped into my hand. I caught one of the perfect spirals. It unspooled in my fingers as I stroked it, still soft even though I could feel the hairspray.

"Uno! Fucking move your ass," Nads screamed.

I looked over my shoulder and watched him start off toward the next shop. I looked back at Thomas, still holding on to the curl. He smiled and pulled the strand of hair I was holding from my hand. He stepped closer again and said quietly, "You have my consent for that too. My hair, I mean."

I was almost speechless as he sidestepped me to follow Nads.

❖

"God, I'm so tired," Thomas said.

"Me too."

We turned away from each other coming into the apartment. I looked at him as he started toward our rooms.

"I'm gonna go put my head in the sink," he said. He gestured to the curls in his hair. "I have to see if I can get this out."

I nodded and went to the living room, throwing myself on the couch. It felt amazing to lie down. I got out my phone and responded to some of the fans on social media. I also opened the group chat with my sisters.

Amilia: *oye cabrón, you're pissing Mamá off. Quit making out in the streets with some guy you haven't even brought home.*

Arturo: *What?*

Amilia sent a photo. A fan had taken a picture of Thomas and me, my fingers still in his hair. I honestly hadn't even realized people had been watching us, which, in hindsight, was super ridiculous 'cause we were us. I had designed our social media to make sure people saw us. Did we always stand that close to each other?

I thought about last night and the short kisses we shared. I didn't understand. How could I be sure I was feeling the way I was? What's the difference between new and exciting and romantic? I needed to be sure. I couldn't tell Thomas some half-thought-out feeling. I didn't even know what it was called. How could I match my feelings to a name? I figured I could ask my sisters. Amilia claimed to be in love every few weeks, and Ariana had said it at least once in our adult lives.

Arturo: *Can I ask you guys a serious question?*

Ariana: *I don't know, can you?*

Amilia: *You can, but if you want the answer to be serious, we'll have to charge you.*

Arturo: *How do you know when a feeling is a...love feeling and not a regular feeling?*

I put my phone down. My sisters were the closest people in the world to me. I waited for the notifications to stop so I knew I would have their full answers. I expected them to interrogate me and bombard me with guesses. To my surprise, the phone only buzzed twice.

Amilia: *Yeesh aren't you Latino—our people invented the language of loving feelings.*

Ariana: *Well, the colonizers brought the language, but we taught them how to use it ;)*

Arturo: *Like what?*

Amilia: *Look up any song from our country.*

Arturo: *Like Como La Flor?*

Ariana: *Oof. There's more to Mexican music than Selena.*

Arturo: *Livin' la vida loca?*

Amilia: *I'm going to take a screenshot of this, print it out, and hang it on my fridge then every day I will remember to punch you the next time I see you.*

Ariana sent a YouTube link to a music video, then another link with the translation.

Arturo: *I don't need the translation. My Spanish isn't that bad.*

Amilia: *Your Spanish is caca.*

I laughed and opened the links. It was a good song. In Spanish I heard a reflection of my feelings, the language doing something for me that English couldn't. I *felt* the song as it played rather than just listened to it. It literally pulled memories with Thomas to the front of my brain, and not just since marrying him, but from our whole friendship. If the feelings matched this song, which it felt like they did, then I loved him. Amilia's next message interrupted the video.

Amilia: *Is it Thomas?*

Arturo: *Is what Thomas?*

Amilia: *Your loving feelings.*

Arturo: *I don't know.*

Amilia: *I know.*

She sent screenshots of a conversation from December. I had been complaining to them about how I missed Thomas while he was visiting his family when his dad got sick. He had been gone for almost three months. I remembered them teasing me about having a crush on him. Apparently Amilia was keeping receipts.

Arturo: *I thought you guys were joking.*

Amilia: *Were we?*

Ariana: *You tell us, Artito.*

How was I going to tell them when I couldn't tell myself? I switched back to the internet. I thought about what Chandler said and went back to the site with the different romantic and sexuality discussion boards. If someone else could label it, then maybe it would fit me too. I ultimately got lost down a rabbit hole.

"Hey."

I jumped a little and locked my phone. Thomas was leaning over the back of the couch. His hair was loose and straight again, having been washed and blown dry.

"Hey," I said.

"I...do you want to watch something? I know it's late, but you aren't working tomorrow, right? I'm hungry-ish too, so..."

I wasn't listening. I thought about the atmospheric feeling of being in the van with him. And the gravity I felt when we were on the floor together. I had his consent too. I had it until he said otherwise. I sat up and he didn't move away. His eyes looked bigger when his light hair was down, a shade of brown like a sunny forest trail. With me sitting up and him leaning over the couch, we were exactly face-to-face.

I looked at his mouth and felt that plunging feeling I got when I thought about kissing him. I'd even felt that simple kiss in the hallway deep in my chest. But on the floor! On top of him. I had never felt like that. I wanted to feel that way again. I knew without a doubt all of those feelings were because of him.

"Art?" he said, a small smile on his face.

I hadn't been listening, so I smiled and slipped my fingers into his hair. I had consent for that too. He closed his eyes to the touch as I stroked from root to tip. It was so fucking soft. And he smelled amazing. He smelled like shampoo, flowers, mint, and something else, some natural smell I liked.

"Thomas."

"Yeah."

"Kiss me."

He opened his eyes, and for a second, there were a million thoughts in them. Then there was only one. He kissed me. It was like a sparkler on the Fourth of July. He pulled away. I stared at him. He didn't move. Was it my turn? Was it like, a cue? Did he not want this? Well, I could only trust that he wouldn't be here, doing this, if it didn't feel good to him. I shifted on the couch so I was kneeling, and I took his face in both of my hands. His hands came up to my wrists and he just held me there.

I pressed my mouth back to his, and to my surprise he hummed. What had been a sparkler turned into an explosion. Desire raced all over my body from where we were connected. I didn't know really what to do next, so I chased the first impulse that came to mind. He seemed willing to follow my lead. My lips parted, and he swept his tongue into my mouth. He let go of my wrists and came around my shoulders, warmth tracing along all the nerves in my arms. I pushed into his mouth. He moaned softly. A flush, something akin to hunger, rose up as a reaction. God, I didn't know a sound could do that. The couch rocked as I instinctively leaned on it to get closer.

"Fuck," I said, breathing. Thomas looked horrified, like he was ready to run to the bathroom again. I definitely didn't want that. I laughed and held on to him. "We're going to break this one day."

That made him blush. I went back to kissing him. In a quick move, I hooked an arm around him and pulled him over the couch. His smile against my lips was a reassurance. I was so overwhelmed by my feelings that I could hardly think. I suddenly felt like we were moving at light speed. After a little shuffling, we settled on the couch, entwined in each other. He was almost under me again, the way he had been on the floor.

I kissed him deep, putting a hand on his hip and the other on the armrest behind his head. He pulled my hair slightly as he tried to hold on to me. This time I moaned. Having him in my mouth made me want to rock against him, rub my body against his. I understood these physical and emotional feelings were the whole fucking point, but it had never come together like this for me.

"Fuck, Art. I can feel you thinking," Thomas said, pulling away.

"Really?" I had to blink a few times to focus.

"Yeah, you okay?" His eyes were concerned. He panted slightly and licked his lips. It was immediately distracting.

I laughed. "Sí, muy bien. There's a lot going on in my head, but it's about this, about you. I want…"

"What?" he asked. His eyes narrowed with uncertainty, as if he didn't know whether to be excited or worried.

"I want…" I tried to come up with English words that sounded accurate but not cringy. *I want to hear you moan again? I want to touch all of your skin at once? I want your tongue in my mouth?* The song had made the most sense of my feelings in Spanish. *Maybe I should continue thinking in Spanish.* Of course, my brain landed on "Quiero besarte hasta que te haga venir."

His eyes went wide, and a perfect red tint rose on his face. Then he laughed. He said eventually, "If that means what I think it means…"

I held my breath waiting for him to turn me down. I knew it wouldn't feel like rejection. It would feel like the safest *no* I would ever hear in my life.

He chewed his lip ring as he said, "Okay."

I laughed. He rose from where he was lying to meet my lips. He kissed harder this time. And with it came more and more fire. It was like he was a sun growing closer. He kept pushing until I had nowhere else to go except backward. He followed me, climbing onto my lap. There was a clumsy moment of adjusting to get my feet on the floor and him properly on top of me. When he was where he wanted to be, we both moaned as he rocked his body across my lap.

"Fuck," I said.

He didn't say anything. He kissed my neck and rocked again.

"Thomas, I…" I couldn't find the words. I only found blank space where information about this should be. It wasn't until he was riding my lap that I had to wonder if Thomas had ever been with a trans guy. Like, was it a problem for him that my junk was different from his? I had to figure no because we'd gotten this far, but what happened next? Hell, how could I bring this up now?

He stilled and looked at me.

"You can feel me thinking still?" I asked.

He nodded and settled into my lap more completely. "I can, but it's not a problem. Do we need to have a conversation?"

"I don't really want to," I said with a sigh. The idea of discussing all of this now felt like trying to pull the brakes on a high-speed train.

He nodded once. "Do you want to touch me?"

My blood raced, and the hesitation caused by my own thoughts dissipated. I understood he was giving me a chance to catch up, not just with him but with my own feelings. The pause was as much about consent as it was about time to absorb the experience.

"I do," I said, trying to breathe a little more steadily.

"Wherever you want." I looked at his face. And he looked back at me. He was calm and steady. He knew what he wanted. Stunningly, in this moment, he wanted me. But he was giving the choices to me. *Okay, Arturo, assume he has thought about this. He knows trans guys exist, and he knows you are one. If anything about you was a problem for him, he would stop this. So, he must want me exactly as I am.* It was the only conclusion that made sense with the look he was giving me.

I stroked his thighs. His jeans were tight, and his muscles were hard under my hands. I wondered what his skin felt like there. I wondered if his body hair was as soft as the hair on his head. I moved on, slipping my fingers under his shirt. He shifted slightly, moving toward my fingers.

I looked at him again. He gave me a cocked eyebrow. "Figure it out?"

I laughed. "Shut up and kiss me."

He did. Our bodies weren't flush, so there was room to feel his skin with my hands. I had seen his body enough to know what tattoo I might be touching. I found the scar on his ribs from when he fell out of a tree. Even though grazing his nipples was unintentional as I traced my hands up his chest, I would never forget his grunt of pleasure.

I had meant it. I wanted to make him come. I had only the vague awareness he masturbated since our rooms were just across from each other. He had never brought anyone home. We had never talked about anything sexual. For all I didn't know, I desperately wanted to know what getting him off was like. My hands seemed to know where my mind wanted them without me thinking too hard about it. I traced back down his chest until my thumbs grazed the waist of his jeans. He rocked forward. I could see his hard dick, bulging against his jeans.

"Thom—"

"Yes, please, yes," he begged against my mouth.

He sat back again, giving me access to his fly. I looked at his face as I undid the button and adjusted the denim to free his dick. His eyes weren't on me, though. They were closed. He seemed so tense. He was reserved most of the time, which I knew people mistook for indifference. I don't think many got to see his excitement. But I saw the way he chewed on his lip ring, the way he clenched his jaw and fists. Maybe I should have said, "Quiero verte venir."

Starting at the base, I stroked my palm over his dick, closing my fingers loosely around him. He gasped and looked like he was trying not to rock into it. Touching his cock was as comfortable and familiar and revolutionary as kissing him had been. I stroked back and forward again, and he rocked his hips slightly to match. He closed his hand around mine, adjusting my fingers into a tighter hold as he set a pace. That easily, he had shown me how he liked it.

"Shit, fuck," he said when I had it right. He let me go and put his hands on my shoulders, his forehead falling against mine. I watched him enjoy this. His thighs tightened against mine as I worked his dick. His hands drifted. Slowly, they slipped down my chest to my thighs. His fingers gripped my thighs, and his thumbs traced over my crotch.

It took me a few breaths to say, "You can touch me back."

He froze, and his eyes opened wide, as if he never would have expected me to say that. He didn't let either of us say anything. He kissed me, his hands running through my hair. As he kissed, he rocked, using my hand to stroke himself. That felt weirdly powerful. It felt like kissing me was enough and my hand on his dick was enough and his hands in my hair were enough. Maybe I should just get him off.

"Art, fuck, this feels so good," he said, his forehead pressing against mine.

"Se siente rico."

"Okay," he said. I couldn't tell if that was for him or me. But he nodded and put a hand on my wrist to stop my strokes.

He looked at me with a calm, clear expression. "Show me how."

I considered his request. Without a word, he had shown me the way he wanted to be touched, what felt good. Okay, I could do that. I put my hands on his hips and maneuvered him to somewhat standing. He helped me pull my joggers down as soon as he realized what I was doing, not to move him off completely but enough to give him access. Then I pulled him back to straddle one of my thighs, one of his in between mine. As I pulled his hand down to my crotch I held my breath. Maybe it would have been less terrifying if he weren't looking at me. But he was, and I wasn't going to back out now. Thankfully his expression was intent. I maneuvered his fingers into place and stroked.

When he repeated the movement without my guidance, I suddenly couldn't move. The feel of his strong fingers was paralyzing. His hand was hot, slipping over me. My eyes closed without my permission. I couldn't do anything except feel him.

"Qué chingón. That feels amazing," I said.

His forehead came back to rest on mine. "Fuck yes."

A moment later he said, "I...do you...what should I say?"

I had never thought about it, so I spoke on instinct. "Say what you would say to any other guy."

"I love stroking your dick," he said.

My whole body reacted. I had never really thought about what words I wanted used during sex. Him saying "dick," though, did something to me. It shut off the last reservations I had. I pulled him into a kiss, his mouth crashing against mine hard enough to hurt. I put my hand back on his dick and pushed my tongue into his mouth. I wanted everything. He moaned, his hips thrusting, and let me have the parts of him I wanted.

He fucked into my fist, stroking me in time with the way I stroked him. I wanted to see him. I put my free hand on his hip and pushed him back slightly. He went with the same understanding he always had when we silently communicated to each other. From this angle, it was awkward for him to keep touching me, but I didn't care that he let go. I looked first at my hand, then at his face.

"Keep rocking like you were," I said. "Use me. I want to watch."

He did, bracing himself by holding on to the wrist of the hand I had on his hip. I adjusted my grip and added the slightest movement, helping in a small way to get him off.

"Almost," he moaned, his breathing shallow. I didn't say anything. I held on to him and watched. He came with a staccato of moans and a death grip on my arm. Cum spread over my hand in warm lines. I steadied him and he relaxed against me.

"Dios mío."

He took a few breaths and looked at me. His smile was full and perfect. He looked so fucking free, no masks and no reservations. His hair was everywhere. I put my clean hand in it and pulled him down for more kissing. He met my mouth eagerly. His hand was on my dick again. He stroked and I rocked instinctually.

"Fuck." I had to hold on to his legs. "Faster."

He sat back long enough to lick his hand before it was back between my legs. I wondered if I should have done that for him. That question was lost as he stroked, working up to a speed that was more perfect than I had ever given myself. He trailed kisses across my jaw, bit, then sucked my neck, just under my ear. My orgasm came with a blinding speed. I knew there were sounds and squeezing and his breath on my skin, but I didn't register most of it. I only held him on my lap as my body burned out like a flare. Slowly, the fire was replaced with a hazy satisfaction.

"Fucking hell," I said, opening my eyes to look at Thomas.

He didn't move. He looked at me, maybe waiting to see what I would say or do. I wanted to tell him I had never experienced that. I wanted to tell him I hadn't even known it was possible for sex and orgasms to feel that encompassing. Doing what we just had was reality shifting for me. I blinked at him. I could think it, in Spanish and English, but the words wouldn't form on my lips. *Say anything!*

I said, "I, um…think you were saying something earlier, maybe about food."

He laughed and nodded. He sat back as if we hadn't just gotten each other off. He crossed his arms. "We have frozen pizza and chicken nuggets."

"My favorite combo."

That made him laugh more. He went to move, but I didn't let him walk away without another kiss. Then we cleaned up and made food.

CHAPTER ELEVEN

Thomas

Maybe I died? Maybe the board hitting that screw the other day actually caused my head to collide with the corner of the coffee table. Then the last few perfect days with Arturo were just my last neurons firing before my brain finally stopped.

Since the couch sex, Arturo had become completely uninhibited with his touching. I thought he was touchy before, but after Wednesday, it felt constant. I was tuning into his hand in my hair or his arm around my shoulder or his hand on my leg more and more. It was fucking perfect. Unfortunately, we both had to work a lot over the next two days, so we didn't get much time in the house together. The moments we did cross paths were full of small kisses and skin-on-skin grazes. The serotonin dump was fascinating. If I got any happier, people would start to notice.

You still haven't told him that you're in love with him, though. So, gaslight yourself all you want.

That thought and the countless ones like it racing around in my brain always brought me back to reality. I blinked and looked around as if that joy-bursting thought had come from someone nearby and not my own head. I was on the train home. Even the usual disheartened end-of-the-workweek crowd didn't seem so bland in the light of my happiness. I made eye contact with a woman a few seats down, and she sneered at me. I waved. I wished I was the type of person who knew how to hold on to joy.

I was actually thinking of starting a conversation with her when my phone rang. It was my brother, Al. I waited until I got off the train before I called back. "Hey."

"Hey, I was callin' just to check in on you."

"Why?"

"Well, it's a pattern, brother. When you do something wild, you stop calling as much as usual, and my social media notifications explode. I can only think the worst sometimes. Word on the street is that you're divorcin' Arturo and are now goin' after that guy that won gold at the Olympics in skateboarding."

"I hate people. Also since he's Japanese, I don't know when we would've met."

"I know havin' people speculate on your life can take its toll, and you have a long history with speculators. I wanted to see if you needed anythin'."

"I'm good."

"Teach," Al said, not believing me.

"Al."

"How…are you mindin' your heart in all of this?"

That was a question. "What do you mean?"

"I think you really like this guy."

I was instantly defensive. "What makes you say that?"

"I like to think I've gotten to know you much better in the last few years. You don't talk to anyone the way you talk to him. On the phone you sounded…I don't know how to explain it. But am I wrong?"

No, you just have annoying timing.

"Finish your sentence."

Al laughed and thankfully continued. "*And* I know how quickly marriage can change things. Even if it's not supposed to be real, something'll be different because of it. You have the advantage of knowin' Arturo longer than I knew Dani before we got married, I'll give you that much, but even with that, I think I put more thought into plannin' the marriage. Either way, we're pretty reckless about tying the knot. I'm offerin' to talk about it."

I hadn't realized how similar things were for me and Al. Outside my building, I had to dodge a woman with a shopping cart before I could hop into the doorway. I didn't go in, though. I leaned against the cement entry, not thinking too hard about the spiderwebs erected in the corners. The city was at its most divided at this hour. In one direction people like me walked toward their homes after work, in the other people poured toward downtown to start their Friday club-hopping and bar crawls. Maybe they were on their way to the stadium for a baseball game. *Where Arturo is.*

How are you mindin' your heart? I wasn't. Obviously. It had broken the minute Arturo asked me to kiss him. The half that was still beating was creating this euphoric state of rosy sunshine I was currently living in. The other half was black and lying on the bottom of my chest, waiting for everything to fall apart. That would happen the minute Arturo made it clear he didn't actually want to be with me.

"Did…did your feelings for each other change over time? Like, when did you know it was love, like the long-term kind?" I asked. I thought about the day I met Dani. I could see how in love with her Al was. They had been married for a while by then, with a kid well on the way. Then there was his other partner, Lucas. He still acted smitten around that guy, and it had been over a year.

Al said, "Um, my short answer is yes. I don't think I knew it was long-term love until probably Ysabel was born."

Ysabel was Al's second, born almost two years after he married. "That long?"

I could almost hear Al shrugging. "Yeah, like I knew I loved her, but we learned kind of slow how to communicate that love to each other in a way the other understood. Like, I get her flowers all the time, and that's my way of tellin' her I love her. One way she says she loves without saying it is she's constantly touchin' the people she loves. You would think that was obvious, but it wasn't really. I thought most people touched each other, but around the time Ysa was born, we went to that reunion with her extended family. She would hug people, but her little pats and scritches weren't there. When she's mad at me I know it 'cause she won't even shake my hand. And yeah, all of that continues to change over time."

I thought about Dani, constantly patting my shoulders or brushing back my hair. I took it as mothering, which I guess is a form of love. I felt the hope inside me like the buzzing of fluorescent lights. I wanted the increase in Arturo's touching to be a sign of his changing feelings for me. *Hope is gonna kick my ass.* Seven syllables.

"I think I show people I love 'em by avoiding them," I said.

My brother laughed, then sighed. "Yeah. I know that was a joke, but riddle me this: Avoiding hurts too, doesn't it?"

"Don't call here again," I grumbled.

"All right, all right. Well, I'll go back to your question. Now, with Lucas, it's different. He wants time together. And I think that's true for me too with him. I guess what I'm sayin' is it can look different for everyone and can change over time. Dani and I have matured a lot in our relationship."

"What about if you're friends, then something changes?" I asked.

"I don't think I've ever been friends with anyone, least not until after they broke my heart by telling me they weren't into me." Al laughed. "You know my history. I guess there's one guy I've only been friends with, but we were rivals first, at least in my own mind."

I laughed too. "Useless."

"Don't I know it. But unless I'm reading things wrong, you haven't thought of Arturo as just a friend for a while now."

"Jefferson curse, I guess."

"Naw. Well, kind of. I think you went into it with friendship in mind and somethin' changed. The beauty of life is stuff's supposed to change. There's a lot of good in changin' too. Just think about how bad things were sometimes and how bad they haven't been for a while. Things get worse, Teach, and you know that better than anyone. But, little brother, things get really good too. Maybe you should ask him if things have changed for him. I bet they have based on the way you two stand there making puppy-dog eyes at each other."

I wanted so badly to believe his feelings had changed. Hell, he had even said during the interview that he wasn't straight. I guess I also learned that firsthand this week, since it had been hard for us to keep our hands off each other. But I also had fucked a few guys who claimed straightness even to this day. I didn't tell him any of that.

"What if it's good now and gets bad?"

"Even as friends, it can go south and you could just not be anything anymore. Dani and I know things could change for us. But in the grand scheme of things, you end up with less if you never go for more. The important thing to do is try for the happiness where you can."

"Fuck me."

"Now, if you feel satisfied with that conversation, I have a few more questions. When was the last time you went to a doctor?"

"What's that got to do with anything?"

"You also got a bill here for your credit card."

"I'm hanging up," I said and did.

I went into the apartment and turned on everything that would make a sound so I wouldn't have to think.

❖

The drive to Arvada would have been short if we hadn't gotten stuck on the highway because of an accident. We had plenty of time, even accounting for delays, but that didn't stop Nads from grinding his teeth and cussing as he tried to weave through traffic that wasn't moving. I was looking out the back window, sitting too close to Arturo in the back seat of the SUV. There was a cooler where I usually sat since there were two bikes shoved into the back where the cooler usually was. I managed to sit so I faced Arturo without coming in too much contact with him. Looking at him was easier than touching him. I couldn't touch him without smiling like an idiot anymore.

He didn't seem to notice the impact he was having on me. My left hand rested across my lap, and in the relative seclusion of the back seat, Arturo slid his hand toward me, his fingertips slipping beneath mine. My whole body warmed at the contact. Then my blood went icy as Flip turned around, tossing an arm over the back of the seat. She looked right at Arturo. I didn't move. But neither did he. I wasn't ashamed of how I felt about him. I wasn't ashamed to have his hand in mine. I was terrified Arturo would feel ashamed, though. He didn't even flinch.

"So, what do you think the Anything With Wheels will be this year?"

Uno laughed. "I think kids' scooters, like the plastic kind, and wheelchairs."

"Really? A wheelchair seems kind of insensitive."

Uno thought about it. "I guess, but I don't give the competition much credit for being sensitive."

"I liked when it was shopping carts," Rocky added, looking at Flip.

She grinned, then looked at me. "What do you think it will be?"

I waved my free hand. "Won't matter, Uno has it covered."

He beamed.

"Yeah, well, I need you to get the same confidence on blades," The Major called to me from shotgun.

I groaned. "I hate blades."

"Then ride a bike, and Rocky can blade," The Major said, tossing their hands up.

"I hate bikes more."

"Don't worry, I'll make us look good," Flip said, turning to face the front.

I tightened my grip on Uno and watched traffic finally break.

The Saturday morning crowd was dense. This park wasn't surrounded by much. There were a few houses but mostly it was open space, not including the two fields the city organized into temporary parking lots for the crowd. Between the fans and the food trucks, the brown grass was turning into a horrible dust. Despite the Dust Bowl era feel, I liked this park. It had a lot of street and transition features, which made it one of the easier parks for the biking and blading event. Flip was still the top blader, and Nads, despite his constant constipated mood, was third overall in biking points. There was a lot of pressure on them as our featured participants. The rest of us were just supposed to try and get any points we could.

"Shit, this is a lot of people," Rocky said, leaning over Flip to look at the flow of people through her window.

"Looks like way more than last year," The Major said.

We were directed to park with the other teams and given stickers to designate us as competitors. This time there were formal-looking black chain barriers between the teams and the fans. As we walked to the park, assorted people in the crowd called to us. We waved back. Some were even wearing T-shirts that matched ours for the campaign. We were wearing modified versions. The sponsor had sent us new shirts with all the same information but now with DropCloth and Bored Skateboard logos on the sleeves, though they were smart enough to send Rocky a tank since he would have cut the sleeves off anyway. An unfamiliar emcee waved us over, so we started toward her.

"Morning, Major Leaguers, I'm Addy Rose. I'm helping Waste today." She was dressed like a pin-up girl, her tight jeans and tucked-in tank making for a distinct look compared to the grungy Waste. We waved. She pursed her very red lips. "I was told to remind you of sportsmanlike conduct. I don't think that will be a problem, since certain parties won't be in attendance today. But just keep that in mind."

We nodded. After she walked away, Nads glared at Uno.

"What did she mean, did Mickey's team drop out?" Rocky asked.

"The roster hasn't changed," The Major said, scrolling through their phone looking for any news about team changes.

"Either way, we got this," Uno said.

"Just keep your head in the game. This place is a circus," Nads said. People with clipboards continued to usher us along with the other competitors.

"At least we're headliners and not sideshows," Uno said to him. He tried to pat Nads on the back, but Nads shook him off.

Nads turned to him. "Can you focus for once? There's a team within two thousand points of us. Do you even know how many points the winner of this event gets?"

"Four thousand?" Uno answered. He at least *looked* like he was taking Nads seriously. And knowing him, he probably was.

"Right, so if we fuck this up, we lose first place," Nads said. "Quit fucking around."

Uno looked like he was going to say something. I brushed the back of his hand with my fingers. He looked at me, and I knew he heard what I was saying. *Leave it alone, Art.* He nodded. To Nads, he said, "Don't worry, there's a lot of points here today. We got this."

Nads just groaned and marched on. Uno turned back to me, winked, then started to follow the others.

"I forgot something in the van. I'm gonna go get it, and Pirate is going to help me," Flip said, backing out of the crowd. She grabbed my arm and started pulling me.

"Don't be fucking late," Nads warned.

I shrugged at Uno, then turned to follow Flip.

"Don't you need the van keys?" Uno shouted back.

"No," Flip said.

I guess that was message enough. She didn't leave anything behind. She obviously wanted to talk.

"You good?" I asked when she finally stopped back by the SUV. There were a lot of people around, so she took me to the other side. We were sandwiched between it and an expensive-looking truck. I leaned on the SUV, and she leaned on the truck.

"Well?" she asked.

"Well."

"What happened between you and Uno?" Her smile was knowing and excited.

"Nothing."

"Bad?"

"It wasn't bad," I said, quick to defend the experiences I had with him. I would defend Uno to the grave. She knew that, so she was forcing my hand.

Her smile broadened. "I literally saw you guys holding hands."

"Fine. We kissed."

She cheered.

"I'm not going to tell you anything else because I didn't ask him if I could," I said, using politeness and respect to avoid the bashfulness I would have felt telling her about it.

"There's more? Damn your ethics. I wanna know." She grabbed me by the shoulders and shook me. "That's fucking cute. What did he say when you confessed? Are you in love? Can you at least tell me that much?"

I half nodded, half shrugged and then started picking at my fingernails. I had redone the black two days ago, but the job yesterday had—

"Pirate?"

"Flip?"

She squatted down so her face was in my line of sight. "You did tell him, right?"

I shook my head.

"Why not?" She hugged me. I was surprised. She really could see right through my defenses if she knew the right thing to do was hug me.

"I don't know." *You do know. You're scared shitless. You will never be happy because you always choose misery.*

"If you didn't tell him, how'd you end up kissing?" She held me at arm's length, her tone all concern. There were voices all around us, and the air smelled verdant and coated my sinuses in dust. It somehow all felt dire, and I thought vaguely of the weather before a storm. I felt exposed to Flip but relatively safe in the tiny space between the massive vehicles.

I watched some fans pass. "It's a long story."

She sighed. "Okay, that's fine. Well then, how are you doing with all of your worries?"

"What worries?"

She laughed, but not because she thought I was funny. "You've got to be kidding. You had so many concerns."

I didn't say anything.

"Pirate, I know you know what I'm talking about."

"Flip, I know, but what does it matter? I mean, how can things be different really? In the grand scheme of things, we didn't marry for love, so why would anyone ever believe we'd hook up for it too? Maybe we're just touch starved. Maybe it's an experiment. Maybe it's just a story that sells. I don't know. I don't want to know."

She looked at me like I had said the most disappointing thing she'd ever heard. I sighed and looked at the ground. It really didn't do Arturo any justice. He was absolutely amazing. If it weren't for my own overwhelming fears, I probably could tell him every detail of my life.

Maybe in the end it was the idea of him staying with me that felt the most terrifying. You can only be hurt once by someone leaving you because they're gone after that. If Arturo loved me, his ability to hurt me grew every day. Even considering what Al said, it didn't change my fear. Flip and I stared at each other, and she looked like she was trying really hard to understand what was going on in my head.

At least you know what your fucking problems are now.

"I—"

"Hey," Uno said, coming around the SUV.

We both snapped to attention, surprised to see him.

"The emcees are reading the rules. I didn't want you two to miss team roll call." He was smiling and his voice was warm, but something was off.

"Uno," I said, reaching out for him. He didn't dodge me per se, just took a step toward the crowd. *Or a step back.* "Come on, we have some ass to kick."

I couldn't tell if Flip noticed the weird vibe behind Uno's voice, and I didn't get the chance to ask. We followed him. He didn't say anything on the way, and we crowded in with the rest of the team as the emcees started calling team names.

"Hey," I said, brushing my hand down the back of Uno's. He jumped a little as if I had interrupted his thoughts. I didn't think I had ever seen him that distracted at an event like this. I asked, "You okay?"

"Sí. I was just thinking." And he turned away.

My heart started to race. Uno's tone and expression were so off. I would have said more but it was game time. Nads shoved a pair of blades into my arms and I tried my best to put them on where I was standing. I tossed my shoes into the duffel The Major was carrying and tried to breathe. The emcee called the team members up for the potpourri round, which was Uno's event. We screamed, chanting *if you know, you Uno* with the crowd. For a second, Uno seemed himself as he waved and trotted to meet up with the other competitors in the designated area. When he got there, though, his expression went far away again.

"Is he okay?" Flip asked me.

I started gushing questions at her. "What if he heard? What if he knows I have feelings for him? Do you think he thinks I've lied?"

Flip shrugged. She put her hands on my shoulders, we were about eye to eye with my skates on. She was only half in hers. "Pirate, it's okay if he heard or didn't hear. He's your friend. Take some deep breaths and find out what's on his mind."

"Don't do that," I said, blinking at her.

She grinned at me.

"What're you talking about?" Nads asked.

"Nothing," we said together. The crowd roared when the competition assistants hauled out a wagon full of those wheely squares kids used to play with in elementary school gym class. Uno took one of the innocuous-looking toys without much expression.

And we watched him do the worst of anyone in the group. Most people's first instinct was to treat the thing like a board, and they skated out across the park. Uno did that too and went for a nearby rail. That sent him sprawling, though. He recovered enough to fail at dropping into a bowl, and then ate shit on some stairs.

Everyone in this round got a cursory five hundred points because it was a shitshow of a round that was purely for fun. The winner got fifteen hundred points. It wouldn't be Uno this time. He moved to the edge of the roped-off area, staying with the other skaters who didn't place. He watched as the top three in the round tried to complete tricks with industrial dollies, the big flat square kind. I didn't watch them. I watched Uno.

The worst part was not that he had failed to land anything, it was that he wasn't his bright, playful self. He usually treated fuckups as fan service. He'd make a show of it and still walk away as endearing and loved as if he'd won. So, to have him lose so badly and not even ham it up was almost terrifyingly out of character. After it was said and done, Uno came back to us five hundred points up and bleeding from a palm. I immediately reached out to him. He didn't let me have his hand, though. I guessed it was okay. I wouldn't make him touch me. Not that it didn't hurt a little. I was about to talk to him when Nads stalked over.

"What the fuck was that?" Nads screamed at him, pushing him a little.

"Fuck off, Nads." Uno sighed, pushing past Nads and me, heading toward the van. There was a first aid tent, but Uno didn't look like he was going in that direction.

"Hey," Chandler said, coming through the crowd. "That was something to see. How's your hand?"

Chandler stopped in front of Uno, and Uno let him see it. It took a second to shove down my own jealousy. Standing there with Chandler made it easy for Nads to catch up. He grabbed Uno by the shoulder and turned him to face him.

"Come on, man, where's your head?" He wasn't quite yelling this time.

"Fuck you. I just had a bad run." Uno tried walking away again, but Nads grabbed him.

"Nads, leave him alone," Rocky said, catching his cousin's arm. I tried to put myself between him and Uno, but Nads pushed me out of the way. I regretted putting my skates on. It made it hard to follow them in the crowd.

Nads wouldn't be deterred. "Oh, okay, so you can focus on fucking politics, but when we need you to get your head out of your ass and do your job, you fuck it up. And your only reason is a *bad run*. Uno, this round was the only reason you were on the fucking team."

Uno turned. Instantly The Major, Rocky, and I stacked ourselves between him and Nads. Uno shouldered past me and The Major but couldn't get past Rocky. He pointed at Nads. "Go fuck yourself, Nads. What points have you even earned, man? I can earn more on my worst days than you on your best. What's your problem?"

"What's my problem? That's funny since it's everyone's problem when your fucking shitshow of a life turns our place in this competition into a political drama and then you blow the one round you really mattered in." Nads was red faced and almost foaming at the mouth.

The Major and I had managed to get back between them. The Major was trying to push Nads back, but they were failing. I faced Uno, but I didn't touch him. He looked past me, past us all as if no one was there.

"Stop it, Nads. Uno and Pirate are the only reason we have been ahead at all," The Major said.

"And sponsors," Uno snapped. Chandler added himself to the line of people trying to keep Uno and Nads separated. Flip was doing her best to keep fans from getting involved.

Bringing up the sponsors somehow elevated Nads's rage to an unheard-of level. "Fucking great, nice to have 'em and lose 'em. They won't keep us if we lose. And what would all of this fucking shit have been for? The shirts and getting the other team kicked out of the comp? All for the Uno show. Your politics are risking everything, and you don't have the decency to skate well. Decided to take the whole team down with you, I guess."

"Bro, chill," Rocky said.

Where Nads got more animated, fighting his way out of The Major's arms, Uno went still. In a soft but passionate voice I'd never heard from him before, he said, "Sure Nads, fuck me and my life—*my politics*—right? You're the straight, white, cis dude here. You get the privilege of being boring and doing the least, and no one questions your place on this team, in this sport, or in this fucking city. You think *I'm* making my life political? Why the fuck would anyone ask for this? This is just how it is for me every fucking day, man. Good or bad. My life will never *not* be a part of some shitty political agenda in this fucking country. It's so great to know me and my one bad day are no more important to you than my life is to the assholes who called me Mr. Green Card. Nice to know that as soon as you start to worry, you have someone to blame it on. Glad I can play that role in your life, Nads."

Nads looked like he was going to say something, but The Major shoved him. They shouted, "Nathan."

Nads looked at them for the first time, surprised to hear his given name.

The Major said, "Walk the fuck away."

Nads looked around at all the faces staring back at him. No one was on his side.

"Fuck you guys," Nads said and walked through the stunned crowd.

By the time the rest of us turned around, Uno was gone.

We ended the night three hundred points short of first place. For the first time, we weren't leading the competition. The only reason it wasn't a five hundred point drop was because Flip and The Major bladed perfectly, and Rocky biked like a god. I was absolutely shit on blades and would have busted my face open if it hadn't been for my helmet. I still was able to get at least a few hundred points. The only other person to win cursory points was Nads. Despite being a humongous dill-hole, he was poetry on a bike, his tricks technically perfect even if he wasn't the most creative. But his perfect round ended when he lost both tires on a rail that had been chewed up into a sharp point along one side. Since it was a hazard of the competition using skateparks as is, he didn't get to redo his attempt. At some point, Chandler told us all that Uno had Ubered back home. The drive back to Denver was silent.

By Friday, I was convinced Arturo was avoiding me. When I got home after that disastrous night, his door was shut, so I let him be. Then he was gone almost all the next day. When I did try to talk to him throughout the week, I got back a lot of vague answers like "I'm going to be late to this" or "I have to go to bed for that" or "I'm going to be out for a while." I couldn't blame him for his mood. Even if I took myself out of the equation, his fight with Nads was enough to send anyone into a depression, even the ever-optimistic Arturo. So, while I tried to engage with him, I also tried not to be pushy.

He did his part for the competition, though. Since all hell broke loose before he took pictures for our socials, he spent the week retweeting and sharing anything positive that had any of us in it. I wondered how much of it he was doing to salvage his portfolio. And I wondered how much of it was to salvage the team and his respective relationships with the others. Rocky had his back and liked or commented. The Major, Flip, and even I did what we could for our online Hail Mary at keeping up the momentum of fans we were building. Nads was silent, and despite the posts, Arturo was silent.

I could not shake the idea it had something to do with what he might have overheard me telling Flip. I felt two ways about that. First, I was paralyzed with fear that he knew I was in love with him and that was making him avoid me. And second, I was paralyzed with shame for thinking his mood had anything to do with me when his fight with Nads was more important. I was fucking stuck either way. But I missed him. He was still my friend. By Friday, I was determined to go into the weekend on speaking terms with him. I decided to confront him as I heard him come home from work. I was desperate to get back what had suddenly gotten so far away.

I was in my room when I heard the door open and close. I felt nervous, so I grabbed the mug I had been drinking coffee from and went to talk to him. *Yeah, the mug will definitely help keep me from taking emotional damage.* My brain reworked the sentence into a 5-7-5 as I went down the hall. It was soothing, and I landed on the right order by the time I stepped into the kitchen. *My only defense/from emotional damage/is a coffee mug.*

He was leaning into the fridge and didn't acknowledge me walking up.

"Hey," I said.

He jumped a little and looked at me. "Hi."

His smile was fake, which was discouraging, but I pressed on. It seemed rude to just up and ask him why he'd been avoiding me, so I asked, "How was work?"

"It was okay. Look, I'm just gonna order a pizza, then go to bed. I'm fucking exhausted."

He started to walk past me, I presumed to go to his room. I grabbed his arm. "Art. Are you avoiding me?"

There! Out in the open. No turning back. I let him go and went back to holding the mug. I was actually squeezing it for dear life. I was surprised it didn't break in my hands. It took a moment for him to turn and look at me. His face was a wall, like something I would expect from myself. It looked so out of place on him. He sighed and sank back to lean on the counter across from me.

"No, at least not specifically."

"Why does it seem like it, then? I mean, where have you been?"

He flapped his arms a little. "No sé. I thought I had something in the team that maybe I didn't."

See, Thomas, not about you. I sighed, disappointed in my relief, and put the mug down. "I'm really sorry about what happened. Nads is an asshole and shouldn't have said any of that. He also doesn't speak for the whole team."

"No one's said anything to me about it."

You haven't really been approachable. "I bet they would if you give them a chance. We all should've done more in that moment to stand up for you. I can't speak for the others. It just, lately, feels like every time I try to talk to you, you walk away. Even just now I had to stop you. Are you not responding to the others' messages or calls too? None of this is an excuse for not offering support. We want to talk to you about it—I want to talk to you about it. I guess it just looked like you needed space more than anything. I'm sorry for wrongly assuming that."

He nodded, his hair flopping along. He crossed his arms at his chest, and he looked almost like he was folding in on himself. Then he fixed a stern gaze on me. "Do you agree with him?"

"Who? Nads? Fuck no, man. You're my best friend and the best person I've ever known. I wouldn't have anything if it wasn't for you," I said, surprising us both. "Besides, team stuff is for Uno and Pirate to work out, and Pirate will always choose Uno."

"And Thomas?" he asked.

I love you. I hesitated, afraid those words would come out of my mouth. It was too vulnerable, and it didn't seem like the time to talk about this. So, I found something else. "I missed you."

He smiled, and his walled expression caved in a little. "I'm sorry. I wasn't avoiding you. I have a lot to think about. I *was* taking space, I guess. Maybe I needed it even if I didn't want it."

"Okay. That's cool. I get that. I'm glad you're getting what you need. I'm here too if you want to talk."

He shook his head. "I don't want to talk."

I tried to reach into my bag of therapy lessons for something resembling comfort. *Where's your shitty advice when I need it, Richard?* I was so used to being comforted by Arturo, bolstered by him, that I didn't know what would help him besides talking. He usually always said yes to talking.

"You want a hug or something? Coffee?" I said, presenting my cup. "I mean, what would help you feel better, if anything? I could buy you the pizza or at least order it for you."

He laughed, genuine and real, and a sound I had missed. "Yeah, I'll take the hug."

I crossed to him, slipping my hands around his waist, putting the mug down on the counter he was leaning on. He threw his arms over my shoulders. I didn't know what to do next.

"Arturo? I—"

He exhaled forcefully and squeezed me tighter. I got the impression he didn't want me to look at him. "Thomas, can we just not fucking talk about anything ever again?"

"Hey Google, how do you say 'what do you want on your pizza' in sign language?"

He laughed, the depth of it sending a rumble through my chest. And we both laughed when the robot voice of Google answered with a video link. We ignored it. Instead, I looked at him. I wanted to see the brightness in his face that came with his laugh.

His face wasn't bright. Instead, there was confusion. He started to ask a question. "Are…we…is…"

Fuck me. I was terrified of what he was going to say. But he never finished it. Instead, he leaned in and kissed me. The heat and force of it made my head swim and my knees weak. I practically collapsed against him. He pushed back, taking my space until my ass hit the counter. He crushed me against it. He kissed like he knew exactly what he wanted and was taking it. It was hard to admit to myself how much hope I put into that kiss. Even if he had overheard me and Flip talking, maybe it was okay. Arturo wouldn't lead me on.

I'm the one leading people on.

"Art, I—" I said, pulling back just enough to speak. I kept a tight grip on his hips, though.

He looked at me. His lips were parted and he was breathing hard. With his mouth and his hands and his hips in contact with me, it was hard to think. I had to think. I had to tell him. We had to talk.

"You want to go to my room?" I asked him. *That's not what I, your brain, said to do, you trashcan fire of a human.* It was going to be fine. I could tell a different conversation was going on, one beyond words. He had trusted me with himself sexually, and I was lucky for that, especially after everything he had said in our interview. I knew what a great distraction and a great comfort sex could be. Arturo's expression of relief wasn't a surprise. He nodded. *Why bother having a brain if you aren't going to use it?*

I led the way to my room.

CHAPTER TWELVE

Arturo

Thomas was like a GPS through a dark forest. I was grateful for his direction and his distraction. Everything inside me had gone cold for a while after the shouting match with Nads. If what he said was true, it wouldn't have been the first time in my life I didn't understand some interpersonal connection. I had to wonder if I'd crossed some social boundary. I wanted to be his friend. At the same time, it was hard to believe that Nads could be on the same team with us, be best friends with The Major, and not understand the money wasn't worth trading the dignity of our identities for. The cycle of wanting to be his friend and wanting to write him off as a bigot was like running on a hamster wheel, going nowhere fast.

Between Nads and what I had overheard Thomas telling Flip, I had yet another new feeling. Was it rejection? Heartbreak? The words I had overheard echoed in my head. *We didn't marry for love, so why would anyone ever believe we'd hook up for it.* It was mostly surprising how much it hurt to know he wasn't in love with me. I hadn't thought he was, but I must have been hoping. I had been so fucking preoccupied trying to figure out my own feelings I got blindsided by his. But he insisted we were still friends. Then he was in my arms. And he was warm in a way that I hadn't felt in days. I decided that ultimately him not loving me didn't change anything even if it hurt to know it wasn't shared. So, what really was different now that I knew? *Besides me and everything.*

As he walked down the hall, I stared at the spot at the back of his neck, exposed under his high bun of hair, and wondered if I should tell him. I was sure it was love. The pain in my chest cleared up any doubt. The hurt didn't stop me from thinking about being with him, though. His mouth still felt right on mine even if everything else in my life was a little wrong. And that was a gift in and of itself since I hadn't known I could feel so much for someone.

We stepped into his room and I looked around. Thomas was a tidy guy, no clothes on the floor, no debris, even his bed was made. The decor was black and cool grays. There was some red as an accent color, his sheets were red, and the rug he put down had thin lines of red thread that made the round gray rug look almost like a baseball. I watched him go to a side table and pull things out, setting them on it before turning to me. Around him I could see lube and condoms.

My heart stopped beating. "You want to have sex—like penetration?"

He smiled a perfectly cocky smile. "If you want, you…me… neither…both…I'm not picky. Just prepared, I guess. Besides, that stuff is good for other things too."

"I don't have objects for penetration."

He didn't react. "I do. Feel free to use them on me. I even have a harness."

I stared at him.

He turned red under my gaze. "There are a wide variety of people in my past. I just wanted you to know what options exist. I'm going for full disclosure. Don't overthink it. I never do."

I blinked and tried to find my center of gravity. I didn't know if I was ready for that.

He crossed to me and put a hand on my chest, pressing in a way that was reassuring. "Anything is okay. Even 'not right now' is okay. This offer isn't going anywhere." Indefinite. It *felt* indefinite. That was important. I knew enough about Thomas to know he wouldn't give just anyone that kind of permission. I didn't know if he meant just for tonight or if it was like his kisses. Okay, even if he wasn't in love with me, maybe he loved me on some level, something in between.

Thomas slipped his hands around my waist, sliding under my shirt so his fingertips brushed my bare sides. His hands were warm and familiar. I closed my eyes and followed his movements in my mind. He smiled as he traced his fingers up my chest, pulling my shirt up with them, then over my head. The strap-on he mentioned wasn't on the nightstand, but I assumed it was in the same drawer the lube had come from. What the fuck was the next step?

"Art?" There was hesitation in his voice even if there wasn't any in his touch. He was holding on to my waist, rubbing with his thumbs.

"Yeah?" The feeling that passed from him to me was a general sense of honest vulnerability. Even with his greater experience, he was as open and exposed as I was.

"There really is no pressure," he said.

I nodded. I wanted to explain that my hesitation wasn't pressure or fear. I was just sorting instructions in my head. But I couldn't really find the words. I stepped closer to him, leaving only a sliver of space between us. "Te desco, pero I guess I'm just slow."

I reached up and pulled his hair loose from the ponytail. Then I sank my fingers in it. With a gentle pull, I tipped his chin up and kissed him. He gripped me, almost too hard, but I liked it. The fire he generated within me flared brighter, like a fine blue flame. I had a small picture of what many kinds of sex with him could be like, and I wanted all of them.

I stopped kissing him long enough to get his shirt over his head. With the fabric gone, he leaned into me until he was completely flush with my body, kissing the part of my neck that was level with his mouth.

"God, you're so warm," I said, wrapping my arms around him.

"Are you cold?"

I snorted. "No, never mind."

I pulled him down on his bed until he was lying on top of me. I wasn't willing to let him go, so he squirmed until he was straddling me, nuzzling kisses as he got comfortable. I was so focused on the way his chest felt against mine and the way his soft hair grazed my skin that I almost forgot there was opportunity for more. I could have just lain together forever.

"What do you want to do?" he asked. He shifted enough to lie almost full bodied against me, his head propped on his hand, which was resting on my chest.

I stared at the ceiling and thought about it. I was also choosing to believe, completely, that there would be other times like this, other ways to explore him, other places—even my room. I had really enjoyed seeing him in my shirt the other day, so I figured seeing him in my bed would be ten times as great. But the most important thing was it didn't all have to happen tonight. Maybe he wasn't in love with me, but this wasn't nothing.

"I think it'd be fun to do something different from the other night, but not penetration." I tried to get through the statement without being embarrassed, but my face warmed anyway.

He smiled. "Sounds good. I have a few ideas. How naked do you want to be?"

There was almost no embarrassment in his voice. The only thing I heard was flirty confidence. I had only ever seen him this sure of himself when skating. I liked it. Him unbothered by embarrassment or shame was beautiful. He tongued his lip ring and slipped a finger just inside the waist of my jeans.

I wasn't a naked type of guy generally, but in the last year I had gotten pretty lax about clothes mostly because of Thomas. He was one of the only people who I felt saw me exactly as I wanted to be seen, no matter my scars or differences. I pulled him to me, kissing him, feeling his skin and muscle and bones where our torsos met. He felt so thin in my arms.

"Yup," I said, "I definitely want all the way naked."

He nodded once, resolutely. He kneeled and started undoing my fly. The only part of him I could really reach was his legs, so I ran my hand along his thighs as he worked. He focused only on what he was doing. He was so gorgeous he was hard to look at. I closed my eyes and tried to breathe.

"What position did you have in mind?" I asked.

When my pants were out of the way, he started to work on his own. He had to stand to manage it. I opened my eyes. The fabric slid away, revealing red briefs and strong legs. Almost all the way bare, he would have made the perfect cover model for a tattoo magazine. He didn't notice me watching him. He was thinking, staring at the wall as he removed the briefs. I hadn't known the tattoo that started on his ribs went all the way down his thigh.

"There's a sort of cowboy meets doggie position. The idea is to get off by rubbing your dick along someone's ass crack," he finally answered and his eyes met mine.

He crossed his arms casually. I laughed. His explanation was so matter-of-fact, he seemed almost ambivalent. I, on the other hand, had never heard those words in his tenor voice. It did something for me. He seemed amused by my laughing and waited me out. When I overcame my shock, I thought about it.

"Um, so you on top?"

His answering grin was devilish. "Works for everyone."

"How do you know?"

"Friends…research…a willingness to watch a wide variety of porn."

I trusted him. He was naked, looking at me like this was the most ordinary thing to ever happen, and that was trustworthy. It was also very sexy. I sat up a little.

"Come back," I said.

He came slowly, crawling. His eyes never left mine. He came all the way for a kiss, his body spreading over me. Him being on top was different. I constantly felt like I wanted to trap him under me forever, safe and happy. He didn't treat me the same. He hooked an arm under my head, half to hold himself up, half to get a hand in my hair, and that was the only entrapping thing he did. His free hand roamed over my chest, but he stayed neatly in my arms. He wanted to be held. Physical intimacy was like everything else between us. There was no competitiveness, just feelings that complemented each other, wanting to hold and wanting to be held.

I flipped us. I wanted to kiss deeper, hold tighter. He gasped, and his legs came around my waist. His dick was hard between us. I pressed my whole body down on him. It was like lying down on a bed of coals. I kissed his neck and caught his hands, pinning them above his head.

"Fuck," he gasped, the word followed by soft moans as I rocked my hips, grinding our bodies together.

Genitals were fine, sure, but I especially loved his hands and lips the most. I thought of our first kiss and how obsessed with his mouth I had become since. Then I thought of him slipping the ring on his finger and the feel of his dick in my grip. One of his hands slipped mine and raked through my hair. He bucked his hips.

"Shit, I could come just like this," he murmured, his voice a rumble in my ear.

I paused and tried to catch my breath. "Fuck."

Thomas gave me a surprised look. "Why are you stopping? This feels fucking amazing."

"Sí, pero…I want to do the cowboy doggie thing."

I don't know what I expected him to do, but he just shrugged. "Cool."

"Okay. Do you want to go first?" I asked.

He shook his head. He smiled up at me lazily. He added a wink. "Have fun."

"*Cool? Have fun*?" I laughed. "I'm gonna need you to find more excitement, por favor."

"Estoy caliente. Vamos!" he shouted. He put his hands on my chest and pushed me away. I peeled myself away from him and sat back on my heels. He rolled over and made himself comfortable again. Seeing him like this short-circuited my brain. He looked at me over his shoulder. I wondered again how to start.

"Want a suggestion?" Thomas said, turning over enough to look at me more straight on.

"No," I said indignantly. "Sí."

"Just straddle me and adjust, it'll all slot together."

His nonchalance was fucking attractive. I was still hesitant.

"Do you like this? Like, it doesn't turn you off."

"Fuck no, you'll see." He smiled and rolled over. "You don't have to keep your briefs on if you don't want to. And the lube is there if you want it."

Lube was probably a good idea. I reached for it and fought with the plastic seal round the bottle. He didn't move, but I could see his smile. I straddled him, more on his thighs than his ass. He tensed, and I trusted that it was from excitement. I applied some lube to myself and tossed the bottle away. On an impulse I traced a lubed finger down his ass crack. He moaned into the bedspread and jerked his hips.

"Christ," he said.

He really did seem to like this. That obliterated the last bit of doubt I had in my mind. *Vamos.* I moved to be more on his ass and ran my fingers down his back as I put myself where I figured made the most sense. He flexed his ass as our skin made contact. I understood all at once what he meant as soon as I was all the way seated. I adjusted and then my dick was between his ass cheeks.

"Oh fuck," I gasped. I followed the instinct to grind into him, rocking my hips. I closed my eyes and held on to his shoulders as my urge to thrust increased. It was somehow getting better as I moved, like our connection was becoming more seamless, fitting together more completely.

"Yes, fucking yes," Thomas answered.

He put a hand behind his back and gestured for me to take it. I did. Suddenly I had leverage to add to my thrusting.

"Am I hurting you?" I gasped, not stopping as I waited for the answer.

He moaned and flexed. "Hell no. I love it. I want to feel you come."

"Fuck yes." I groaned. I rolled my hips, picking up pace, picking longer strokes. The sounds he made when I found the rhythm I wanted made my brain block out everything except for the reality of fucking him. I had to wonder if a brain alone could orgasm.

"God, Arturo," he said, squeezing my hand. The orgasmic sensation moved from my mind to my chest, like my heart was exploding from the joy of being with him. It was him. Thomas. The first real love of my life.

"I'm close," I said.

Thomas's whole body reacted, tensing and almost thrusting beneath me. I let go of his hand and slipped my arms under him, his back hot and solid against my chest. Holding him sent the orgasm rocketing down my body. I tried to keep moving to keep up with it, but I quickly failed.

"Arturo," he said.

The orgasm was so sudden and total that I froze, my entire being completely focused on coming. I moaned against Thomas's skin as it passed, squeezing him as close as I could.

"Fuck yes," he gasped, squirming. "Fuck, I want to come so bad."

"I can—"

"Sit back," he demanded. In fast synchrony, I sat back kneeling, orgasm still tingling along my nerves. He didn't turn, he just knelt and leaned against me back to chest. He pulled my hand around him, asking without asking for me to touch him. I did, wrapping my arm around his chest and my hand around his dick. He thrust into my fist, using my body behind him as support. I could see every part of him, my view over his shoulder perfect. I kissed and sucked his neck as he fucked against me.

"Fuck, fuck, fuck."

Warmth coated my hand, a moan catching in his throat. He

covered my hand with his again and together we stroked him through it. When he was spent, he sank back against me. I sat back on my heels to support us both.

"Jesus," he said in a breath, wiping sweat off his face.

"It's pronounced *Arturo*," I whispered into his ear.

"Shut up."

We stayed like that for a few seconds. Shivers followed his fingers over my skin where he caressed me. When our breathing was close to normal, he turned slightly in my arms and tipped his head up for a kiss. I gave it to him.

"How was it?" he asked. Now that we had both come, his cockiness was gone.

"More amazing than I could imagine."

He smiled and his face pinked. I wanted to touch his cheeks, stroke his hair. But I was very aware I had cum on my hand.

"I need to wash my hand. There's also a lot of lube making my southern hemisphere tropical."

Thomas laughed and shifted. I started toward the door, snagging my briefs along the way. He stood and grabbed his towel off the floor. He said, "Hey."

I turned to him.

"Come back? I mean, do you want to hang out with me? Here? Tonight? After we clean up?"

The want on his face was clear. Now that I knew my feelings, I understood that our relationship had always been love on some level. It was like one of those memes—*you can't unsee it.* I couldn't unsee how into him I was, and I had always been able to see how much of himself he was giving me. It was stupid how having sex with him hadn't produced nearly as many stomach butterflies as him asking me to stay did.

"Yeah, sure...okay..." I stuttered. Then I ducked away, truly excited.

We ended up ordering pizza and lounging half-dressed together in Thomas's bed. We didn't talk about anything serious, and he put a movie on his laptop. Sure, we had a big-ass TV in the living room, but I wouldn't have moved if someone had paid me. I even made him go get the pizza when it came to the door. When one movie ended, he just started another one. I didn't know I was asleep until I woke up.

He had cleaned around me and had even put my phone on a charger by his bed. I noticed all of that before I realized I was holding him while he slept. I snoozed my alarm. I had to go to the stadium, but I allowed myself a few minutes to watch him.

Lying with him, I texted him the details of my morning, and that I would meet him and the rest of the team at the Commerce City skatepark for the last day of CASST. I added that Chandler had agreed to swing by and grab me. I would send the group chat the same info so the team would know I was going to be late. Not that I was skating today—only The Major, Flip, and Thomas were. It was up to them to get the points we needed to place. I wasn't following the math after the last event, but I was sure we wouldn't make enough points for first. It was funny that both Nads and I were useless now, despite the show he made at the last event.

I noticed a message from The Major. I opened it. *Uno, I'm so fucking sorry about Nads. Not making excuses, he's an asshole. I love you and love having you on the team, and he really does need to get his shit together. I'll try to keep him off your ass today. I need you both, okay?*

It was so easy for The Major to just toss out phrases like "I love you" and "I need you." I didn't respond even though I appreciated it. Thomas had said to give the others time. And I guess he was right. While I truly believed no one could speak for a group, my heart seemed to believe The Major spoke for Flip and Rocky. Thomas shifted against me, breaking my thoughts, and I watched to see if he would wake up. He didn't, he just snuggled in deeper. My phone alarm went off again. I couldn't stay.

"Adiós, mi amor," I whispered, peeling myself out of his bed.

I dressed and got on the bus to the stadium. It took me less time than I thought to sort out my timecard with my manager. They were confused by some of the shifts I had traded so I could take CASST events off. I had to show them emails and texts between me and coworkers to vouch for us both. It was a terrible system, but I got it done.

I sat on one of the planters outside the stadium when it was over to wait for Chandler, using my board across my lap as a table for my phone. I checked my messages. There was a thumbs-up from The Major and Flip in the group chat, what I assumed was a fart emoji from Rocky, and a sleepy face from Thomas. Chandler texted: *on the way, 15 min*. The red alert bubbles on all my social media apps were a burden sometimes. Since last weekend, our social media had been a shitshow over the fight with Nads. I had dozens of DMs on every platform about it. Even the sponsors wanted to know what was up. I would get to them all eventually or at least put together some statement. *Someday*. I texted my sisters instead, shoving down thoughts about my portfolio. The media wave we had been riding all competition long was probably crashing down around me and I was actively ignoring it. So much for that.

Arturo: *Hey*

Amilia: *Hola, hermano.*

Ariana: *Artito!*

Arturo: *I had sex with Thomas.*

I got a kick out of watching their messages come in. At first, they were excited, then they were disgusted. Their repulsion wasn't that it was gay sex, for them it was just because I was their baby brother. It took no time at all for them to get over that and to start demanding details. Someone behind me cleared their throat.

"Are you Arturo Ortiz?"

"The one and only—oh." Two cops were standing behind me. "Shit."

CHAPTER THIRTEEN

Thomas

I checked the time on my phone. It was forty minutes past when I expected Arturo. And my last few messages to him had gone unanswered. I thought about texting Chandler, but I was probably overreacting. Right? I looked at The Major. They were looking around too.

"What's up, boss?" I asked. They had been quiet since we met up. Nads was coming from work and wasn't able to pick us up, so everyone had been on their own to get to the park. The Major looked worried but was doing a decent job of keeping it together. Rocky was filming because Uno had asked him to. The Major and I had both taken time with the fans in between our heats. Now that we were done with our final round and neither Uno nor Nads was present, maybe it was time to panic. Flip was waiting with the other bladers for her last run.

"When was Nads supposed to be here?" I asked them.

The Major shrugged and crossed their arms over their chest. I watched them squint at Flip, who was only a hundred-ish yards away, as if to focus on her. They said, "I don't fucking know what his problem is. He said, 'I'll get there when I get there.'"

I sighed. "We're falling apart, Maj."

"Don't remind me." Then they turned to me. "By the way, I'm sorry for what happened between Nads and Uno."

"Why are you telling me?"

They uncrossed their arms and shoved their hands in their pockets. "I just know how close you and Uno are, not to mention you're married.

I told him too. I realize you guys came into this together, not that you aren't important individually, but well, you guys came *together*. It's hard for me to think about this team without Nads since we came into it together the same way. But lately he's been a royal bitch. Anyway, I'd take any beef with him as a beef with me—in most cases. So, I wouldn't blame you for making Uno's beef with Nads your own. Besides, you've put yourself between him and harm more times than I can count. I really love this team, even Nads. I don't know who's shit on his breakfast, though."

"Trouble at home?"

The Major laughed. "Maybe. He's been really weird, the last, like, six months. I've never known him to be like this. But he won't tell me what the fuck's going on."

I hadn't actually expected The Major to answer that question honestly. "Shit, I'm sorry," I said. "And you've known him for..."

"Ever. He was my—"

"Hey," Nads said, coming through the crowd. He was breathless and a little red-faced.

"Glad you decided to show up," The Major snapped.

I didn't say anything.

Nads grinned. "I wouldn't miss them telling us we won."

"Well, we won't know that until—" The Major stopped and faced him. "What the fuck are you on today?"

"What?"

"You haven't been half this happy in weeks, dude."

He didn't say anything, just flipped The Major off and looked toward where the skaters were about to start their heats. He *did* seem happy. He even continued smiling a little as we waited for the emcees to announce the round. No one pressed him, though. Even I gave up on wondering about him and watched Flip. She made the other bladers look like amateurs. She completed her last skate for the competition with a perfect backflip. The crowd around us screamed.

"Geez. See how much better we skate without Uno?" Nads said, clapping.

"What the fuck, man?" I said. "Those two things aren't related."

Nads rolled his eyes. "Aren't they?"

"Hey, fuck you," I said. "No, they aren't."

"It doesn't matter anyway. Let's get closer so we can see who won this thing."

He was so calm, it set off alarm bells in the back of my brain. He wasn't even shouting. His voice was devoid of tone, angry or otherwise. I didn't follow him. I checked my phone again to see if there was any word from Arturo.

"Hey," Flip said, rolling up to me. "Is Uno here?"

"Not yet."

"That's not like him."

"Maybe I should call him," I said.

"I'm surprised you haven't." She was shiny with sweat and her smile was tight.

"You were fucking amazing out there," I said, remembering myself.

She laughed. "I don't need you to tell me that. Call your man."

"I've been calling, but he hasn't answered."

"It's not like you'd burst into flames if you tried it again."

I pressed call. As the phone rang, the focus of the crowd shifted toward the stage where the DJ had been set up. Emcee Waste trotted out onstage and started recapping the competition, interrupted only by cheers from assorted teams and fans. I got Uno's voicemail twice before I gave up.

"Shit. I'm gonna try Chandler."

Flip nodded and crossed her arms to wait it out. I selected Chandler's number and waited. Again, I was sent to voicemail. But this time it was different. It didn't ring enough. It felt like he had forwarded my call. Or maybe he was on with someone else. Maybe they were somewhere in the crowd, being blocked by fans.

"What the fuck?" I sighed.

"You okay?" Rocky tossed an arm around my shoulder, pointing his phone camera at the stage.

"Fine."

"They'll turn up," Flip reassured.

I nodded, but I didn't feel it. I let Rocky and Flip lead me by the shoulders toward Nads and The Major.

"Here we go," Nads said over the rumble of the crowd. He was the happiest I had ever seen him.

Waste's voice was almost too loud as he shouted into the microphone. "All right, all the final points are in, and we have the final scores for each team. As we call your name, come up and collect your prizes. We'll announce the team winners and then the individual prizes."

I stared at my phone, willing it to ring. Waste pressed on. First team up was the last team in the competition, tenth place. It wasn't who I thought it would be, so that meant some of the teams had climbed since I had looked at the scores last night.

"Did you call him?" The Major asked.

"He didn't answer. Have you heard anything?"

"Nothing."

I wondered if I should call his family. As questions mounted in my head, teams climbed the stage, collected small prizes, and left. Minutes were fast becoming an hour, but it felt like the slow crawl of centuries. My heart started to hammer, and an anxious sweat broke out on my skin.

"Fuck," I said. I scanned the crowd, seeing no one.

"All right, folks! We're down to the top three teams." Waste paused to wait for the crowd to stop screaming.

"Now according to my math, this should be us," The Major said. We were third. That wasn't bad. It wasn't as much money but—

"In third place, G House Gas."

I froze.

We all froze. *The Eco Guys?*

"What? How?"

The Major scrolled through the notes they had in their phone, counting on their fingers. "What'd I miss? We were at least three hundred points behind those guys."

"See? I told you. I made sure we'd win," Nads was telling them, shouting over the cheering. *Win? To win we would have had to—* My gut dropped into my shoes as I met Nads's eyes. He was smiling, but it faltered when he looked at me.

"In second place, Taste of Spring."

That wasn't us either. That was a team from Colorado Springs. They were standing near us, and their shouting was a mix of excitement and disappointment. They went to the stage to collect their second-place prize. Something serious had to have happened for them not to take first. There weren't enough points at this event alone for us to have gotten ahead.

Rocky and Flip were cheering their asses off because that could only mean we were first. Fans started to close in. I felt shoulder pats and heard offers for high fives. I heard my name shouted. I reacted to none of it. I couldn't take my eyes off Nads. Nads was there, Uno wasn't, and we had somehow won. I had a bad feeling as to what the reason could be. In two steps, I was face-to-face with Nads.

"What the fuck did you do?" He might not have been able to hear me, but the tightness around his eyes made it clear he knew what I wanted. I had the front of his shirt in a fist before either of us realized I had moved.

"What the fuck did you do, *Nads*!" I screamed.

I could almost feel the cameras in the crowd turn toward me. There went even more of everything the team stood for and the reputation Uno had tried to build for us. Then again, it was probably on-brand for me in the grand scheme of things. The Major tried to get between us, but I shoved them away. Nads had fifty pounds and six inches on me, but I would claw through his rib cage if I had to. He shoved me off and stared me down.

"Now, you already know who the winner is. In a landslide victory, they managed to land three of the biggest point prizes in the competition. First, they caused a spectacle at the opening ceremony when two of their members got married on the spot, and just today, in a Hail Mary, we have confirmed Arturo 'Uno' Ortiz has successfully Visited A Jail even though he had to get arrested to do—"

My fist connected with Nads's nose before Waste finished his sentence.

"You fucking called the cops on him?" My voice broke as I shouted down at Nads, who was on the ground, already starting to bleed. The crowd oohed and backed up. Nads got on his feet and ran at me. He drove his shoulder into my stomach as his tackle connected and we went sprawling, taking The Major down with us. The force of his body colliding with mine, then me hitting the concrete caused a horrible pain to flash along my spine. It felt like my ribs were being zippered together. Breathing was almost impossible.

"I did what I had to," Nads said, defending himself. "I told you both I wouldn't let us lose."

I got an arm free and tried to punch him again, but he caught it, trying to pin me down. I bit his arm before he could. He screamed, and his elbow connected with my nose. He was a harder hitter than the bigot guy had been, plus it was my nose, so my eyes filled with tears, and I thrashed blindly. Only a second had passed before we were both gasping, bleeding, and intent on killing each other. In another second, Rocky and The Major grabbed Nads under the arms and pulled him off me. Flip got me to my feet. The crowd around us was loud with surprise and confusion.

"The Major Leaguers?" Waste's voice echoed.

"Pirate!" a familiar voice said. I almost didn't hear it. I wanted it to be Uno so badly that it took a second to connect the face to the name. Through the tears, I could see Chandler. He was practically climbing over people to get to us.

"Do you know what happened?" I shouted, shaking off my team-mates and running toward him.

"Yeah, I came to get you. They wouldn't let me near him, but I thought you might be able to help."

"Let's go."

I tailed Chandler out of the crowd, not looking back to see if anyone else followed.

❖

I was almost arrested trying to get into the police station. A bunch of fans had followed us and were messing up any attempt Chandler or I made to talk to someone about Uno. It left me screaming mad. At some point, the rest of the team came—except Nads, of course—and even more fans joined. When the media showed up, the cops came out and sent everyone home.

Defeated, I let the others into the apartment. Flip was on the phone with someone she knew who worked for a lawyer, and Chandler was talking to some connection he had in the police station. The apartment was loud with activity, but I felt like I was trapped in a fog. It had all become such a blur of phone calls and trying to talk to the police that I didn't even realize it was dark until The Major came into the kitchen and turned on the light.

"Fuck, Pirate," they said, walking to the far end of the kitchen then back. "I didn't know he was gonna do that. I fucking told him—"

"I believe you," I said with a sigh.

"You want some of this?" Rocky asked, pointing to the coffee-maker. He looked distraught, like he needed something to do. I nodded and handed him the coffee from the freezer.

"I don't know what his problem is, you know?" The Major said, opening cabinets like they lived here. "He's never wanted to win anything this badly. He didn't even think about the damage he could cause Uno."

"Yeah, he's been a real dick lately," Rocky answered, his tone tight but neutral.

"This is so far beyond being a dick, Rocks. He's going to pay whatever it takes to get Uno out, once we figure out who to talk to." I watched them hand mugs to Rocky, who was carefully placing coffee in the filter basket. I suddenly felt alone in my own kitchen even as they talked around me.

"With what money, Maj? He never has any."

"His winnings, I guess. How can he not get why I insist we never fuck up around the cops?"

"I don't know."

I walked away from their conversation and out the front door, wandering to the end of the hall. It was at least quiet. Each apartment had a light over the door as if this were some quaint neighborhood street, but the hall had no lights otherwise. We were the last of four apartments on the floor. At the end of the hall was a narrow window leading to a fire escape that looked more dangerous than a fire probably would be.

I leaned on the glass, staring down the two floors of rusting and broken metal. There were supposed to be shops below us, but no one seemed in a hurry to finish gentrifying this part of town. Most of the buildings around us were shitty apartments and empty stores. *There is nothing more/unhelpful right now than me/to you. I'm sorry.* My phone rang. I answered without looking. "Hello?"

"You okay?"

"Hey, Al," I said, surprisingly relieved. "Keeping up with the news?"

"Yeah, I'm…I…well, I'd offer help, but the person I'd've thought to call is already there."

"Who?"

"Chandler."

"Oh right." There was a small, busy silence as we searched for something to say to each other. I found something first. "It helps that you called."

"Any word?"

"No. There's no way to get hold of anyone. When we call the station, we get the runaround. And he hasn't called anyone. I don't think you can call cell phones from jail."

"Naw, you can. When a friend was arrested, he called me, but that was because he couldn't remember anyone else's number."

That was fair. The only numbers I knew by heart were Al's, my sister's, and a defunct landline that hadn't been used in a decade and a half. I wondered whose numbers Arturo remembered. His family's, for sure. Hell, he probably was like Al and memorized everyone's number. I thought of all the people Arturo knew. I could try to DM his sisters on social media, see if he called them. Then I remembered another number.

"The cop," I said.

"What?"

I was almost ecstatic. "I have the number for a cop in Boulder. I don't know how it works, but I could call her. The worst thing she could tell me is she can't do anything about it."

"Don't let me get in your way," Al said. We said a quick goodbye and hung up. I started back down the hall. I knew Uno had the number on a card in the apartment somewhere. I just had to—

I looked up just as someone turned into the hall. Our eyes met, and I might have shit myself with joy.

"Arturo," I said, rushing toward him. He let me hug him. "Fuck, how?"

"They dropped the charges and let me out or whatever. I don't think there *were* charges."

I stood back and put a hand to his face. I thought if I stopped touching him, he would evaporate. He rubbed his cheek against my palm and sighed. He looked infinitely tired.

"I'm so fucking sorry. As soon as we found out, we—"

He sighed. "Mira, I just want to go in and shower."

"Everyone's here. Well, everyone except Nads."

He squinted at me. "Why?"

"We were fucking worried. Christ, we were all trying to figure it out. No one else knew that Nads was going to do that. I've never seen The Major so mad. They all wanted to help. Rocky's making coffee."

He found that image as funny as I did, and his face broke into a small, worn smile. "Okay. But help me get rid of them? I'm not really in the mood for a crowd."

I nodded, surprised. I moved to open the door, but he stopped me.

"Why is it you insist on stopping fists with your face?" he asked, inspecting my cheek and chin under our door light.

"I don't *insist*. That's just where they're aiming."

"Duele?"

I shook my head. "I don't know that one."

His almost black eyes met mine, and his smile crept into them. "Does it hurt?"

I sighed. "Fuck yes."

He kissed my other cheek. I breathed him in. After a heartbeat, he let me go. When he stepped back, I let him into the apartment.

"Hey," he called, and I could see him put up a mask as the others rushed toward us. That's what my sister called it at least, a mask. I had never seen him use it.

The others peppered him with questions and pats on the back. They told him they were happy to see him and they were sorry. I don't think he really heard anyone. He did answer their questions, though. He told them the same thing he had told me and took a cup of coffee from Rocky. While he went to talk to Chandler, I went to The Major.

"Would y'all mind leaving?" I asked. "I don't think he's up for a crowd."

The Major nodded. "Trust me, I get it. I'm just glad he's out. I hope he sees that the rest of us didn't want this." They didn't wait for me to answer. They shouted at the others, "Right, Flip, Rocky—let's go. I have to work in the morning. I'm glad you're home, Uno."

While The Major negotiated with Flip and Rocky, I went to Chandler and told him the same thing. He nodded and said a few things to Arturo. He was the last to leave. Then it was just Arturo and me.

Chapter Fourteen

Arturo

I collapsed on the couch as soon as the house was empty. I couldn't bring myself to do anything except feel the dull ache radiating through my body. It felt worse than having skated for three days straight. I have never hit pavement hard enough to feel as bad as I did when I landed on that couch.

"Um, Art?"

"Yeah?"

Thomas stepped into my line of sight. He looked terrified or maybe worried beyond reason. I loved him for it. I had spent the day staring into the dead or hateful eyes of the cops. It was nice to see someone who cared. I shook off the thoughts and blinked.

"Lo siento," I said. "I didn't process what you said."

He sat on the arm of the couch as if he was afraid to get too close. "I asked if you wanted me to leave too."

I stared.

He let out a long breath. "I didn't know if you just wanted the rest gone or everyone. I don't mind. I get needing space."

I found myself shaking my head before he had finished his sentence. Thomas was the only one in the entire state I actually wanted to see. And I could tell by his relief he wanted to stay as badly as I wanted him to. But it was also impossible to sit there with him looking at me. We would have to settle on being in the same house for now.

"I think I'm gonna shower," I said.

He looked like he wanted to stop me for a moment, but then he nodded and let me pass. I went through the motions of cleaning myself. It had been insanely hot in the holding room, and the way I sweated made it torturous. The memory made me turn the water to cold. Instead of thinking about the hours I had lost sitting alone in that room, I read the shampoo and conditioner bottles. Then I counted the tiles on the wall. Then I was freezing. Numbly, I finished showering, put on clean clothes, and went to the living room.

"Hey," Thomas said. He was sitting at the dining room table, scrolling on his phone.

I looked at him. His face was almost too sympathetic. I didn't know how to take it. Was he pitying me? Did he think I was weak or fragile or broken? I wanted it to stop. I backtracked into the kitchen and poured some hot coffee into the cold one that I had abandoned earlier. Then since it felt like a normal thing to do, I sat with him at the table.

"Do you want anything? Food? I think we have some pizza—"

"No, gracias," I said.

He nodded. "Do you want to talk about—"

"Fuck no," I snapped. I sipped the coffee.

"Art?"

"I don't want to talk." I moved too fast trying to put the mug down. It tipped dramatically onto its handle, paused, then toppled completely. It spilled a semicircle of coffee, a flood at first, then a river as the mug rolled to the other side of the table. Thomas and I watched the mug clatter to the floor before we reacted.

"Fuck." I tried to breathe as a disproportionate rage surged through my body.

"I can get it," Thomas said.

"No, I got it," I said, moving for the paper towels.

"It's fine," he said, beating me to them.

"*Thomas,*" I snapped. He froze. I had to take a breath before I spoke again. "Please just give me the towels."

He nodded. I took the roll and fought off the urge to tear the whole thing in half. I unfurled more than I needed and tossed it on the mess. I could feel his beautiful and expressive eyes on me. I didn't want to be mad at him. I didn't want to be mad at all.

"Thank you," I said. "I just need a minute, okay?"

He made a small affirmative sound. I looked up at him.

"How about this?" he said. "I'm going to go chill in my room. The door is completely open if you need."

I nodded. "Okay, thank you."

He backed away and disappeared down the hall. I sighed to myself and tried to focus on cleaning rather than thinking. When the coffee was cleaned, I picked up the pieces of the mug, then washed the dishes, piled my laundry, and sorted my mail. I searched for any other task to do instead of thinking. I was making my bed for the first time in years when my phone rang. I looked at the name on the ID. *Mama*. I sighed. I didn't want to talk to her, but I knew she would have found out about everything by now.

"Hi, Mama."

She went off in Spanish for a few seconds, thanking God and asking if I was all right without giving me a chance to respond. Finally, she took a deep breath and paused.

"Arturo."

"Ma?"

"Are you really okay? Are you home? What are the charges?" This time she waited for an answer.

"Yeah, Ma. I'm fine. It was just part of the contest. There are no charges."

No one had to tell me it was part of the contest. I had been thinking about it while I paced the holding room. There was no clock, so I tried to measure the passage of time by doing laps. What kind of place doesn't even let you know how long you have been there? I had been wondering how the cops found me. They had called me by name, claiming someone had reported Arturo Ortiz skating around the stadium, bumping into people and wreaking havoc. I had also been the only person I could see with a board. It wasn't random. Only six people knew where I would be, and only one was mad enough to put in the call.

"There are no charges?" my mother said, pulling my focus back.

"No."

"Then why did they take you to jail? Shouldn't they have just left you alone?"

I took a deep breath. I didn't want to tell her about the way I had talked to them. My whole life, my parents said to be careful and respectful. They told me how the cops could be. I had grown up in an affluent neighborhood of Arizona because my parents both worked for the university. But none of that stopped people from treating us like shit. The cops were always called on our family gatherings. Once, they tried to tell my cousin Ricardo he didn't own the car he was driving when they pulled him over for speeding. My own sisters were escorted out of the mall once because they had been in the wrong store at the wrong time.

And that was just my lived experience. I saw the news and the way things worked. Through it all, my parents said to be respectful and polite. The alternative was always worse than any bruised ego. I saw the way my parents talked to the cops. They would have been disappointed in me.

"I mouthed off enough for them to get mad enough to take me in." I don't know why I told her the truth instead of avoiding answering. Maybe I was too tired. Maybe I simply needed someone to understand.

"What? Artito, por qué? You know better."

The room was feeling a little too small. I started to pace. "God, Mom, just the shit they said. They asked if Arturo was my real name. They asked what I was doing outside the stadium—where I work—and when I told them, they didn't believe me. They practically tased me when I tried to get my wallet out to show them my ID. My T-tool, a wrench thing for my board, fell out of my pocket when I got my wallet. The way they reacted, it might as well have been a gun." I realized I was almost screaming at my mother, so I took a breath. "They wouldn't even call me by my name. They kept saying 'boy' or 'son.' At least they gendered me right, I guess. They asked me if I had a green card."

"Mijo, that's what cops do. How did you ever end up in front of them in the first place?"

In a fit, I hung up. I didn't realize I had done it until I noticed my hand was hurting. I was squeezing my phone. I couldn't have broken it—the case on it had withstood my entire skateboarding career. But it hurt my fingers to try. I had an answer to her question: the contest and a shitty teammate. But that didn't matter. I hung up because she didn't understand, and I didn't want to say anything that would hurt her. She expected me to be in charge of everything that happened to me, proactive. It was my fault in her eyes. And I wasn't disagreeing. It would have been impossible to explain to her how we both were wrong in a situation with no right answer.

The conversation with the cops replayed in my head.

"Ortiz? What's that? Mexican?" one cop asked.

"Yes."

"And?" the other asked.

"And nothing."

"Boy, you seem a little tall to be a full Mexican, where else you from?"

I shook my head to clear it, water from my still-wet hair pattering as it struck objects in my room. If I thought about it anymore, I would burn down the city. *How do I not think about it?* My brain responded to that with one word. *Thomas.* I had thought of him while sitting in jail, but only after I had given up on trying to figure out how everything had gone to shit so fast. I let my mom's return call go to voicemail, then I texted her. *Sorry Mama. Lost signal. I have to wait. I'll call soon. Love you.* I hit send, abandoned the phone, then I went to Thomas's room. I knocked on the door even though it was open. He turned and waved me in. There was a lamp on, coating everything in a warm yellow light.

"Hey."

"Do you want me to stop what I'm doing?" He smiled. He was sitting at his desk in the corner. He only used the desk when he was doing something business related.

"No...I don't...thanks." I turned to look at the bulletin board on his wall. There was a calendar displaying the wrong month and a few thousand sticky notes with his little poems on them. I read a few. I had read some of them before, but I knew I would never catch up with how many he wrote. I recognized him in all of them.

"How'd you learn to do this?"

He looked at me. "Um, therapy."

I felt a flush of embarrassment. "Shit, should I not read these? I always do when I come in here. I—"

"It's fine. I burn the ones that can't be read. Or I don't fucking write them down."

He stood and came over. He stopped close but not touching me.

"Some of these are pretty dark, so I can't even imagine what the burned ones say." I scanned the wall, looking for the few I especially liked.

"You think some of these are dark? Which?"

I pointed to one. *Half full or empty/doesn't matter/if the glass is beyond drinking from.*

"Huh, I never thought about it that way. But I guess some are."

"I like this one. *Hold it by the base/proud dandelion, seed ready/blow with all your might.*"

Thomas doubled over laughing. When he could, he said, "You know, that's about blow jobs, right?"

I blinked and read it again. I felt a different kind of embarrassment spread over me. "I thought it was about wishing."

He snorted. "A good blow job is kind of about wishing."

I stared at him. "I think I should worry about you more."

He grinned.

"What were you working on?" I asked, trying to move on from the sexy yet scary poems.

He waved me over to the computer. "I was working on a new board design. Bored has been asking for one. Since I have to replace mine, and I don't like any of our spares that much, I figured I might as well try it. Turns out I'm pretty shit at this."

I had forgotten he was still on a backup board. I looked over his shoulder at the computer.

"Is that the skull from our wallpaper?"

He laughed. "Like I said, I'm shit at it. There's also this one."

He walked me through a few more concepts and asked my opinions on them. I didn't have many, but I was grateful for the distraction. I didn't know how I was going to be able to stand being me, being in my head and body, after everything that had happened today. I felt him stare at me.

"Um, last thing I heard was white grip tape," I said, knowing what his staring meant.

"You look tired. You want to go to bed?"

I shook my head. As I did, his hand came up to my cheek just like it had in the hall. I caught his wrist as soon as his skin connected with mine and held him to me.

"Um, sometimes when I've been dealing with something and I find it hard to sleep in my room, I'll sleep in a different place," he said softly.

I knew that was true because I had woken up to find him curled up on the couch a few times. I considered that.

"You suggesting I sleep on the couch?"

He smiled and shook his head. "I was suggesting you sleep here."

I stared at him. It was a good offer. And it was a real offer. He wasn't insisting, but I could tell he would be happy if I said yes.

I nodded. "Now?"

"Sure, I could be in bed. I can put on a movie or music or just talk to you while you fall asleep."

I thought about it. "Talk to me."

He stood and closed his computer, then he shut off the desk lamp. His room wasn't dark since there were a few things that gave off ambient light enough to see by, not to mention the light from the hall. I watched him walk around his room, doing things. Then he started taking off layers of clothing until he was in what he deemed pajamas, his boxers and a tank. He pulled his hair into a black silk ribbon, winding it into a bun at the back of his neck. Then he looked at me.

"I'm gonna brush my teeth. Do the, you know, thing, to get ready for bed."

I had brushed my teeth in the shower, so all I had to do was undress and crawl under the blankets. I usually slept in whatever shirt I had on and my boxers, but I decided to keep the sweatpants on and ditch the shirt when I remembered how warm he was. I sat on his bed and rubbed my eyes. Then I stared at his window until he came back.

He crawled around me to his side of the bed. *His side.* Well, it was his whole bed, and the one night we had spent together before didn't seem like enough to establish sides. He shoved under the blankets and held them open to welcome me in. I rolled, fell against him, and heard about twenty minutes of his skateboard art ideas before I was asleep.

❖

I hadn't been awake for more than six minutes before my phone rang. I remembered abandoning it in my room, so Thomas must have retrieved it after I fell asleep. I ignored it and simply lay there with an arm around Thomas. I watched through the window as the vague silhouettes of birds landed on the windowsill. There was a nest of sorts there but I didn't think these particular birds were using it. The short buzz for the voicemail notification reminded me about the phone call.

I rolled over and looked at the screen. It had been a call from my boss. *Hijo de puta.* It was Sunday, and I had taken this whole weekend off since I thought we would be celebrating in some manner. Plus, I saw him yesterday. I was probably fired. He probably saw the whole arrest on the news or on the internet somewhere. Or one of my shitty coworkers had sent him one of the countless videos. Either way... I rolled out of bed and listened to the voicemail while I pissed.

Ortiz, it's Dennis. Give me a call when you can. I'm worried about you, but they say you're home. Either way, kid, call me.

"Okay, Denny. Coffee first, though."

It took a stupid long time to make coffee, mostly because my clumsy ass dropped the coffee container and spilled grounds all over the floor. I watched it drip and steam, making the carafe misty. If I focused on the coffee, I wouldn't speculate on what Denny wanted. Things happened without my input for a while until I found myself sitting at the table, coffee in a mug in front of me, waiting for the call to connect.

"Ortiz?"

"Hey, Den."

"Geez, I'm glad you're not locked up."

"Tell me about it. Is that why you called?"

"No, I got a call. Some of the higher-ups are thinking this skateboarding persona of yours is getting a little too big."

"Don't bullshit me, Den. Are they firing me?"

He sighed. "They want me to fire you, but you're one of my best employees."

"What, then?"

"Take two weeks. I'll make sure at least some of it's paid."

"What am I supposed to do with two weeks, Dennis?"

"Figure out what you're doing, Arturo. Figure out if you want to be a skateboarding celebrity or if you're going to continue here."

"That's..." I paused. I hadn't thought about my plan since Nads and I had it out last week. I passively sensed our social media presence was going to shit, and my reputation along with it. My portfolio would take some serious energy to spin back to positive. But I didn't *have* the energy. I didn't have the energy for the stadium, either. I didn't have energy for skateboarding or the team. I didn't even really have the energy to hope Thomas meant something more by inviting me into his bed.

"Arturo," Dennis said.

Dennis was going out on a limb for me. These two weeks were the closest he could come to a gift. *Maldito sea.* None of this felt like it could be salvaged by a two-week vacation.

"Bien, okay, Den, I see what you're saying." I didn't have much of a choice. "I'll take it."

There were a few more words from Dennis after that, but I didn't hear them. I instead took my coffee back into Thomas's room and got back in bed with him. I tossed the phone back on his nightstand.

"Coffee," he mumbled, probably smelling it.

"It's yours if you want it," I said, charmed by his sleepy face.

He put up a hand, not moving.

I put the handle of the mug in his hand. "If you're not awake enough, though, you're going to get coffee on your bed. It's hot still."

"I'm way better at drinking things in my bed than you could imagine," he said. Eyes still closed, he maneuvered the mug to his lips and sipped, then he made a face. "We have to start buying better coffee."

I tried to rouse a laugh, but I couldn't. Instead, I closed my eyes. I could sleep through the next two weeks. My phone rang again. I looked at it.

"Fuck me," I said. "It's Weise."

"Want me to take it?" Thomas asked, managing to roll over and not spill any of the coffee.

"No, it's fine." I left the bed again and answered the phone again. "Hello?"

"Uno, what the fuck is up with the underwhelming social?"

I took a breath. "What do you mean?"

She said the company had been waiting for the celebration posts. I didn't explain that there hadn't been any celebration, that there had hardly been anything to celebrate. I listened. They had expected more from the event yesterday. The few images Rocky had posted were holding their own, but there was nothing from us on the win or the arrest. The fans were posting pretty regularly and were still engaged. But she was disappointed we hadn't used either to our advantage. I had zero thoughts on the matter.

"First, you're posting everything, and now you're posting nothing? What was the point of the stunt if you're not doing anything with it?"

"I have a plan, I promise. Just give me another day or two. Like you said, the fans have it under control on their own. We're building suspense." I was lying through my teeth, but it came easily enough.

About half an hour's worth of *uh-huh*s and *yeah sure*s later, the call was over. And I had been given the job of getting something media-worthy together on our socials before the sponsor forced our hand. Knowing them, it would be something terrible like a pool party—and not even one where we skated the pool, but a wet bash worthy of mid-2000s MTV. I groaned and let my head fall onto the table with a thump.

"What was that about?" Thomas asked, coming into the living room. Distractingly beautiful, he flopped down on the couch. I had to clear my throat to explain.

"God, can't they figure something else out?" Thomas said when I was done.

I sighed. "They can. And they will—if I don't drum up something fast, then the media turns over to them."

He blinked like that was no big deal.

"That would hand them everything. That means the team page and our personal pages too. Everything would have to go through their people. If you wanted to share a post from your own brother, it'd have to go past them."

"Ew," Thomas said.

"Besides, I'm supposed to want to do this for a living."

"Richard the Therapist would say there is no 'supposed to.'"

That wasn't a dismissal but an invitation to debate the point. Since that debate would really be me advocating for my plan and Thomas advocating for my sanity, it was better to evade. Luckily, while staring into Thomas's perfect face, stubbly and sleep fresh, a plan did come to mind.

"I think I know what I can do, but it's going to be fucking awkward."

"What?"

"Chandler has the contact info for the photography team who did our first article photos. And he still needs material for his piece. I think we can do a victory shoot, set up a sort of reenactment of our best tricks, pose with some trophies, etcetera. No sé, I'm not a photographer, but…"

"How are you going to pull that off with work?"

I shrugged, not feeling like explaining. "They gave me more time off."

"You have it so made at the stadium." He looked off in the distance as if trying to picture the event. "I guess it could work. It'll look weird with just the five of us."

"Who are you leaving out? Me?"

"Fuck no, Art. I was talking about Nads. Are you telling me you could hang out with Nads right now?"

"Not hang out, but if we stage it all, I wouldn't have to interact with him. Like I said, it'll be awkward."

"You're better than me. I'm not done kicking his ass. Can't we leave him out?"

"Nope, we're contracted as a team. The sponsors don't know he went rogue. They think this was one of my stunts."

"Fuck the contracts. Why protect him?"

I silently asked myself the same thing. But again, the battle of career versus sanity wasn't winnable. I knew my hands were tied. I didn't want to hand over the team socials and all my work with it. I had worked too fucking hard. Besides, the money was finally good. We won, and that came with its checks. And maybe Thomas didn't know it or he was ignoring it, but he had won Best Trick, which had a small cash prize of its own. I had won most points overall. I had learned that in the Uber from the police station. I looked at the results almost automatically when I was released. I also watched the fan footage of the fight between Pirate and Nads. I didn't know what to do about Nads. There was so much on the line. It had already cost more than it was worth.

CHAPTER FIFTEEN

Thomas

After only two days, Arturo's restlessness started to give me anxiety. I thought I was thorough when I stress cleaned, but I had never seen anyone do the things he did. One day I came home to him vacuuming the oven. I felt compelled to disrupt his mood. I tried to text him throughout the day, but his responses were terse and sparse. I suggested he try to watch TV or cook something he hadn't made in a while, or even take a walk. He never followed any of my suggestions. Even when I got home, the nervous energy remained and he would follow me throughout the apartment, picking up anything I set down in the wrong place.

I had one last idea before he started breaking and entering to clean other people's apartments. I changed out of my work clothes on Wednesday afternoon without bothering to shower. I could do that when we got home—hell, I would need it by the time we got home. I threw some snacks and waters in a backpack, then I summoned an Uber.

"Come on," I said, trading him the vacuum for his board.

He pulled his headphones off and looked at me. "Qué?"

He looked at the board like he had never seen one. I turned off the vacuum, set it to the side, and closed the junk drawer in the kitchen. All the junk was on the counter and he was vacuuming the drawer.

"Let's go, the Uber's here," I said.

"Where are we going?"

I didn't answer. I pulled my board through the straps of my

backpack and headed for the door. It took a second before I heard him follow. He didn't say anything as we got in the car and headed out of the city. I watched him stare blankly at the passing world. I wanted to hold his hand. I figured it would comfort him, but we had never done that sort of thing in public. Sure, we had spent the last few nights together. But in public? I didn't know. So, I did nothing. When the Uber stopped at a small neighborhood skatepark and I started to get out, Arturo stopped me with a hand on my wrist.

"Why are we here?"

I smiled at him. "To skate, duh."

He actually rolled his eyes, his frown becoming more of a grimace. He did get out of the car, though.

"Why here, I mean?" he asked, looking at the "park." It was five times smaller than Denver's and had hardly any elements. There was a funbox, two rails, a three stair, and a scattering of other objects only a city official would guess belonged in a skatepark.

"Well, I'm pretty sure I would've kicked your ass in the tourney if fucking Mickey hadn't been such an A-hole. So, now I'm challenging you to a game of Skate to prove it," I said with a grin, trying for a charming tone.

He side-eyed me. "You think so?"

I smiled. *Got him.* "Besides, we've been skating for a lot of different reasons recently, and I'd like to skate for fun for once."

That earned me a smile. With Arturo, if competitive banter didn't work, cheese sure would. He loved inspirational togetherness and *enjoy life* crap. I loved him for it.

"Okay, challenge accepted on one condition."

I put my helmet on. "What condition?"

"There's only one attempt, not two."

I rubbed my hands together. "I won't need any more than that."

He laughed, throwing his head back and crossing those perfect arms over his chest.

"Kickflip down the three stair," I said.

"Five bucks says you miss."

I didn't miss.

We skated until each of us had won and had to call the third round a draw since it was getting dark. A neighborhood patrol person told us the park closed at dusk and that we'd better get home. I laughed. They probably didn't know we were closer to being thirty than being teenagers. I waved the guy off and looked at Arturo.

He was stunning. He rolled through the park, his hair windswept and gently curly. His smile was bright. He was wiping sweat off his face with his shirt, the black trail of hair down his belly stealing my attention. He stopped in front of me, oblivious of how into him I was.

"Fuck, I almost had that," he said. I had called a frontside tailslide on a ledge and hadn't landed it. He was trying to show me up, but he didn't land it either.

"My ass you did."

He grinned at me and winked. "I'll take it."

I rolled my eyes despite the surge of want his words generated. He looked at me, full on and intensely, and stepped off his board.

"You did this to make me feel better?" he asked.

My stupid face warmed. "I…you're my husband. What else am I supposed to do when you're not happy?"

I had picked "husband" because he was so much more than just my best friend. I looked away, unable to keep meeting his gaze. He nodded and seemed to be tearing up. If he lost it now, I would lose it with him. Then we would be two fucked-up, skateboarding adults crying in a strange neighborhood. I was surprised when he wrapped his arms around me. I hugged him back. He held me tight and hard for what could have been five minutes. To me, time had stopped. I had stepped out of reality into an empty zone where he and I alone existed. Then a car drove past, breaking the moment.

He took a small step away, his hands falling back to his side. Then he kissed me, throwing me slightly off balance. It wasn't making out, nor was it a peck. It was just a whole and complete kiss.

"Besides," I said, even more bashful when the kiss ended, "I'd have flipped a table if I had to listen to the vacuum for another night."

He laughed. "Hungry?" he asked.

I nodded. He treated me to dinner, then we went home and went to bed together. For the first night since he got out of jail, he smiled and teased me. He was his annoying, playful self. I'd missed it.

❖

Unfortunately, all the normalcy I had managed to help Arturo find didn't last. I hadn't known but during the day, Arturo and Chandler had been putting together the photo shoot he had promised the sponsors. It depleted his energy. So, after the next planning meeting, he was back to shuffling around the house, his expression pinched and guarded. He didn't vacuum while I was home, though.

By Thursday night, he had put together a master file for the shoot with Chandler's article notes, a social media calendar, strategic sponsor shots, and a million other things I had no idea about. Then he sent out the details to everyone else. The shoot was Saturday, so it was short notice. Everyone confirmed they would be there, even Nads.

I volunteered to help Friday morning, so I called out of work to help Arturo and Chandler with final problems. Then I spent the afternoon watching them discuss the industry like two old philosophers. I didn't give any shits about what they were talking about, but it was interesting to see them work. Chandler surprised me by how in tune he was with Arturo. They proved a formidable pair. Chandler could also speak to him in a way that I couldn't. As a cis, white person, I stayed out of the way of some of their conversations. I knew it was important for Arturo to have that, and since I couldn't give it to him, I was grateful to Chandler.

I was not looking forward to the shoot. I hadn't heard much from The Major, Flip, or Rocky since Saturday. They had all checked in at some point, and I let them know Art was okay. I didn't want our team to fall apart. I had no skills in keeping it together. I didn't have a lot to give after the last month overall. Richard the Therapist once said energy was a limited resource, like money, and I was going broke pretty quickly. I knew it would probably take what I had left to keep myself from beating the shit out of Nads at the shoot.

Arturo and Chandler had been smart about it, though. Everyone on the team except Nads was showing up at the Denver skatepark at five to take individual shots. Nads was coming at seven to take the group shots. The rest of us were scheduled to be out of there at seven fifteen, then Nads would do his individual shots after we left. From what I could tell by eavesdropping a little on the calls Chandler and Arturo made, the others were still just as pissed at Nads as I was.

I had never looked less forward to a Saturday, but it came anyway.

"Ready to go?" Arturo asked me, interrupting my thoughts.

I looked between him, Chandler, and my plate. I had finished my early dinner/late lunch ages ago, but the waitress had never come back for the scraps. I blinked a few times to get oriented, then I nodded. Chandler had treated us to lunch "off the record," as he put it.

"You all right?" Arturo asked.

"Yeah, I was…reflecting."

"Bien, let's go."

I followed them out of the restaurant into Chandler's rental.

"If anyone needs to tap out, just let me know," Chandler said. He was vague, the invitation for both Arturo and me.

"Thanks," I said from the back seat. Arturo tapped away on his phone, his face scrunched. The drive was silent after that. We arrived at the park without much fanfare by design. Uno had put on social media that the team was doing a shoot starting at six thirty to give us at least an hour's peace to set up and get some shots together before the fans.

Since this was for the benefit of the sponsors, it put a heavier obligation on us to behave. I had been given strict orders not to punch anyone. The fans and sponsors wanted the winning team to be just that: a team. And even though we were all pissed as hell, we somehow weren't broken up. So, this shoot would just perpetuate the idea we were a team, even down to the outfits. Uno and Chandler told us to wear black pants and simple white shirts. It was the fastest way to make things look cohesive.

When we arrived, Chandler went ahead to make sure everything was ready while Uno and I unloaded gear. Uno hadn't talked on the drive to the park, and he still wasn't saying much. I glanced at him as we walked to the section we were able to rope off for ourselves. There was a small crowd gathering around the caution tape, but it was just the skaters who had already been in the park. The photo and video crew were also inside the tape.

"Art," I said.

I was so surprised by his face. He looked so irritated. I felt like if I said something clichéd, he'd club someone to death with a skateboard. So, I said something that wasn't clichéd.

"You're fucking amazing. I can't believe how fast you can pull some shit together. It's God tier, bro."

He did crack a small smile at that. "Cállate. Your blasphemous shit is gonna get me smote. I know it's impressive, though."

I laughed.

"*Uno!*" Rocky screamed from across the skatepark. He ran full speed toward us. Uno let out an exasperated but affectionate sigh. Rocky almost jumped into his arms. He was all cheer and energy as per usual.

"Hey man," Uno said.

"This is gonna be sick, bro. I know it's shitty how it happened, but still, fucking rad that we were the number one team and you were the number one skater. The Major says even without the last points it would've been you anyway. You pulled off some sick shit this year."

We both let Rocky keep talking. It was his character flaw most days, but today it was a saving grace. He could carry the team with his enthusiasm. Having his continuous hype made it easier to walk across the park. Flip and The Major arrived within seconds of each other. They had a lot to say to Uno, most of it encouraging. I didn't think Uno was listening, though. They were animated and friendly as he stood there, staring at his feet. Eventually I was pulled aside for makeup. My individual photos would be first. I didn't want to leave him, but I had to. The sooner we got this over with, the sooner we could go home.

"Hi, I'm Golden," the very beautiful makeup artist said, offering me a hand.

I grinned and shook it. "I'm Pir—"

"I know who you are." Golden's voice was coy and deep.

"What are your pronouns?" I asked before I said something stupid.

"Any are fine," they said, smiling. "Thank you for asking."

I nodded and sat where they pointed.

"Then again, after everything I've read in Chandler's articles, I shouldn't be surprised you'd ask. Your team leader is NB, right?" Golden set to work, tucking tissue of some kind along my neckline, presumably to keep makeup from getting on my shirt.

I nodded. "Yeah, but be surprised. People know that The Major uses they, them, but most people don't know how to ask respectfully."

"Well, you still have the leg up on most, I guess, since your husband is trans too."

I didn't answer them. Golden put a soft hand under my chin, tilting my face toward a portable light. Within the glow of that light, Golden really was golden. Their skin and hair and eyes all radiated the same warm sun-kissed hue. Their jumpsuit was covered in gold rhinestones. They were very distracting.

"What're you going to do?" I asked, eyeing their worktable. "I didn't know we would need makeup."

"*We* don't…just you. I'm doing some touching up. Don't like makeup?" they asked, holding up a purple powder in a tiny case.

"It's fine. Never been my thing, though, which surprises some people because of the hair and the gayness."

They took a tiny paintbrush and dipped it in the powder.

"It's not part of this scene, so it makes sense to me. Dress for the job you want, right?"

"You must want to be the sun," I said.

They laughed. "Don't flirt with me, Mr. Married Man. And don't even try to sell me that it's 'fake' because I'm not buying it."

I shrugged, which made them smile at me. When they put the purple-covered brush to my face it was not on my eyes, but under them, right around where I had been punched.

"Let me know if it hurts," they said.

"Being married?" I looked for Uno in the crowd. *It does hurt. It hurts to be married to him, to kiss and sleep with and eat next to him and care about all of him, without being able to confirm my truth or receive his.*

"I meant the bruises."

"Oh. No, that doesn't hurt. Are you covering them?"

"Enhancing them."

"Why?"

"They want to make sure it shows up on camera. Chandler has some plan or other. My job was to make anyone who looks tired look wide awake and to make any bruises look like nice Hollywood bruises. Which, no offense, is you on both accounts."

"What's a Hollywood bruise look like?"

"They're purple and pink, none of that awful green and yellow that happens sometimes."

"Oh."

"You really are charming, though, and if it weren't for this…" they said, tapping the ring on my finger with the back of their brush, "I'd let you flirt with me all you wanted. I can't even get a guy to respond to a text, let alone throw some punches on my behalf."

I considered the ring. "Well, I was throwing punches long before Uno. He just makes 'em count."

Golden made a cooing sound and covered their heart. "My God, that was beautiful."

I smiled and found Uno again in the crowd. With Chandler around to direct and make their vision come true, Uno had been demoted back to just a skater. He was surrounded by the rest of the team. I could see the protective way they were looking at him. He didn't seem to notice.

"I'm going to touch up the one by your lip, so try not to talk," they said.

That wouldn't be hard. I let Golden work. I think Golden knew the same thing that I knew, that Flip knew. I think Golden could see my feelings were real. It seemed like everyone who didn't need to know knew, and the one who should have known didn't know anything. I could tell him. I waited for the voices warning me of all the consequences to fill my brain, but surprisingly they were silent.

I shifted in my excitement. Suddenly, I realized I could tell him now. The consequences were gone. What if I told him I loved him? I didn't think he would walk away from me. I had held him in my arms as we fell asleep, I had kissed him, I had shown him love in every physical way, and he hadn't walked away. So maybe he wouldn't walk away from the words of love.

On top of that, the team couldn't really fall apart, as it was already in shambles. Instead of pushing one or both of us out, they were rallying around Uno, trying in their own ways to comfort him. Even Nads, who had done something worse than fall for his best friend, wasn't off the team. Everything I was afraid of was either never going to happen or had already happened. I could tell him. I wanted to tell him.

I watched Flip walk to a refreshments table and return to the group, handing everyone waters. She must have said something funny because everyone started laughing, even Uno. I could tell him. *But maybe later.* I had a good reason to wait, for once. The shoot was no place to confess my love. So, I would wait. But knowing that I could do it, feeling safe in that for the first time in my whole relationship with him, felt monumental.

After Golden dismissed me, the photographer dumped me and my board into a bowl and started shooting. I skated without a helmet for the sake of the cameras. The whole camera crew were a vibe, they were hyped to meet us and cheered as I made a trick or encouraged me when I missed one. It was nice to just skate. I actually got lost in the momentum. Then, as easy as that, they called a wrap, and I got the privilege of watching the others each take a turn.

Uno was the last to skate, and he was in his element. The crowd of fans had grown, and the cheering that had been a gentle rumble for me and the others turned into a dull roar for him. He was more than just a local celebrity. I could see his spirits rising as more fans showed up. And his skating was amazing. At some point, a cameraman had said the trick didn't have to land to look cool in a photo. So, Uno took that and ran with it. He attempted tricks he wouldn't usually try. He even impressed everyone when some of those wilder tricks landed. I knew I probably looked as in love with him as I felt while I watched him.

For as great as the crowd was at lifting everyone's spirits, they also made it jarringly obvious when Nads had arrived. It was some saving grace that everyone didn't start booing. A few fans wanted us to get rid of Nads. We weren't doing that. When Nads arrived, the cheering stopped. As a team, we followed the crowd's stares to where Nads was riding up. He got off his bike and stood at the edge of the park. Uno was about to drop into the bowl, but he stepped off his board and watched Nads too.

Nads at least had the decency to look like shit. His bruises were darker than mine, and he also looked like he hadn't slept in a while. I proved my humanity to myself and found a small moment of empathy. He had wanted to win so badly, he had ostracized himself from his friends. Even if you didn't count Uno or me, it's not like The Major or Rocky went over to greet him.

I took a step in his direction, but Chandler of all people caught my arm. He whispered, "Let me have the board."

"Why?" I asked.

He smirked. "You don't need a weapon."

I sighed but turned over the board.

"All right," Arturo shouted. He trotted over and stood on the stone barrier that fenced in the park. I was surprised by how calm he seemed.

He looked like he was talking to everyone, so we all turned. "Now that we're all here, let's do the group shots. Derek will direct everyone."

He hopped down and crossed through the photographers and crew members until he got to me.

"You okay?" I asked him.

He shrugged and turned to listen. If I tried to focus on Derek, I knew I would inevitably focus on Nads, and if I did that, I would want to throw him and his bike into the South Platte River. So I focused on Uno. And it was easy. I didn't look away when his eyes snapped to mine as if he sensed me staring at him.

"Qué pedo," he said.

"Nada," I answered in Spanish, just to annoy him. "Qué estás mirando?"

He grinned at my generic and poorly pronounced question.

"You're the one looking at me, güero."

"I think you mean guapo."

He smiled. "I mean, you need to pay fucking attention."

"Why aren't you paying attention, you're the one talking to me." I crossed my arms and pretended to suddenly be interested in what Derek was saying.

"I already know this shit—I wrote it. You're the one who needs to know the poses."

"If I *pretended* to learn them, would that make me a pose poser?"

Uno audibly groaned and hunched over as if my question had injured him. I laughed. We drew the attention of the others. I waved and tried to shut up. Uno just sighed and shook his head. When everyone turned back to Derek, Uno turned on me.

"You're going to get us in trouble," he whispered, leaning toward me.

"With who? You're in charge," I said.

He smiled. He was close enough to kiss, but I didn't. After a heartbeat, he went back to his own space. I did note that wanting to kiss him in public didn't give me anxiety.

As we listened, Golden made Nads look less horrible, then they came around to touch up the makeup I'd sweated off. They winked at me when they finished. Derek made one last remark, shouting it as if to recapture anyone whose attention had wandered, and then people scrambled to get where they needed to be.

Shooting the group photos was awkward, but the camera crew really knew how to read a room, and that helped it be less terrible. Derek made it feel more like he was teaching us about photography and magazine life rather than posing us. He talked through every picture, making us stand here or *like this*, because of some photogenic reason or other. We paid more attention to him than to each other. Even though no one was really expected to smile, Derek managed it with some well-timed jokes.

It helped that people were always between me and Nads and between Uno and Nads. The Major was front and center of the group. Flip was usually near them since she was almost as tall as The Major, especially with her blades on. That left me and Uno winging one side and Rocky and Nads on the other. After a dozen different poses, Derek announced he was going to start smaller group photos.

Uno and I were pulled aside to take what Derek kept calling "wedding photos." We mostly stood together with our boards trying to make each other laugh. Then Flip, Nads, and Rocky did one highlighting the three sports, and that was actually a cool shot. We had gotten clearance from the city to have the bike on the park as long as Nads took the pegs off. After thirty minutes, Derek said that was it. I was surprised when it was over. It had actually been fun.

"Is there anything I need to do before we leave?" I asked Chandler and Uno, who were having a final discussion.

"Naw, I'll make sure the rest gets done," Chandler said.

"Thank you for doing this. Hopefully it's enough to keep the sponsor off our asses," Uno said.

"I already know it is," Chandler said. He tapped on his phone. "While you all were doing the group shoots, I dropped some of Derek's unedited photos into a mock layout with some of my headlines. Then I did the same with the posts we discussed. Take a look."

He turned his phone to us.

"These look fucking amazing," Uno and I said together.

"Agreed. And the sponsors think so too. I don't usually do this much, but I like you guys, and what happened was fucked up. I wanted to help."

This was the first time Uno seemed to comprehend the support he was getting from the people around him. His eyes were big, and his mouth was scrunched in a way I had come to understand was him radically accepting something, which in this case must have been kindness.

"Thank you for everything. We'll talk soon," was all he said, though. We shook hands with Chandler, hugged the rest of the team goodbye, sans Nads of course, and got a Lyft home.

The day ended with me too mad at myself to fall asleep. The urge to tell him I loved him was stronger and freer than I had ever known, but I still hadn't said it. I had had plenty of opportunities since getting home. I could have said it when we got into the apartment and he hugged me. I could have said it when we stood by the sink doing dishes side by side.

He went to his room to talk to his mother, so I went to mine just to have somewhere to go. I tried writing some haikus, but the words weren't there. For the first time in a while, the exercise felt forced instead of necessary. I was happy, yet distressed and wildly annoyed with myself. So I just lay in bed on my phone.

Later that night Arturo asked me to sleep with him in his room. I agreed and followed him to bed. Watching him fall asleep was like watching someone come into focus through a camera. The phone call with his mother seemed to exhaust him, and maybe the magnitude of the whole day finally overwhelmed him. But as he slept, the suffering and sadness fell away piece by piece until his sleeping face was as light and unburdened as I remembered.

I was nowhere close to sleep. I reviewed the day and how I hesitated every time I tried to open my mouth. Even whispering it to him while he slept was impossible for me to do. Why couldn't I do it? I tried to think about what Richard the Therapist would say, but maybe it had been too long since I had seen him because I couldn't even conjure any of his past messages. What the fuck was my problem? It was like my jaw locked shut and my brain system dumped any form of language I had ever known. *Arturo, I'm in love with you!* Why was that so hard to say?

CHAPTER SIXTEEN

Thomas

When I came home from work the next day, Arturo was sitting on the couch. The TV wasn't on. There were barely any lights. Our eyes met as I stepped into the doorway of the kitchen. He had an I-have-something-to-say-you-aren't-going-to-like look.

"Hey, Art," I said, trying to be cheerful.

"Can I talk to you about something?" he asked.

I nodded and strolled over. I pulled my uniform shirt out of my jeans and hoped I didn't look like a total dick. Receiving bad news while dressed like an employee was worse than just getting bad news.

"What's up?" I asked, sitting near him.

He looked like he was about to just spit it out, then veered off at the last second. "How was your day?"

I sighed. "Art."

He put his hands out to stop my protest. "I just talked to my mom. She offered to fly me back to Tucson for a while."

That was all he said. That was the end of his news. I had to wait for a feeling to surface. Was he leaving because of the events? I mean duh, but did I have something to do with it? Was he leaving me? *Why wouldn't it be about you?*

"Uh, like a vacation?" I said stupidly.

He half smiled and let out a breath. "Yeah. I'll be back here, but I don't know when."

"What about work?" *What about me?* I didn't ask.

"When I said they gave me more time off, what I meant was they kind of temporarily fired me."

"What! Why?"

"The arrest. They said I could keep my job if I could prove I was dedicated to the company, which mostly means they want me to quit skateboarding."

"Fuck. Why didn't you tell me? Can they do that? I don't think they can do that."

"No sé. I didn't tell you because I didn't want to talk about it or fight it. It's fine. It'll be nice to have the time. Claro, considering everything that's happened, I need to figure some shit out. I haven't been keeping up with my portfolio plan, for example."

I felt my face warm with anger. I was mad at his job. He loved working at the stadium. I was still seething with rage at Nads, and his pathetic expressions yesterday hadn't changed that. I took a few deep breaths. My rage couldn't help him. I didn't want him to leave, but I did want him to heal.

This isn't about you, Teach. Sometimes people needed time and distance, just simply for the physics around them to be different in order to heal. But I still felt him leaving in my chest. I hoped it didn't show on my face. I realized I had been quiet too long. "When would you leave?"

He looked down at where his hands rested in his lap. He was playing with his wedding ring. I don't think he noticed he was doing it.

"Mom was able to get a flight for tomorrow at four. I can take the train."

I opened my mouth to protest. It was too soon for me, but it probably couldn't come soon enough for him. I stopped myself from speaking.

He filled the space. "Look, I don't want you to worry. I'll CashApp for my share of the rent until I get back. I mean, I still want to be here. This trip really is temporary."

"Art," I said.

He let me take his hands. His shoulders sagged and his floppy black hair fell over his face. His beautiful nearly black eyes were shiny. I smiled at him. "I get it. I understand. I was gone for a while with my family, and you kept all of this together for me. I can do this for you."

He smiled shallowly and rubbed his eyes with the backs of his hands, mine still held in his. "Thanks, man. Fuck. I feel so fucked up right now."

He obviously needed this trip, needed me to not burden him with my feelings, needed someone to manage things for once so he could sort everything out. So, I centered myself around his needs. "What can I do to help?"

His hands fell away, and when he looked up, he mostly looked tired.

"I have to pack," he said.

"Want help?"

He nodded.

Packing went fast enough, especially when he got out of my way and let me fold everything into a bag for him. Then I found us some dinner. He was silent again. That was the hardest part. I was so used to him filling spaces and making noise that his quiet, pained presence made me hyperaware of him. It felt like he would disappear into the ether at any moment.

He moved around listlessly, picking things up and putting them down again. I didn't know how to reach out to him. I wondered if I should talk to him about anything that came to mind. That had worked to get him to sleep the last few nights we spent together. That was pushing my limits a little. I didn't have a lot to talk about, and I had already told him as many baseball facts as I think he was willing to listen to. I guessed I could move on to facts about baseball movies.

It also didn't help that some of the questions rolling around in my head were the ones people usually asked me. Those were a *whole* different type of question. My sister asked me every day for a year if I had *a plan*. I was almost ninety percent sure suicidal thoughts weren't a normal part of Arturo's brain landscape. Then again, all the brochures and afterschool specials said it doesn't hurt to ask.

I was doing the dishes, watching Arturo touch things in the living room, when my brother's voice came to me. I remembered him talking about his wife, and her touches that meant love. Arturo had been a touchy guy. Maybe that would help me ask. *Okay, so what, you just hold the guy and ask the love of your life if he is thinking of hurting himself? So great. Happens every day.* I guessed if I were the love of someone's life *and* they knew it was important to ask sometimes, then it could happen often enough. Despite my sarcastic brain, I was committed. I dried my hands and went into the living room. My heart fluttered and I stepped into Arturo's path. With a ghost of a smile at me, he tucked his hands under his armpits.

"Hey," he said.

"Hey." I put my arms around him. He didn't untuck his hands, but he nuzzled against my shoulder. I stuttered through the words, my voice sounding too loud. "Art, I have to ask you something. It's a weird question, but I can't *not* ask it, I guess."

He looked at me.

"Are…have you…are you thinking of…hurting yourself?" I was squinting already, so I closed my eyes.

To my surprise he kissed me. It was soft and reassuring. And when I opened my eyes, there he was, really him: Arturo undistracted and unconcerned and wonderous. "No, Thomas, but thank you for asking."

I gulped a laugh of embarrassment and relief. We both knew it revealed something about me to think to ask. People didn't think to ask that question without hearing it a few times. I could tell he could see the years I spent hating myself behind my thoughts.

"Do you want to watch something?" I asked him, desperate for a subject change. He moved to the couch. I turned the TV on and clicked through to a movie I had seen a million times. Then I went to sit next to him.

He lay on the couch and threw one leg over the armrest, which meant his head was nearly in my lap. I wanted to keep touching him, and the easiest thing to do was pet him. I raked my fingers through his hair, gently, slowly to test if it was an okay touch. He didn't say anything. I did it again.

"You don't have to do that, you know."

"Do what," I said, pausing with my fingers buried in his black mane.

"Comfort me or whatever."

I shrugged and opted for sarcasm rather than compassion. "I'm doing this because I like it, so keep it down if you don't mind."

He huffed, then fell more completely into my lap. I could both stroke his hair and rub his back. He lay like that for a while, watching the movie. He caressed my leg too, not in a sexy way but in a stim way, like it was comforting him to do it.

"This does feel nice," he said softly.

"I really do like doing it," I said, trying to match his tone.

He sat up and looked at me. "Thomas...do...when we...had sex..."

I knew my face looked surprised. "What about it?"

He blinked and his mouth fell open. Then he shook his head. "Never mind."

"Wait, I want to know."

"It's nothing."

I paused the movie. "You really don't have to tell me, but I have no judgment and I want to know."

He sighed and sat up to face me. It was nice to see his usual urgent expressions. I liked the way his pushy, curious thoughts made his face look bright and eager. There was almost a smile in his eyes.

"Do you really like touching me? Did you like what we did?"

"Fuck, yes to both questions," I said without hesitation. *How can you feel okay saying shit like that to him, but you can't just tell him you love him?*

His eyes turned sad, and his mouth was crooked in a way that made him look a little suspicious of me.

"That all you want to know, or do you want me to go into detail or something?" I pushed.

He let out a surprised laugh, then looked at his hands. I fucking loved his hands. The way he played with the ring on his finger made the muscles along his arms bulge and twist. I had loved sharing a bed with him. He was perfectly warm, and his arms were thick and his body was hard limbed with a soft middle and—

"Why are you asking?" I said to distract myself a little.

He shook his head. "I was thinking back through some things and thinking about how comfortable I am being with you. I haven't asked you what you thought about it."

"Loved it," I said. I could have said *love you* if I weren't the worst coward I knew.

He smiled bashfully. Then he had a thought and squinted at me before asking. "It wasn't penetration, so did it seem basic to you? Like were you bored?"

Excuse me, Mr. Ortiz, would you like to hear my thirty-slide presentation about how every part of that experience was exquisite and not at all basic?

"I was the exact opposite of bored. And it wasn't basic to me. I guess if you thought so, we could always try something different."

And the award goes to Thomas for having the only mouth that works without a brain. I know logically he was looking for answers, not an invitation, but I was a man of opportunity. He stared at me. I shrugged. Well, I wasn't going to take it back. And if he said no, I would go back to watching the movie. But the longer he was quiet, the more I faltered. Finally, I said, "I mean, assuming you wanted more."

"Absolutely."

"Physically." I finished my sentence. His expression changed a few times as he thought about it. He stared at me hard, and I tried to match his look, but I was distracted by the way he chewed his lip while he thought. Again, my mouth wouldn't stop. "It's been a lot the last few days, so I get if my offer's inappropriate. And it doesn't have to be sex."

"Don't."

I froze.

"Don't apologize for it. I want it. I'm just trying to sort out my own thoughts. Wanting it this much is new for me. And I guess I never really thought about what kind of sex life I'd have. I feel like I'm thinking about you constantly. It's maybe like describing your favorite movie but it's only available in German. I'm more than willing to learn the German. I just have to catch up, you know?"

"That is a wild analogy." I laughed to play off my alarm. *Christ Almighty.* In that moment, it sure felt like he loved me. *Sex isn't love, dipshit.* I opted to smile. And I couldn't find anything else to say. He seemed lost for words too, so I put us both out of our misery. I leaned over and kissed him. My body flushed, waves of warm and cold, as the feel of his lips made my pulse race. He kissed back, softer than usual. Most other kisses up to this point had so much energy and urgency behind them. Now he was almost waiting.

I pressed farther into his space, parting his mouth with mine, entering with my tongue. He breathed into it, sucking in return. His hands came around mine, and I understood. He wanted to feel wanted. All the rejection of the last few weeks by the sport, by his job. No wonder going home made sense. *Go where you're wanted.* I wanted him. I wanted him in my life, in my line of sight, in my bed. I knew I probably wasn't enough to make him stay. I couldn't even tell him

I loved him without the threat of a panic attack, but I could tell him I wanted him in this way.

"Fuck," I said when I paused for a breath. "You're an amazing kisser."

He didn't say anything. He just took my hair out of the bun it was in. That's when I remembered I was dressed like a middle manager. I had never changed or even showered from work.

"Damn it, I'm dressed like a dillhole." I groaned, looking down at my work shirt.

"I don't think so, but that's an easy fix." He pulled the shirt over my head.

I thrilled at the way his eyes appraised my body. I took his mouth back, scratching my fingers through his hair as he ran his hands over my skin. It was an ego boost for me to have hands exploring me. He pulled me on top of him. But now that I had thought about it, I couldn't get the idea that I needed a shower out of my head. I paused again. "Art. I want to keep this going, but I feel weird that I haven't even showered from work."

He took a steadying breath and his hands tightened on my body. "Um, okay. Pero, I don't mind one way or another."

"Or you can join," I said. *Yup, fucking keep talking. You're not embarrassing at all.*

His eyes widened, and I could see him thinking about it. He stroked my skin, leaving electric tingles in his wake. I wanted to touch his skin too, run my fingers through his wet hair, watch trails of water run down his body. I swallowed a mouth full of drool. "Shit, I may be thinking about it too hard."

He considered me. I didn't move. I wanted to beg or coax, but I also wanted him to make the decision on his own, without influence.

"I've never showered with anyone else," he said. He had moved on to stroking my hair. I waited, unsure of what to say. "What do people like about it?"

I laughed. "Sorry, I'm not laughing at you, I'm just surprised. For me, I like the way water makes people look—shiny and wet. Plus, it's a shower, so it's relaxing. Um, I saw a T.A.T.U. music video in, like, 2003 that was a sexual awakening for me. There were a lot of people standing in the rain. I haven't been the same since."

He smiled, genuinely. "Weren't they women?"

"Lesbians. Any gay person at the time was enough to trigger my own gay synapses. Besides, I think ties are universally attractive no matter who they're on."

He laughed. Then he again stopped to think. He seemed to land on a memory of his own. When he refocused on me, I knew his answer before he said it.

"Bien. Let's go."

I kissed him before letting him up and leading him to the bathroom. It wasn't until I got the shower running to warm up and was watching him strip that I wondered why he never once questioned my intentions—or his own, for that matter. What the fuck were we doing this for? What the fuck was *he* doing this for? I knew my reasons. I get living in the moment, but I knew what consequences I was facing. *One fat, bleeding, broken heart.* What was at the end of this for him?

Then he smiled at me, and his eyes raked over my body, and that alone was everything I wanted in a lover. *Perfect. So glad you can just fuck and be fucked. Glad you didn't learn any lessons from all the other people.*

I needed that voice to shut up. *Naked guy no clothes/a sexual fantasy/don't overthink.* Not my best, but it did the trick. I kicked off my boots and undressed myself the rest of the way. He watched and I didn't mind. Then I stepped into the water. I put my whole body under the hot stream and closed my eyes. I used the moment of wet warmth to calm down. I had never come just from looking at someone, and I didn't really want now to be when I learned if I could. I didn't open my eyes until he ran his hand up the length of my back. There was a tattoo along my spine, I figured he was following it.

"Now what?" he asked.

"Now I stand here and forget work," I sighed, enjoying the water. "You stand there and wait your turn."

"So, you get to hog the water?" We both laughed, and I pulled him into the stream to kiss me.

"We're going to drown," he said after a few seconds.

I shrugged, which made him laugh more. After that we washed, and he insisted on putting shampoo in my hair. I let him wash it. We didn't say much. He seemed to be relaxing, though. When he had the water to himself, he stood with his thick arms crossed over his chest and his head thrown back. He was beautiful. I leaned in, enticed by the rivers of water flowing down his throat and chest, pooling in his arms. I kissed his neck.

I turned us, pressing him up against the wall, the water flowing down my back.

"I can name some things we could do, now, here if you want."

"Here?"

"Oh yeah. You could trust me and tell me to stop if I do something you don't like. Or we could wait."

Once, Richard the Therapist had asked me what I wished my other lovers had said to me. I told him how lost and powerless I felt the first few times I had sex with someone new. I had only ever been with guys way more experienced. I told him I wished they'd said to me exactly what I was saying to Arturo. I had wanted options and a safe way out. I didn't know if he needed it like I had, but I couldn't see how it would harm him to have it said. His first response was to kiss me. It was slow and total, his tongue and breath breaching me. It felt perfect, like all my feelings were one of his perfectly crafted plans.

"I'm following your lead. I don't really know what I'm doing. So, I'll say stop."

I nodded and pressed my whole body against his. "You'll see that these things often go how you think they will."

He smiled. He held my face in his hand. I kissed his wrist, then his lips. He hummed happily. My hands met his body at the hip and traced in to where his thighs met his crotch. I massaged a little, rubbing where his legs joined the rest of his body, before I moved my hand low enough to cup him, then stroke his dick. He gasped and sank a little. I stroked him slowly and bit his shoulder, timing the pain from the bite as my palm massaged his dick.

"Fuck."

"Tell me if you like it," I half demanded, half asked.

"I like it," he breathed.

I kissed his mouth and stroked and pressed closer, letting him feel my dick and legs and chest. He pulled my hips, but I stayed far enough away to keep stroking him. He moaned softly, rocking to chase my hand.

I slid my hand through his legs and around to his ass, barely grazing his entrance. He gasped and froze. I froze too. He looked at me, his eyes wide but not unhappy. Then he kissed me hard, like the erotic sensations were a flood, and my mouth kept him from going under. I loved the look of surprise and pleasure he had given me. I wasn't going to push in, even though I wanted to. I massaged and he pressed down into it, physically demanding more sensation.

"Damn it, Thomas, this feels amazing."

I liked the sound of that. I brought my other hand to his dick, rubbing it along the top, focusing with my first hand on his hole.

"Fuck, wait."

I waited. He breathed and wiped water from his face. The steam of the shower made him look dreamy and ethereal. His hair was slicked back, giving him a roguish appearance.

"I don't want to come without you," he said.

I scanned his face. His expression was hopeful and bright. He really did want to come together. I could never come again and still be thrilled to touch him.

I grinned. "I thought you were going to trust me."

"I want—"

I interrupted. "Can I be inside you?"

He closed his eyes and tightened his grip on my body. I still felt electrified with excitement. I kissed along his collarbone while he thought about it.

"Yeah, front hole."

"Turn with me," I said.

I moved us so he was more in the water and I was against the wall. He braced his forearms on the tile by my head. He stared. I smiled. My dreams were coming true, so I didn't know what he was expecting to see in my expression. I placed one hand back between his legs, the other on his chest. I lingered on his dick before I entered him. He sucked in air, one of his hands gripping the back of my neck. He grabbed a fist full of my hair, sending a sharp burst of lusty pain down my spine. He rocked into me, my hard dick grazing along his thigh.

"Fuck, Thomas."

I answered by licking his throat, sucking the water there. He moaned, fucking my hand.

"Your mouth is amazing."

I considered saying something, but I didn't. At this point, I was mostly holding still, letting him thrust and grind against me. I braced against his force with my leg between his. The steam from the hot shower was total now. It made the room feel unreal. It made me free. I watched Arturo enjoy himself. I caressed and rubbed and licked and bit. He rocked against my body.

"God, I like this. How does this feel so good?" he asked, probably more to himself than me.

He brought his other hand up to hold my face. I caught it, entwining my fingers with his, rubbing my cheek on his palm. His hands were the most erotic thing in my life most days. Even in the shower, naked and together, I still wanted more of his hands. I had wondered for a long time what they would feel like on my skin, around my dick. Now I knew, and it was better than I had ever imagined.

I could feel him watching me. I kissed his wrist. I closed my eyes. He watched me lick his palm, along the length of his middle finger, then sucked both it and his ring finger into my mouth. He lost it. His thrusting became erratic for a handful of small strokes, then in one final hard thrust against me, his eyes squeezed shut, he came. I sucked his fingers again before letting his hand go and wrapping my arms around his waist to support him.

"Dios mío," he said. He loosened his grip after a few seconds and looked at me.

I looked back. But he didn't say anything. I waited. The hot water had held out this long, miraculously, and I knew it wouldn't last, but I didn't feel the need to move. He put our foreheads together and finally relaxed all the way. It would have been the safest, easiest thing in the world to tell him right then that I loved him. I even felt like I was about to, which was delusional because I was still scared frozen. I closed my eyes and took a deep breath.

"Thomas." He put his hands on either side of my face. "I want to be inside you too," he said.

My brain stalled out. I searched for something cheesy to say. What I said instead was, "Who doesn't?"

He laughed and shook his head, water splashing me a little. He took a step into the water and used it to slick his hair back. He was observing me, studying me in that intense, calculating way he had. When he had seen whatever it was he needed, he came back to me and crouched in front of me. He wasn't kneeling, which made the experience something unique. I suddenly had no idea what he was going to do.

He went back to observing my body, his hands kneading my thighs. I closed my eyes and put my hands against the wall, unsure. His finger was the ghost of a touch at first, a quick brush on my hole. I couldn't hold in my gasp.

"Fuck."

"Te gusta?"

"Absolutely," I answered.

He hummed and pressed with his fingers. I couldn't help myself. I chased the pressure and the overwhelming pleasure that came with having him inside me. He was slow enough, holding inside before pulling out and inching back in. It was exhilarating on its own, but it was more so because I could tell he was still watching me.

"Stroke yourself," he said.

"Jesus Christ."

I had imagined him saying every dirty thing I could think of, and *stroke yourself* was by far not the filthiest. But him half asking, half ordering me to touch myself with him watching! If I never heard anything ever again, I wouldn't be mad about it. I did as he requested and lasted three strokes before I was coming, overflowing and hot, like a volcano. When I was spent, he carefully left my body and stood. His grin was victorious and eager. I rolled my eyes. He laughed deeply.

❖

The numbness I felt the next day watching him get on the train to the airport wasn't a total surprise. I had been left behind. Me and everything else.

CHAPTER SEVENTEEN

Arturo

Arriving home didn't disrupt my mood like I had expected it to. My dad picked me up at the airport, and my immediate family was at the house to meet me. My parents lived in a two-story adobe house on a small ranch near Tucson Mountain Park. They'd bought the property because there was a room for everyone, including my mother's parents.

It was great to see my family, even if the reunion was muted. Mama had recently gone blond because she wasn't ready to be gray. Amilia was punkish, but in a neat business way, and Ariana was all athleisure. Recent depictions of Mexican families in cartoons and shit didn't do my abuela justice. She was movie-star gorgeous. Papa was round bellied and warm faced. And Abuelo Navarro was a tidy old man who liked to wear traditional clothes to "annoy the Americans," his words not mine. The most I had going for me, compared to the beauty of my family, was I was the tallest, even taller than Papa, who had held that title until I went through puberty.

"Mijo, it's good to see you," Mama said, wrapping me up in her arms. I sighed and rested my chin on her head. She kept talking, of course, half in English, half in Spanish, but I didn't listen.

"How was the flight?" Abuelo Navarro asked.

"Bien," I told him, shaking his hand around my mother.

Amilia and Ariana hugged me once Mama let go. Well, Amilia punched me, then hugged me. Abuela gave me a lipsticky kiss on the cheek.

"Please, tell me what happened?" Mama asked as she pulled me inside.

"I already told you."

"I know but, Artito—"

"Mama, por favor, not now."

She sighed. "Fine. There is dinner in the microwave for you. Don't cook it in there, just put it in a pan."

I kissed her forehead and walked away. She let me go, but I didn't eat dinner. I went to bed in my old room turned guest room. No one bothered me. I slept for a few hours, the ringing in my head caused by being on a plane fading slowly. Even though it was still early, I didn't get out of bed.

For once in my life, I wanted stillness. Even the smell of someone making tortillas didn't move me. The hues of everything looked off, like the bright red and green world of Arizona was dull. Had Denver looked dull? Home did have the advantage of not feeling like it was spiraling out of control.

I didn't love the silence, though. The house was full of people, but talking to my family today had brought on the spiraling feeling. On the other hand, I was here to experience them, so I should want to talk to them. I argued with myself about it for a while. By ten p.m., I was so fed up with myself that I dug my phone out of my pocket. It was at three percent. I scrambled for a charger, looking first where I would put it, then I remembered Thomas had packed my bag. So I looked where I thought he would put it, and there it was. I plugged in the phone.

Then I froze, staring at the bright screen. All the apps on my homepage were social media. On any given day, I had a few hundred notifications across three major apps. I knew I would have thousands by now. Today they'd posted the first few photos and a teaser for the article. I had scheduled it all through a third-party site so the campaign would launch as planned without my involvement. The rest of the engagement I had assigned to Rocky.

I stared at the messenger app. I could reach out to the team. But the idea of them apologizing for the ten thousandth time was almost as cringy as the idea of them not apologizing for the ten thousandth time. They had said a lot already, but none of it matched what I was feeling enough to be a comfort.

The idea of comfort made me think of Thomas. I had indulged in him probably a little too much already. He had let me sleep with him, and we had *slept* together. He helped me through action and not with words. I had wanted to feel loved, and he had made that happen— which in the long run was only hurting me since he wasn't actually in love with me like I was him. Even then, I still wanted to talk to him.

I sent him a message.

Arturo: *Hey, I made it in a few hours ago. Then I got distracted.*

Thomas: *You fell asleep.*

I laughed.

Arturo: *Maybe.*

Thomas: *I'm glad you made it. I hope it feels nice.*

Arturo: *It feels like family.*

I paused, waiting for a response to come. One didn't. I was rarely at a loss for words. When he had gone away to be with his family when his father was sick, I had kept up easy and constant banter with him. I knew it was what he needed.

"What do I need?" I asked the empty room.

Downstairs, my abuelo put on his favorite band, and the mariachi music filled the room with muffled, nostalgic harmonies. I didn't have any response to send back, so I didn't send anything. I closed the phone, opened it again, closed it again. I finally turned on a movie I had started with Thomas a few days ago and had fallen asleep through.

❖

My first few days home were foggy. I felt like I was present and living them, but when I was asked to recall something from the past few days, I couldn't grab the memories. Actually, every day since the Saturday of the arrest was foggy, with a few bright spots, most of which had Thomas at the center of them. I missed him enough to wonder why I had bothered to come home. Not only was it painfully hot, but everyone kept asking me if I was all right. It was no better than my teammates constantly apologizing.

I wasn't all right. I was still raging mad. I had never felt so angry, I had the urge to find the tallest building and just start throwing punches until I made it collapse. I didn't know how to tell them that. The only difference between Denver and Tucson was that in Tucson I didn't run the risk of seeing anyone who knew about the competition. And that was a relief.

I found a box of my old stuff in the garage as well as an old skateboard. I spent the days doing whatever my mother asked me to do and skateboarding on the back porch. I slept a lot too. Being angry was exhausting. Why was I still so angry? It had been days. It was over. No more damage was done than a few hours wasted in a holding cell. And everything was right enough with the sponsors and the article and the team. So, what was my problem? I wasn't used to not knowing what to do next.

I took a lesson from Thomas and found solace in boarding. I would skate around the neighborhood at night when it was cooler or go to the skatepark until someone kicked me out. During the day, though, it had to be on the back porch under the awning. Boarding away my anger worked well enough to a point. It felt like the only time I got a break from the thoughts tornado-ing in my head was when I was on my board.

But, of fucking course, that was short-lived. I was practicing kickflips when I heard that fatal crack of a deck separating from itself. My board slid apart from the center, nearly making me do the splits.

"Fuck me," I said. What the fuck was I supposed to do without it? I had only the one in the house from years ago because I hadn't been able to work out how to get one on the plane from Denver. I picked up the pieces and Frisbeed them into the yard with a roar. They landed amongst the chickens in a way that was funnier than it was satisfying.

"Oye, Abuela's going to shit if you kill one of her chickens," Amilia said, coming through the back door. She pulled it closed behind her just for it to slide open again. Ariana came out onto the porch in a huff.

"And you couldn't hold the door for me?" Ariana said, smacking Amilia's arm.

"You have hands."

"Don't you two have jobs somewhere?" I grumbled.

"It's Sunday, dipshit. Come on," Ariana said, pulling my sleeve.

I rolled my eyes. "Come where?"

"I want to try a new hair mask."

As the little brother, I knew all too well what that meant. "Ari, I don't want to put anything in my hair."

She grinned. "You won't have to, I'll do it for you."

I caved because of course I would, and I let her pull me into the bathroom that split their rooms. My sisters sort of came and went when they wanted. If it had been up to my mother, none of us would have left. But at twenty-seven and twenty-eight, they wanted independence. They shared a two-bedroom closer to downtown where they spent their weekdays. Then they would come home to be with the family when they were free. I knew they were mostly hanging around the house these last few days because I was home.

Ariana sat me on the toilet, and Amilia plopped herself down on the edge of the bathtub.

"So, what's new?" Amilia asked. I glared at her through one eye because Ariana was misting my hair and water was getting in my eyes. Amilia shrugged. "What? You haven't told us what you're doing here."

"You already know," I mumbled. I fiddled with the ring on my hand while Ariana drenched my head with a spray bottle.

"No, hermano, we know why Mama wanted you here. But why did you feel the need to come?"

"Seemed like the right thing to do. There's support here," I said, mostly paraphrasing our mother.

Ariana yanked my head up by a fist full of hair. She was sectioning it off with a comb and pulling it up into ties. Our eyes met. She added to Amilia's question. "There wasn't support in Denver?"

"I'm not sure."

"Your teammates seem supportive on Insta," Amilia said. She was filing her nails now.

"I haven't been on much."

"Isn't it your job?" Ariana asked.

"Here, give me your phone. Let me go through it to show you," Amilia said.

I held it out to her, then snatched it away when I realized. "You just want to snoop."

"I want to snoop and help. I can do both."

I gave her the phone. I recognized my own need for help, and I didn't mind her snooping. Amilia had always been the information finder. She was naturally suspicious. Ariana was all business. She wanted to know what you'd done, what you were doing, and what you were going to do next.

"Hold still," Ariana said.

I watched her pour some goop into her hands. She lumped it onto my head and started massaging it in. I liked the touches. It was comforting. So many days spent with the three of us crammed in the bathroom while Ariana tested one product or another.

"Ah, mira," Amilia said. "The one called The Major told fans the team did not support the way you were treated and wanted to give back the points, but then the other teams said no because you deserved them because it happened anyway. Most of this community supports you."

"Why didn't they say anything to my face?" I asked.

"That face," Amilia said, then made a disgusted sound.

"They probably didn't want to overwhelm you. These things are tricky. They don't know you like we do. They don't know to push you," Ariana said. "Some people think space is better."

"So, you have support there. Why come here?" Amilia asked.

I sighed. "I don't know, Ami."

"I *know* you don't know. Cálmate. I'm trying to ask metaphysically. I want to help you figure it out."

"Be more direct. You're metaphysically getting on my nerves," Ariana said.

"I wish your breath were metaphysical so I wouldn't have to smell it."

"You would, in theory—"

"Aren't you guys almost thirty? Shouldn't you be more mature?"

Amilia made some rude sounds, then shifted closer to me. "Artito, I know you don't know. We are going to figure this out together, okay? So, what does home have that Denver doesn't?"

I sighed. "I think it's like Ari said. No one there knows me like you do. Maybe it's about relating. All that I have in common with anyone else is skateboarding." I was wincing through the words because Ariana was scraping a comb through my hair.

"Did you try talking to them, telling them?" Ariana asked.

"No."

"What do you want them to do? Read your mind?"

I didn't answer her.

"What do you want people to relate to? The situation? Your feelings?"

"I guess feelings. I'm angry. I don't know why I'm so angry. I usually can let things go. But I can't let this go. It's just in there. Now my board is broken."

"So, you want someone who can understand your anger?"

"Yeah."

"I think they can, Artito. Rocky posted he was as mad at the cops as he was at Nads." Amilia showed me a post from a few days ago.

"I don't know. What am I supposed to do, just blurt out how pissed I am?"

"Yes," they said together.

"Here, I'll help you." Amilia turned my phone back to herself.

I didn't stop her. While Amilia was silently typing on my phone, Ariana finished gooping my hair.

"Now we wait thirty minutes," she said.

"That's too long."

"What else are you going to do?" She stared at me. "What are you doing with these eyebrows?"

"*Nada.*"

"*Nada.* Por qué nada? I can tell, huevón. Being a guy doesn't mean being ugly." She stood and crossed to a small box on the counter. "I'm going to wax them for you."

I groaned. "Guys don't—"

"What color?"

"What? Why?"

"Artito!" She added under her breath, "Dios mío."

"Fine. Black."

While she was melting black wax, Ariana put on some music and hummed along. I closed my eyes, wishing I were asleep. I couldn't really move because of the crud on my hair.

"Here," Amilia said a while later. She handed me my phone. She had started a group chat with me, Rocky, Flip, and The Major. She had set up the group on my phone, added herself, sent the first message from her phone, then she removed herself. Clever.

> Amilia: *Hello, I'm Arturo/Uno's sister. He is emotionally constipated and wants to talk to you but doesn't know how to start. Tell him about why you are angry about his getting arrested.*
>
> The Major: *hello.*

(Amilia left the chat)
The Major: *okay goodbye.*
Rocky: *was she real?*
Flip: *Uno is in this chat so she must be.*
Rocky: *UUUNNOOO. She was right, I'm pissed.*
The Major: *I have a list, let me find it in my notes.*
Flip: *Boi if you're emotionally constipated, you about to get a tea laxative.*

Flip was right. Message after message came in, filling the screen faster than I could read.

"Why isn't Thomas in this?" I asked. It's not like I was going to thank her. I was still her little brother.

"Oh, I guess I thought he was different since he's not just a friend anymore." She winked at me.

"Is there something going on with him that we don't know about?" Ariana asked, bringing over a tub of warm wax and a little spatula.

"No, he's been great." Then I thought about it. "He hasn't said much since I've been here, though."

"Why are all men like this? Even the gay ones. Give me the phone back. We have more work to do." Amilia snapped her fingers at me to put the phone in her hand.

"No kidding. I'm going to call you Frida from now on with these eyebrows." Ariana usually let Amilia do the prying for information while she focused on less emotional aspects. Amilia would crack you open and spread out your contents. Ariana would make sure you got scooped back together. They were so much. But I felt loved.

Chapter Eighteen

Thomas

I was expecting the knock on the door to be my takeout, so I was more than a little surprised when it turned out to be my brother and his boyfriend.

"Teach," Al yelled, pulling me into a tight hug.

"What the fuck?"

Al shook me a little, picking me up out of the doorway to make room for Lucas. Lucas smiled at me over my brother's shoulder and held up my takeout.

"We might've scared the delivery guy." Lucas laughed.

"I bet," I grumbled.

Al let me go, and Lucas dropped the bags of food into my hands. I watched them look around my apartment for a few seconds. I was having a hard time believing they were real. I had been alone for days. After putting Arturo on the train to DIA, I only worked, slept, and ate, the last two being half-assed at best. *Who are you kidding? Work is being half-assed too.*

I had barely talked to Arturo. He did text me, but I couldn't bring myself around. He was gone, and it was growing harder and harder every day to believe he wasn't trying to get away from me, even in a small way.

"This is really cool," Al said, his voice breaking my stupor.

He was looking at the wallpaper. I trudged into the living room, leaving my dinner in the kitchen as I went. "What the fuck are you two doing here?"

Al rolled his eyes. "Well, if you'd look at your phone every now and again, you'd know I was comin'. I told you."

I glared at him, unsatisfied with that answer.

"Kyoko's in California for work, and she asked us to meet her out there. She was able to secure some equipment or something, so they needed drivers to shuttle some of it back. Plus ROAD TRIP." Lucas cupped his hands around his mouth, making "road trip" horribly loud.

I blinked. That didn't make it any clearer. "So, you stopped here as like a pit stop?"

"Naw, you were out of the way by about five hours," Lucas said, nudging me. He went past me and pulled the fridge open.

"Then why are you here?"

"I was worried about ya, and we had the time," Al said, coming closer to inspect me.

Alexander Jefferson was tall, broad, blond, and the guy everyone thinks they want. Really, they just want to be him. Maybe I was biased because I wanted to be him. He was always so cool to me. But I knew early on I was going to be small, thin, and in his shadow. He never made me feel like that, though. Richard the Therapist helped me figure that out. Al was also annoyingly modest about himself. But with his beautiful family, two partners, and overall contentment, it was hard to take his humility seriously. Lucas was the perfect complement to my brother. He was just as tall and broad. He was also handsome as fuck. He had soft, brown skin and was growing his mohawk back. He was covered in some of the coolest tattoos. They were like two big novelty bookends.

"What're you worried for?" I asked obstinately, my accent deepening in the wake of my brother's.

"Well, you weren't answerin' your phone. You also had a huge, public fight with the only people you know out here, and you look like shit."

"Fuck me, I guess."

"I'm sorry. But I really am just worried."

"Well, stop, I'm fine."

"You don't look fine."

"*You* don't look fine," I snapped, reverting to seven instead of acting twenty-seven.

"I bet I look fine," Lucas said. He was cracking open one of the fortune cookies from my dinner. He winked at me. Al and I both just flipped him off.

"Al—"

"Listen, Teach, you can keep shoutin' if you want, but I planned to be here for three days and I'm stickin' to that plan. So maybe you might just accept it and pick some different questions."

God damn it. Three days? He was never going to believe I was fine since I also had an appointment with Richard the Therapist tomorrow. In a moment of clear-headedness yesterday, I called Richard the Therapist and took his next available opening. Then I slept through to today, skipping three meals by accident. So, now, on top of everything else, I was starving. I glared at Lucas.

"Fine, but quit fucking eating my food."

Al laughed. "There's enough here for everyone. Were you planning a party?"

"It's meal prep," I said, which wasn't a total lie. I was living off ordered meals and whatever leftovers those might produce.

"I hate that you just said that," Al said.

"It's at least balanced, so he'd be fine," Lucas said taking the bags over to the table. "We can buy you more food tomorrow."

I watched them crowd around my table and felt a burn in my chest. It was my heart starting again. I did love Al. And I loved Lucas. And having them annoy me and fuss over me was adding a few more heartbeats. And I would never tell them, but I was grateful for the company. I grabbed plates and silverware and landed in a chair.

"How long is Arturo gone for?" Al asked.

"I don't know."

"Have you talked to him?"

"A little."

"Is he doin' okay?"

"Al, if you want to know about him, why don't you call him?" I instantly felt bad, so I let my head fall to the table, hoping the thump of it against the wood would be jarring enough to make me feel better. My head didn't hit the table, though. It landed on something not quite hard but also not soft. I shifted, and Lucas pulled his hand away. He had blocked me at the last second.

"Don't do that," he warned in his kind but stern nurse's voice.
I glared at him.

"So, you never told him how you feel, then?" Al said.

"No."

"Why?"

"Never seemed like a good time." It wasn't a full lie, but I also didn't have to tell them everything. I didn't have to tell them I couldn't get the words out of my mouth even though I wanted to say them. I had tried typing them too, and even that was a brick wall.

"Any time's a good time to tell someone you love them," Lucas said.

"Gross. And false," I said.

"Well, how's everythin' else, then?" Al asked. He finally seemed to get that I didn't want to talk about Arturo.

"Like what?"

He groaned and looked like he wanted to slam his head on the table too. *Must be genetic.*

"All right, guys. How about we eat and I talk," Lucas said. He used one of the spoons to dump some of each carton onto my plate, then onto Al's. He moved on without waiting for Al or me to agree. "I called Chandler the other day to see if he was still here in Colorado. He's not, but guess where he went?"

I didn't listen to Lucas's story. He and Al talked with each other, and I shoved food I barely tasted into my mouth. I was having a hard time holding on to my anger. Which was fine because I knew I should let it go…well, I was working on letting it go. But what was left when the anger was gone was just a raw, exposed, lonely nerve, and I knew how to deal with that less than my anger.

You're just as pathetic with your brother as you are with everyone else. Look at those two. Lucas is barely older than you, and he has his shit together. They already think you're pitiful, so it's better not to tell them more. They'll tell you to be a man and deal with it.

Richard the Therapist once said that if the voice in my head repeated anything my mother used to say, I should do the opposite. This voice sounded so much like Wynona Jefferson that I could have been a ventriloquist.

"I know neither Arturo nor my team—*friends*—are leaving me. But I don't know how to let them stay either," I said, interrupting Lucas.

They both looked at me, and I met their eyes for a few seconds. Then I looked at my plate.

"It's really hard when something disrupts relationships," Al said. I tried not to roll my eyes at his empathy. "It can also be scary to have people start living up to your good expectations—the ones people have disappointed you with in the past."

"What are you most worried about?" Lucas asked.

"That it's a trick. That I'll let my guard down, and then they'll abandon me anyway. That I'll be right about them abandoning me, but also stupid for not seeing it coming."

"That sounds like a lot to deal with," Lucas said.

"Do they know how much you care about them?" Al asked.

"I doubt it."

"Waiting for the other shoe to drop is a really challenging aspect of trauma and is one of the hardest things to heal," Lucas said matter-of-factly.

"That sounds like some bullshit," I said.

Lucas laughed. "It's not. There're whole books on the matter."

"Don't mention it to Dani unless you really want to be pestered into reading," Al said with a sigh.

"I guess I'm just fucking tired of working on things. Is there ever a time when you get to *be* and not have to work at it?"

"Yes," Al said.

"No," Lucas said.

They looked at each other.

"You don't have to work at it with me, little brother," Al clarified without looking away from Lucas.

Lucas shrugged. "I don't have siblings, so that could be a thing."

"I don't think that's it. I think we're just good right now. Like you and Chandler right now," Al said. "In this moment, enough work has been done. It might not last, but here we are."

"I guess. Yet, you never really fuck off when I tell you to."

Al blinked at me. "I guess I never thought you were serious. Do you actually want me to fuck off?"

"No."

"Do you want to keep talking about this?" Lucas asked.

I didn't get to answer. The doorbell rang. Lucas and Al both looked at me.

"I don't know who that is," I said. I stood to go answer it. "I swear if it's Betsy Ross, I'm jumping off the balcony."

"That's not funny," Al said. "But…same."

I went to the door and looked through the viewer. It was fucking Nads.

"Christ Almighty, why?" I groaned, banging my head on the door since no one was there to stop me.

"Who is it?" Al asked. He was closer. I looked behind me and saw Al and Lucas standing in the hall. Instead of answering, I opened the door.

Nads looked up at me, unsurprised. "Hi."

"What do you want?"

"I came to talk to Uno." He looked calm until his gaze shifted from my face to behind me. "You hire bodyguards?"

"Does he need to?" Al said.

I looked over my shoulder in time to see Lucas and Al crack their knuckles in unison, their side-by-side presence blocking the whole hall.

"Arturo isn't here," I said, ignoring the show of force.

Nads's expression fell farther, and he shrugged. "Oh. When will he be back?"

"I don't know. He's out of town."

"Well, do you have a way of reaching him?"

"*I* do," I said, hoping to imply I would not be sharing it. Nads considered his options during a long, awkward pause. I stepped back to close the door.

"I…" he said, halting me.

I looked at him.

"I want to apologize to you too. Can I come in?"

I looked back over my shoulder. Al gave me a look that let me know he would carry Nads to the curb if I asked. Lucas's expression, on the other hand, said something much more sympathetic. I stepped back from the door, leaving it open for Nads to follow.

"In my room, on the right, in the closet are some sheets. Why don't you and him go fix up my room so y'all can stay in it," I told Al.

He looked at me with genuine concern. "Are you sure?"

"I can handle this."

Al tried to hug me, but I dodged it and went back to my seat at the table. There was still food spread out, and I felt a little like a boss in a gangster movie dismissing my henchmen. Going with that energy, I pointed with my spoon to where Nads could sit.

"Pirate—"

"Call me Thomas."

He blinked and raked a hand over his somewhat greasy hair, making it stick up in the worst ways.

"Right, Thomas. I…I'm so fucking sorry."

I stared at him. He did look sorry. "For what?"

That made him huff. "Are you kidding?"

"No, Nads."

"Nate."

"Nate. I'm not kidding. I think I need to know exactly what you think you're sorry for. Was it having Arturo arrested? Fighting me? Saying any of what you said?"

Nate slumped in his chair. "Honestly, I'm sorry for the whole goddamned competition."

That was surprising. "Why? You got what you wanted."

He shrugged. "Yeah, but now that all the pressure is off, I can see what it cost me."

I stared. I had never heard Nate sound like this. His voice was quiet and weighted with a maturity he hadn't expressed the entire season. He even looked older sitting in my dining room. "What the fuck happened to you?"

"What do you mean?"

"Bro, you've been a ripe asshole for weeks, and now you're just sitting there like some old man. Cut the crap. What the fuck is so different now?"

"Everything, man. Okay, look, I'm gonna explain, but I want you to know I ain't making excuses. I know I was a ripe asshole. But all I can do is answer your questions and try to make it right."

I gestured with my spoon for him to go on. I wasn't really sure if what he had to say would sway my rage. But I did love gossip as much as the next gay, so I was willing to hear him out on those grounds alone.

"We were going to lose our house. We'd gotten behind on payments by a few months. I got us an extension, but I needed the money from the competition for us to keep the place."

He was silent after that, looking at his hands. I waited, but he didn't go on.

SANDER SANTIAGO

"Is that it?" I nearly shouted.

"What do you mean is that it? That's a big fucking deal, Thomas."

"Yeah, sure, but I don't think it's an excuse to be an asshole. Why not move or get the other people living with you to help?"

"I already told you I wasn't making excuses. The other people living with me are my mom, who barely makes enough to keep the girls fed, and my little sisters. They're ten and six. Mom's shitty boyfriend, Harry, took all their savings and bailed. I tried to get it back. When that failed, I did the next best thing. That's it."

"Don't you have a job? Where was all your money going?"

"Helping with everything else, but Mom didn't tell me about the house. I found out because I answered a phone call from the bank and pretended to be Harry."

"Why not let them take it and get something you can afford? Denver is the worst market!"

Nate looked at me like he had never thought about it. "It seemed like I had to do this. To save the house. We can probably move now that we can sell it, but we would've been out on our asses with nothing before the winnings."

"Why not tell someone? Why not tell Rocky? Or The Major? Fuck, Arturo would've done a billion things."

"I know, I know. I was scared. I didn't want Sung's mom to find out."

"Sung?"

"Sorry, Rocky. His mom has tried to take the girls before."

"Right."

"And if word got out because of something the team did, then my aunt would've figured it out."

I stared at him. It was a good enough reason to keep his problems to himself. I needed to stop yelling at him for how his family handled their business. I knew I wouldn't want someone poking around about Wynona. I thought about the parts that were relevant to what he did to the team.

"You wanted to prove something, that's why you kept it from us. You could've told us to keep quiet, and we would've. Arturo and I, I mean."

He blinked and shrank until he was no more than a head above the table. "Yeah. I think everyone would've. But Harry got in my head."

"You understand now where you went wrong?"

"Yeah."

"How'd you figure it out?"

"The Major's been lecturing me for days. And Sung too. It was like I couldn't see how I'd been acting, I could only see the problem. Then I got home from the bank. I was so fucking excited to be free of the problem, I wanted to tell someone. Then it all sort of sank in."

I stared at him, waiting.

"I know I betrayed your trust. I said a lot of shit that I didn't mean. I was so stupid. I called the cops thinking only of the points. It seemed like the fastest, easiest prize to get."

"And revenge?"

"Not revenge, but payback maybe?"

I blinked. "What's the difference?"

"I don't know. Revenge is what I would get on Harry if I could. I don't hate Arturo. I wanted to annoy him at best. Since he was annoying me. Then of course, The Major reminded me how bad I fucked up. What I did was way beyond payback since Arturo is a person of color. I fucking know better. I swear I do. I just wasn't thinking. I really was excited when you guys joined the team."

"Not gonna lie, this is a lot of words."

"I know. What can I do to prove to you that I know I fucked up?"

"Get therapy."

That was an off-the-cuff remark I hadn't fully thought through. Nate laughed. He really did look different. While he didn't look good, his stressed rage had been swapped for self-pity and sadness, and it was a weird improvement. His skin was still as mottled as mine was from the fight.

"Will you tell Arturo—"

"I'll tell him I saw you, but any apology you're going to make needs to be to his face."

"Fine. I'm just grateful you heard me out."

I waved away his gratitude and decided I could say something that was true without sounding like I forgave him. "I don't want the team to break up."

"I don't either."

We stared at each other for a minute. I felt like I was talking to a stranger. How lost had this guy been? How far can you really come in a few weeks?

"Can we come out now? I wasn't done eating," Al shouted after a small span of silence had passed.

"Fine," I shouted back.

"Are they like military or something?" Nate whispered to me.

I smiled despite myself. "Fuck no. The white one is my brother, Al, and the hot one is his partner, Lucas."

Nate looked surprised, like he was going to ask questions, his face brightening for the first time. But as Al and Lucas approached with grim expressions, Nate didn't ask. He instead put his hands in the pouch of his muscle-shirt-style hoodie and slumped against the table.

"I'll walk you out," I said.

He nodded and followed me back to the door. I opened it, and he stepped through.

"Nate," I said.

He looked at me.

"This was a start."

I somehow managed to sound hopeful and threatening. He nodded gratefully and started back down the hall. I shut the door and went back to the table.

"I don't like that one," Al said. They were both scooping food straight out of the containers, not bothering with the plates anymore.

"I did. Maybe I will again," I shrugged.

"I didn't know you wrote poems," Lucas said.

I went to lie on the couch.

Lucas whispered to Al, "What? Some of them are really good."

❖

I wasn't a stranger to Arturo's room. I had slept here with him. But at the end of the day, with Al and Lucas in my room, I was hesitant to make myself at home. Arturo had been more than thrilled to let me stay when I messaged him about it. That didn't mean I knew what to do in his space without him. I did a lap around the room looking at the things he left behind.

You can't pace all night, just go sleep on the couch.

I set my phone on the nightstand next to my laptop and sat on the bed. The scent of him wafted up around me. It was alluring. I flopped back, hoping to create a second wave of his smell. I wasn't disappointed. It wasn't long before I was wrapped in his blankets with my head on his pillow.

"See, just a bed."

I reached out to play a movie, but instead I hit my hand on the edge of the nightstand. It rocked and my stupid laptop crashed to the floor, taking with it a stack of Arturo's crap.

"Fuck." I dove after it and the stuff I had toppled.

The computer was fine, though it wouldn't have mattered if it wasn't. Arturo had been offering to help me pick out a new one for months. I set it down on his side of the bed. I started to straighten the rest of the crap that had fallen. It was mostly papers. I restacked the pages in my lap. The topmost page stopped me.

A: What are you saying?
B: I'm saying: you have consent. Kiss me whenever. Fuck,
I don't know how to explain what that felt like.
Question: Involved? Love?

It was part of our conversation from before the first interview. *Did Arturo write it down?* That thought panicked me somewhat. But I knew almost immediately it wasn't him. He wrote mostly in cursive, oddly enough. Also, why would he make my words *A* when his name was Arturo?

"Chandler." It clicked into place, especially with the question under the quotes. He must have heard us through the door. It was weird seeing that conversation written out. I read it again, my initial surprise gone. My heart thudded, rereading what Arturo had said. *I don't know how to explain what that felt like.* It felt like love to me.

I groaned and flopped backward into the bed, the stuff from his nightstand still on my lap. "How the fuck can you feel it so certainly but not say it?"

You're scared shitless. What if you really are too broken to be loved back? Who would want someone so damaged that he can't even say I love you?

"Hi, brain, if you could just be less of a dick for a second."

I tossed the rest of Arturo's stuff back onto the nightstand and rolled to open my laptop. There was a website that you could type into and build the five-seven-five poem structure without counting.

I grabbed the note I had just read. The writing in Chandler's hand was crammed onto a small page from his journalist's notebook. Because of that, the sentences were broken in a way you wouldn't get on full-sized paper. The way the lines broke, not including the A and B, created two perfect 5-7-5 forms. They weren't very good poetry, but noticing it cleared the landscape of my brain. I put on a movie and tried to sleep.

❖

Even though Al and Lucas insisted on coming with me to Richard the Therapist's office, I was able to convince them to take a walk rather than follow me inside. I sat in the waiting room alone, the piece of paper from Chandler's notes folded in my hand. I was slowly ruining it by folding and unfolding it.

On the hour, Richard the Therapist opened the door and beckoned me inside. I liked him. He had the look of a mid-nineties kids' hockey coach. His beard and his hair formed a mane around his face, broken only by his thick glasses. Today he was wearing his casual Friday look, which was slacks with a button-down, all normal, except the print of the button-down looked like a muted, neon Dixie cup pattern. I knew a few nonbinary bisexuals who would pay him handsomely for it.

"Teach, it's been too long," Richard the Therapist said, plopping down in a leather armchair near his desk.

"I'm sorry," I said, sitting in the one across from it. The chair was in the window so it was warmed by sunlight. I stared out at the office building across the street. Richard the Therapist's office smelled like leather polish and industrial carpet.

"Now, now, I'm here to help you do the work you want to do. I meant that as a greeting."

"Sure."

"What brings you in?"

"Oh, not much."

He reached over to his desk, grabbing his notepad and a plastic Slinky. The Slinky he gave to me.

"Ah, I just got here. Do I really need the conversation Slinky?" I groaned, taking it anyway.

"On the phone you said, 'My husband was arrested, I'm losing my friends, and I can't tell anyone I love them.'"

I laughed.

"Where do you want to start?" he asked.

"I think the friends thing might work itself out, so the love thing."

"Who do you want to say 'I love you' too?"

I watched the Slinky arch a few times as I tipped it from one hand to the other. "My husband."

"How'd you get married if you haven't told him you love him?"

"It's a long story. Kinda moot. But I haven't told him."

"Tell me the story," Richard the Therapist said. I did, discussing CASST and most of the events during the competition. Well, less competition events and more Arturo and me events.

At the end of the story, Richard the Therapist blinked a few times, then nodded resolutely. "Okay, let's focus on the issue you brought up. First of all, *do* you love him?"

"Yes."

"What happens when you try to tell him?"

"My mind goes blank. It's like I don't know any words. My heart races." Our words were accompanied by the swish of the Slinky.

"What are you worried about?"

"What do you mean?"

"Sounds like a freeze response. What reaction could he have that scares you?"

"I don't know."

"We've talked about your history of feeling rejected."

I rolled my eyes. I leaned over and let the Slinky dangle and spring back into my hand slightly.

"You know why we call it the conversation Slinky?" he asked after a few beats of silence.

"I know, I know. I guess a part of me wonders— Okay, let's say he loves me back. How? I know I need to figure out how to let myself be loved or whatever, but I think it would kill me to have Arturo confirm I'm unlovable."

"And proof of being unlovable would come in the form of?"

"Him abandoning me?"

"Ah. I see. Let's talk about this in your preferred analogy."

"Fine."

My preferred analogy was baseball. When I got too in the weeds with the reality of the human experience, Richard the Therapist would concoct these crazy analogies. While they were effective, they were also overwhelming. One day I told him to pick one and stick with it. We landed on baseball. I knew a lot about the sport because of my grandfather and because I had wanted to play ball myself. He knew a lot about it because he was from Boston.

"Okay, so it sounds to me like you're already counting the losses even before you play the game, right?"

I sat back. "Yeah, I guess."

"But you do want to play, right?"

"Right."

"And your husband. Where does he factor in?"

"Um, I guess if I lose, then I lose him, so maybe he's like the championship or the trophy?"

Richard the Therapist whistled. "That's a lofty pedestal to put someone on."

I rolled my eyes. "Where would you put him, then?"

"We'll talk about that. Let's finish setting up the framework first. So, you've already lost this game, lost the championship, to who?"

"I don't know. Non-suicidal people."

Richard the Therapist squinted at me.

I stopped him. "No, I'm not suicidal. But I do think about it, objectively. I don't think he ever has. Don't people want someone who hasn't?"

"No, I think the right people forgive other people their thoughts."

I went back to flopping the Slinky around.

"Okay, so we have this championship baseball game you've already lost to society's image of a good partner."

"Sure."

"First of all, in sports, people generally believe that you automatically lose the games you don't play, right?"

"Right. And by not being able to tell him, I'm not playing."

"But, Thomas, you already have the uniform on. You're standing in the batter's box watching pitches go by. You are already in a relationship with him, aren't you? You're married and you love him. Sorry to say, but the game's already started, buddy."

I blinked at him. "No shit?"

He squinted back. "Does that resonate with you?"

I thought about it. I pictured myself at bat. I used to be scared of pitches—what kid wasn't at some point. But he was right, by the time you're in the box watching pitches go by, you *are* playing the game. And I guess by the time you get to the point where you want to tell someone you love them, you're in the relationship. Not to mention friendship.

"I wish you knew more about skateboarding."

Richard the Therapist thought for a minute. "You're already on the board even if you're not dropping in yet?"

I laughed. "Never mind. Fine, I'm already playing the game. What else you got?"

"Here's where your husband comes in."

I waited. He rummaged through his papers and crossed his foot over his knee, revealing pizza socks.

"You see, Arturo—that's your husband's name, right?—you see him as the thing you're going to win or lose, but I'd like to remind you that baseball is a team sport."

"So?"

"People shouldn't really win or lose other people. That makes everything some huge effort and it's kind of unethical. Instead let's not think about it as a championship game but as the sport overall. And let's make the sport equate to the relationship. You with me so far?"

"Yup."

"The person you are in a relationship with, then, this husband, is *your teammate*, not the prize. You can't have a one-sided relationship just like you can't play a team sport alone. In this sport, you have to commit to showing up, putting on the uniform, and trying to play your position the best you can. But you also have to trust that your teammate will commit to putting on the uniform and trying to play his position the best he can. To me, that's what it sounds like he's already trying to do. He married you, after all."

I froze and let the shape of the game change in my head. I saw myself at bat and a pitch coming my way. And I saw Arturo on deck smiling at me, looking amazing in a uniform.

"Um. Okay, so who's the opponent?"

"Whatever stands in your way. The important thing is that you're a team and you give each other the chance to show up for the team."

"And if we do all that and break up anyway?" I asked.

Richard the Therapist shrugged. "Breaking up doesn't always mean the relationship was bad. Things, wants and needs and people, change. Besides, wouldn't you want to play anyway? Love, even lost, is still love. You're capable of it, loving and being loved."

I stood up and leaned to look out the window. Down on the street by their rental car, I could see Al and Lucas. They were eating ice cream and pointing things out to each other. I was making decisions about Arturo and me without asking Arturo what he wanted. I knew him well enough to know that he would want to be given the chance. *So, what, do I do just blurt it out?* Then what? If I did that, I would be standing at first, watching as he stepped into the box. There was nothing I could do but wait and see. It wasn't the first time I thought of baseball as the perfect sport.

"All right, Richard the Therapist. I'm gonna try," I said.

I crossed the room and was just about to pull open the door to leave when he said, "Hold the phone, you have twenty more minutes on the clock and I have a half sheet of paper still. Come on back here. We have to talk about a bunch of other stuff."

I laughed and did as he wanted. Not that I was as invested as I had been. For the rest of the session I was actually wondering how long it would take to get to Arizona.

CHAPTER NINETEEN

Arturo

"Hold the basket, Artito," Abuela said. She shoved it at me.

"Abuela, this is a stupid shape for a basket for eggs." I fumbled with it. It was a massive slightly concave disc of grass. I had to hold it with both hands under it, otherwise it would collapse.

"Mijo, if I were concerned about stupid shapes, I'd have a harder time looking at your head. Now cállate and hold it."

I stared at her. She had barely gotten home from whatever she had been doing. It looked fancy since she was wearing a bright red skirt and a white blouse, and her salt and pepper hair had been straightened and was flowing around her in a perfect cascade. Even in her nice black shoes, she was ducking into the chicken coop.

"Abuela, don't you want to, I don't know, have different clothes on to go in there?"

"Por qué, mi vida? It's a chicken coop, not a landfill." She popped her head out the door and put three eggs into the basket.

"Sí, pero you'd probably go into the landfill dressed like that too."

My phone buzzed in my pocket, so I shifted the basket, squatting to balance it on a knee so I could get my phone. One of the eggs rolled out and cracked on the ground. The chickens scrambled to eat it. Knowing she had heard it, I looked up to see Abuela staring at me.

"Artito, you better lay a replacement," she said, then she put more eggs into the basket and disappeared.

I looked at my phone. If she thought one egg was bad, my phone almost made me lose my grip on the rest. Thomas had texted me. *I'm coming to visit, expect me tomorrow. It's a long story. Tell you when I get there, trust me.*

"What happened? You look like someone walked on your grave." Abuela put two handfuls of eggs in the basket. Then she took it from me to be on the safe side. She carried it with practiced hands, walking away.

"It was Thomas." I scrambled to follow her.

"Did something happen to him?"

"He's coming to visit."

"Bien, that's nice. I've been wanting to meet this Thomas." She pronounced his name *Tomás*.

I looked at her. "You have?"

"Sí. He's your husband, right? And according to the girls, you love him. That is someone I want to meet."

I actually jumped at her words. "They told you?"

"No, they told each other. They were just not blessed with…cómo se dice, inside voices."

I gawked at her, but I didn't say anything. I wasn't in the habit of questioning my grandparents. When they said something, it was final. She would have been the first to disapprove of me having real feelings for a man, let alone marrying one for a contest. She had said nothing about it. *He's your husband.*

"When is he coming?"

"Sometime tomorrow."

"Bien, I will make food. What does he like?"

"No sé…I mean, anything. He likes what I make, and you taught me to cook. Chicken over beef, though."

Answering her right now was like talking to a video game NPC. I was rushing through the conversation because my attention was on the bigger story. Why was he coming? Did something happen? He said there was no problem, but also to trust him.

Abuela asked me more questions as we went inside, then my mom and dad started asking. Then my sisters. By the end of the day, I had spoken to third cousins and the neighbors about it. I got into my bed bleary eyed and muddle headed. At least all their questions had made the day pass quickly. Lying there, though, I couldn't get my eyes to close. I could only wonder why Thomas would come to me. I decided to message him.

Arturo: *Are you driving through or stopping for the night somewhere.*

Thomas: *We stopped.*

Arturo: *We?*

Thomas: *Yeah, believe it or not, Al and Lucas came to see me. They decided to drive with me. They're on their way to California.*

Arturo: *They'll stand out around here. Aren't they both giants?*

Thomas: *Yup.*

Arturo: *My grandmother was with me when you texted and everyone knows now. I mean everyone. I'm sorry if there's a bunch of people here. Not much family around, but my abuela's friends are nosy.*

Thomas: *Sounds nice. See you tomorrow.*

I said good night and stared at my ceiling.

"Shit."

❖

I had been banished to Abuela's craft room with her and her four friends. They were quilting, and I was supposed to be helping them. Mostly, my mother got tired of me pacing in front of the living room windows.

"Artito, here, pluck this for Tía May," Abuela said, handing me another of Tía May's squares to unstitch. I was sitting on a footstool near the end of the table since all the chairs were taken. I was sitting so low I could rest my chin on the table if I wanted. It made me feel like a kid.

"Artito," Abuela said, flapping the fabric at me.

"Oh sí," I said, taking it.

I had been watching my phone. It was on the floor between my feet. Thomas's last message was from five in the morning saying they were back on the road. I figured they had to be at least halfway, which meant they should have been here an hour ago. If I accounted for them stopping for breakfast and gas or whatever, then—

"Arturo Sebastian Ortiz, if you're going to be in here, you need to work," Abuela said.

"Concha, leave the boy alone. If Chuy were gone and coming home, you'd be just like this," Tía May said.

"Oye, if Chuy were gone, I would throw a party," a woman I only knew as Ticky said.

"If you were gone—" Ticky's sister, Yolanda, started.

"You would cry your eyes out." Ticky laughed.

"Ay, mijo. Don't listen to them. They're just mad 'cause they kick their chichis when they walk and you're still young," the fourth woman, Eloisa, said, patting my shoulder.

"Elo, don't call me when you are strangled in your sleep by your third chin," Ticky said.

They continued insulting each other. It was distracting enough that I was able to pull the stitches for Tía May. These women had known me my whole life. Elo and Tía May used to catch me and put braids in my hair when I escaped my mother. And when my abuela cried after my top surgery, Ticky had said, "Concha, stop crying. Honestly, this will be easier. Getting that child to do anything was like trying to teach a chicken to cha-cha. This way he can just be a chicken." Now they were all waiting around to meet my husband.

"Mama Elo," I said, trying to be quiet.

"Mijo," she said, looking at me over her glasses.

"Is it weird that I have a husband?"

"No sé. Didn't you pick him?"

"Sí, claro, but I'm a guy."

She blinked at me like I was speaking nonsense. Then her face softened. "When I was a girl, a hurricane blew through my hometown, and while we were being rescued, I saw a herd of cows on top of a bank. I know better than to be surprised by anything. Living is the strangest thing any of us will do."

As old lady as that sounded, it was comforting. I was about to ask about the hurricane when Yolanda knocked over a cookie tin full of bobbins. The metal and plastic bits scattered everywhere in a noisy burst.

"Artito," the women all said at once.

I sighed and dove under the table. Then the doorbell rang. My heart jumped into my throat, and I tried to stand. I bumped the table, sending assorted things crashing to the floor or flying into the laps of the women. When I crawled out, they scolded me but were on my heels toward the front door.

I could hear my mother talking to Thomas, and my sisters throwing questions at Al and Lucas. I shoved past my dad and grandfather and stopped behind my mother. The first I saw of him was the hand my mother was holding. I traced it up to his face and found he was looking at me. His smile was soft, and even though he was still nodding at my mother, his eyes never left mine.

"Introduce everyone," my dad said, shoving me forward.

I had to swallow to talk. Seeing his brown eyes made me feel like I was melting—not in a hot way, but it was like his presence was releasing all the tension in my body and I would just fall apart into a pile of Arturo.

"Ay, Arturo. Thomas, Alexander, Lucas, this is Abuela Concepción and Abuelo Navarro. Mama Val and Papa Luis," Ariana said, shoving me out of the way when I didn't say anything. With each shove, she pushed me closer to him. Thomas and the others greeted everyone in turn.

"Hey," Thomas said to me after a moment.

"Hey," I said.

"Arturo, move," Abuela said. And she pulled him away from me.

I watched on the edge of the room as Thomas, Lucas, and Al were introduced to Abuela's friends. The Viejitas loved Thomas's features, telling him how handsome he was. And everyone got a kick out of Al and Lucas, who were a head and a half taller than anyone else in the house. My father kept telling them they should change all the lightbulbs.

"Arturo, go get their stuff out of the car. Come, we have food ready," Mama said, directing Lucas to the kitchen by the elbow.

"It can wait," Thomas said. "The stuff in the car, I mean. I don't want to waste the time on it."

"Psst," Amilia hissed, waving me down. "Go talk to him," she mouthed, pointing.

Thomas and I were the last two trying to file into the kitchen. In a quick move, I stepped forward and took Thomas's hand. He turned quickly. His face was surprised but happy.

"Come with me for a minute?" I asked. A minute would be all we had, too, since my mother and the Viejitas would come looking for us.

"Okay."

He let me lead him into the nearest room, which happened to be the laundry room. We stood just inside the door for a frozen moment, his hand still resting in mine, his eyes on my face. I tried to think of something to say, but nothing came. And I tried to think of something to do, but I had only one idea.

I pulled him to me, and I kissed him. I must have surprised him, because he went stiff, but relaxed when I put my arms around him. He smelled so amazing. He was warm against my body, and his pulse thrummed wildly under my fingers. I was suspended in time. When it became overwhelming, and that fire started to creep into our kiss, I took a step back. I couldn't go out there horny and flushed in front of the Viejitas. Or worse, my sisters. I replaced our kiss with a simple hug.

"Fuck, Arturo what happened to your face!" Thomas laughed, cupping my cheek in his hands. "Is your hair curlier? It's so soft. And your eyebrows!"

I laughed. "Ariana did some stuff."

He grinned and blushed a little. "You always look great, but this is—wow."

His fawning was making me self-conscious. "Why are you here?"

"I—" He didn't get to answer.

"Arturo, vamos, you're making the food cold," Mama shouted down the hall.

"Okay." I laughed.

Thomas smiled and touched my cheek. Unable to help myself, I nuzzled into his hand.

"I'll tell you when we have time. I promise, it's not bad. For now, I'm just happy to see you."

"I—"

"Arturo Sebastian Raymundo Navarro Cordova Ortiz." That was Abuela.

"Fuck," I said.

"I love your family. I think they might adopt Al, though."

"We would finally be able to use the top shelves."

He snorted and wiped his hands over his face. Maybe he was feeling as flushed and overwhelmed as I was.

"Come on, the food does smell good." He led the way to the kitchen.

❖

It took what felt like years for my family to finally get the hint that I wanted to be alone with Thomas. Al and Lucas were our salvation. After dinner and dessert, Al announced that he and Lucas wanted to see Tucson while they could since they would be leaving the next morning. I didn't ask Thomas if that meant he was going too. My family took Al's announcement to mean the Ortizes were playing tour guide. We helped unload their car, then they were all gone.

Thomas and I watched everyone leave from the front door, then I took one of the two bags he had for himself and led him to my room. I put his bag on the bed, and he closed the door. He looked around the room appraisingly. It was just a guest room, so I wasn't surprised by his neutral expression. I felt suddenly nervous. I couldn't imagine why he had come all this way. What couldn't he say over the phone? Maybe the bag around his shoulder was full of my things, and he was kicking me out. Then why would he let me kiss him?

"Thomas," I said at the same time as he said, "Arturo, please let me say this."

I took a deep breath and held it. He closed his eyes and gripped the shoulder strap of the bag. Then he resolutely took it off.

"I'm in love with you."

Since I had been holding my breath, my gasp of surprise was more of a gulp. "What?"

He shrugged, then took on a more purposeful posture, something like Superman meets mosh-pit participant. He said, "I'm sorry I didn't tell you before everything."

"Why didn't you?" I stumbled a few steps closer to him.

He held up his hands like the answer was obvious. "I was fucking terrified."

"Terrified?"

"Yeah, man. I, fuck, I knew I was crushing on you pretty hard, but I was also really into our friendship—plus I thought you might be straight. And we had the team and the competition and your portfolio and a bunch of other fucking stuff. I was afraid of how it would turn out if I told you."

"That I'd leave?"

"Yeah, or at least that's what I told myself."

"Thomas, I'd never—"

"I know you wouldn't. I know it here," he said, pointing to his heart. "But here is a little tougher to convince." He pointed to his head. "And that's because I was afraid of you *not* leaving, too. I've had that not be great either because I don't know, you could resent me, but also if you felt obligated to stay or something. It's complicated but I'm working on it."

"Why'd you decide to say something now?"

He sighed and raked back his hair. "I went to therapy yesterday. I was talking to Richard the Therapist, and he said that you have to…well, it's like baseball. He said you weren't supposed to be the trophy but be on my team. He said maybe I already thought I'd lost and I shouldn't even bother trying to play, but really, we were already playing. He said it all comes down to two things. The first is that you might as well take the swing if you're already in the batter's box."

He took a breath and stared at me. I was not sure how, but I was following him. This scattered analogy was so endearing.

"And the second thing?"

"You have to have faith that whoever's on your team will show up in uniform ready to play just like you. Richard the Therapist said that by not telling you, I wasn't even giving you a chance to prove you cared about me. You always show up, Arturo. You're always fucking ready. And I'm learning to trust that."

I blinked and tried to let it sink in. Thomas kept talking.

"Look, that's not me saying you have to date me or whatever or even *not* be mad at me, but fuck, Art, you're my best friend, and I want you in my life, and I want to be in yours, and I figure, okay, I should treat you like a friend at least and tell you things. Also, I brought you some more clothes because you never said how long you were staying. I also thought you'd want—"

"Thomas." He froze, holding the bag as if he were about to open it. "This feels a little confusing considering what you told Flip at the blades and bikes event."

He squinted at me. "By the SUV?"

I nodded, looking away. He sighed and I heard the bag drop to the floor.

"I thought you might've overheard. What do you remember?"

I closed my eyes to focus. "'We didn't marry for love, why would anyone ever believe we'd hook up for love. Maybe we're just touch starved. Maybe it's just a story that sells.' I might be paraphrasing."

"I was just trying to get Flip off my case. She knew something was up because she noticed us holding hands. Well, she noticed before. Earlier I told her I had feelings for you, and she told me I should tell you, and I told her I was afraid because if you were straight and if something happened, then I'd just be some experiment, and I didn't want that." He paused to breathe and when he started talking again it was slower and steadier. "Even after the interview, I couldn't believe you weren't straight. So that day she had asked if I had confessed and I said no. She said what about all of your worries, and I said what you heard to get her to leave me alone. Her questions were sort of spoiling how amazing it felt to be with you. You didn't marry me for love, and I can accept that. It just wasn't that simple for me, and I really don't expect your feelings toward me to change."

"Wait, you were saying all of that because you thought *I* didn't love *you*, not because *you* didn't love *me*?"

"Of course. Like I said, I've felt this way about you for a long time."

I sat on the corner of the bed. I couldn't even begin to understand my relief. That had been the right question. He was in love with me and that was miraculous, and I was in love with him and that was mind blowing. His explanation was like helium, and suddenly I was floating.

"I'm sorry to sort of dump all of this on you. I'm working on being better, and sometimes you have to rip the Band-Aid off. I'm not here to just say all of that. I do want you to know I'm here for you."

I stood and crossed to him, pulling him into a hug. "God, I missed you so much."

He relaxed and wrapped his arms around me. Him being in my arms was an unexpected combination of hot want and soothing balm. I wanted to breathe him in like a drug and be high on him forever. He loved me, and I loved him.

"I missed you too," he mumbled into my shoulder.

"Can I tell you something in kind of a Band-Aid ripping way?"

He tensed, but didn't move. "Okay."

"I'm in love with you too."

That made him jump out of my arms. "Are you kidding?"

"No."

He stepped away from me, a look of shock on his face. He backed all the way into a chair that lived behind the door. A cat leapt off it just in time.

"Really?" he asked.

I laughed.

"Wh…how?"

I sighed. "According to my sisters, I've been crushing on you for a while, and I didn't see it because I didn't understand what feelings beyond friendship felt like. I think I thought of us as super friends or something. But then onstage, I kissed you for the first time, and that woke something in me. I didn't know that light was out, you know, like you have a room or a house you live in and love and feel at home in. Then, say, someone tells you a bulb is out and so they change it. Then that light comes on and you see how beautiful your house is. It's like I always knew how great things were between us, but didn't know there could be more.

"My mom thinks transitioning confused me, and that all this time I was just waiting for things to sort out. When I was younger, she asked me why I hadn't started dating yet, and I told her I'd have to research it. She thought it was funny until I transitioned. I knew she was worried. She had a hard enough time being okay with me being trans and brown. She kept asking why I made things more dangerous for myself. Now she had to accept that I'm, well, we'll just say pansexual, I guess. And I don't think my gender, or yours for that matter, impacts my feelings… wait. I forgot where I was going with this. Why are you looking at me like that?"

I had been pacing the room, extemporizing casually, so I stopped to look at him. He had a look of absolute ecstasy on his face.

He crossed his arms. "I like when you lecture."

I laughed. I knelt in front of his chair. "The point is, it's my intimate connection with you that brings everything else into the light. I don't want to lose you either."

He groaned and started to sink out of the chair as if embarrassment was making him melt. He rolled onto the floor, his back to the wood and one arm thrown over his eyes. He was absolutely blushing. "Arturo, warn a guy before you say shit like that."

I laughed and lay down next to him. I watched the slowly spinning ceiling fan. The cat came over and made herself at home on my chest.

"I'm not going anywhere." His voice was so soft but also perfectly certain.

"I'm sorry I left you behind," I said.

"Don't be," he said. "I get it, you needed space. I talked with Richard the Therapist about it. I can see how all of it was overwhelming, and sometimes coming home can be healing."

I nodded. "It didn't feel quite like home until just now, with your arms around me."

"Fuck, bro. How about you say that shit in Spanish or something? I can't take it in English."

I waited for a heartbeat before I asked, "Quieres ser mi novio?"

He laughed and looked at me. I watched him think about it, then he shrugged. "Seems like a demotion since you're already *mi esposo*. I guess I could take you to dinner or for ice cream or something."

I laughed. "Fair. Is it weird that I feel even more nervous now?"

"Why?"

"I don't know. What if I'm not a good partner? I've never had one."

He slipped his hand under mine. "Art, don't overthink it. There's a lot of shit we have to talk about, but we'll get there, okay?"

"Right. Hey, can I call you Teach?"

"If you want. Can I call you Artito?"

I snorted. "Sí, pero mi abuela calls me that, so it's not very sexy."

"Art, trust me, you could have any name, and it wouldn't decrease your sex appeal at all."

I looked at him. His eyes were closed. When I didn't answer, he looked at me. His eyes were like wet sand on a long beach. He rolled onto his side and kissed me. Knowing for sure love was in that kiss made it somehow bigger, warmer, softer.

"Mi amor, we have time until my family comes back. There anything you want to do? Shower before they use all the hot water or something?"

He gave me a suggestive look then said, "Guess."

I thought about it. "You want to eat more tamales?"

He rolled with laughter, scaring the cat.

❖

It felt unreal to have him in my house, in my bed, in my arms. It was dark, and the night had gone on later than I think either of us wanted. When everyone got back from sightseeing, they insisted on games and more food. It had been nice to hang out with my family. It was trippy to see Thomas—Teach—mixed in with my people. I thought about his confession and mine. The stunned alarm on his face was charming. I could see he'd been sincere when he said there was no pressure to love him back. I tried to laugh quietly thinking about the absurdity of it all.

"You're still awake?" Teach asked. He nuzzled closer.

"Sí, I was just thinking."

"Want to talk about any of it?" He yawned. I didn't answer and thought he might have fallen asleep. Then he looked at me.

"Why do you think Nads called the police on me?" I said.

"Is that what you were thinking about?" he said. He put his head on my chest and an arm around my waist.

"No, Well, not originally. I was sort of thinking backward through the day and wondering how we got here. I think it would've been hard for me to be in love with you and not tell you at some point. It was even hard to wait this long. I feel like I realized it the same day I overheard you and Flip talking, and then Nads got in my head, sort of adding insult to injury. I had a shitty week, but you were there through it all. I would've figured out how to tell you eventually, but I do think Nads's being an asshole moved the timeline."

"That seems like a more forgiving place to be in than when you left."

"I'm a forgiving guy."

"That makes one of us."

I laughed. "I believe that. But it's not for him, it's for me. I was talking with The Major, Flip, and Rocky about this in a group chat."

"You have a group chat with them?" He looked at me again, suspicion or maybe jealousy clear on his face.

"Kind of. My sisters forced me, pero it's new. Mostly I wanted to talk about this with non-white people."

His expression softened. "Interesting."

"Yeah. I think I was mostly mad at the police walking up to me the way they did. It's *so* different than the police walking up to a white person. If this had been reversed, me calling them about Nads, they probably wouldn't have put cuffs on him. And Chandler was there and couldn't change the situation because it was just as dangerous for him as for me, probably more so actually. I talked a little about this with Chandler too. That's part of why my parents wanted me to come home. They wanted to know I had people to support me, sure, but also people who understood what it meant to be brown and in the path of the police. But I couldn't talk to them until after the group chat, because even they didn't get it. The others did, and it made it easier to sort my thoughts."

Looking back on my anger, most of it was at the world and society for seeing me as different and, in that difference, automatically guilty. For a trans guy I was stealth enough. No one had questioned my gender in years. And the cops didn't know that or that I was in a gay-presenting marriage. The first thing standing between me and the world was always being Mexican.

"The Major was just as mad at Nads as I was. The others too. It wasn't just that he called the cops for the competition. I get that if the world were different, I would've probably volunteered. I knew he didn't understand what I was going through because of all of his comments about the stunt being political. I'm mad at him for that still, absolutely. But I was most mad at myself for *being* brown, mad at the cops for seeing that brownness, and mad at the world for letting being brown matter. That's pretty fucked up, I know, internalized racism and shit. The rage about the world is always under there, sabes?"

"I might not understand about being brown, but I understand about being marginalized. I won't pretend that's at all the same, but I feel you in a way."

I kissed him, tipping his mouth up to meet mine with a finger under his chin. I felt his understanding even if it wasn't the same.

I said, "I wish I knew why he was so desperate that he made that call without the rest of the team. Do you think he really was trying to fuck me over?"

"I know why. He came by the apartment," Teach said, sitting up and turning to look at me.

I sat up too. "What?"

"Yeah. He wanted to talk to you, but you were gone."

"Dímelo!"

Teach scrubbed his sleepy eyes. I felt every emotion as he explained what had been going on with Nads. I felt the same rage and disappointment, but that was buried under worry and sympathy. The guy was on the brink of losing so much and saw me as one more thing pushing him.

"No mames," I said when he was done.

"That's what he told me."

"Why didn't he tell Rocky—his cousin?"

Teach shrugged. "He didn't think Rocky could do anything. Besides, Rocky and Nads might be cool, but their mothers are on rough terms, especially since Rocky's mom offered to take custody of the two younger kids and Nads's mother wouldn't give them up."

"That's crazy. And The Major doesn't know?"

"They know now. Nads said as soon as the competition was over, it all sank in. He regrets it, and The Major was the only one demanding answers at the time."

"That fucker. Wait, why'd he tell you?"

"I think he was ready to tell someone. Everyone he has in his life is mad at him right now. He knows he fucked up, he just…I think he and I were having a similar problem. Richard the Therapist says I confuse vulnerability with weakness, and because of that, asking for help becomes charity. For me, I used to think there wasn't dignity in needing charity. I hear a lot of that for Nads."

I stared at Teach through the darkness. His face was shadows, but I could feel the tension in his body. I pulled him toward me. He came, his forehead pressed to mine.

"But you're more vulnerable now?" I asked, rubbing his neck softly.

"Trying to be."

I laughed. "You're a complicated dude."

He kissed me before sitting back. He didn't say any more. Everything behind Nads's actions unfurled in hindsight. I could hear what he was really saying the whole time. His worry about the sponsors wasn't just about money, it was about security for his family. His rage and misplaced blame over the loss of the lead, the way he was never able to relax, the times we covered meals for him—all of it was a perfect image of pride and struggle. It was so clear a picture, it felt obvious, and it being obvious annoyed me.

I reached for my phone.

"What're you doing?" Teach asked.

"I'm gonna CashApp Nads some of my share of the winnings."

"What? Why?"

"I can't let the guy lose his house."

"But what about everything he did?"

"He's not a bad guy, and you're right, he has some shitty coping skills, but I would help anyone I care about keep their house. He's my teammate, and that counts for something. Besides, if he had told me he needed help from the beginning, I would have helped so much more. I might've even been more careful. I can't really ask him to think critically about the choices he made and not think about my own. And based on what you've said, he seems willing to change. I haven't forgiven him. I don't know when that will happen, but maybe we don't cancel him. Maybe we just let him make up for it or something."

I thumbed to a cash transfer app. "How much more did he need?"

"Uh, nothing now. He was able to cover the bills with his winnings, and now he has a bit more to live on."

"Now?" I squinted at Teach.

He lay back down and closed his eyes. "I sent him part of my winnings already."

"That…Is it possible to fall more in love with someone?" I asked, my heart swelling.

"Yeah and same."

"Crap, how deep does this go?"

"We can find out if you put the phone away."

I laughed. "I meant love."

"Dije lo que dije," he mumbled sleepily.

Chapter Twenty

Thomas

There was a riot of applause as Rocky and Flip performed tricks for the crowd. I couldn't see them from where I sat behind the partition. This was the final interview with Chandler to close out the three-part story he had written on us. It had been about a month since the victory photo shoot and story we did celebrating our win. Fans were demanding more, so Uno and Chandler put together one last event for the season.

I watched as Golden selected whatever it was they needed next for my face.

"How have you been?" I asked.

"Very well, thank you," Golden said with a smile.

"Anything new?"

They laughed. "Stop flirting."

"Who's flirting?" Uno asked, coming up behind my chair. He leaned on it slightly, bumping my side with his hip.

Golden gave him a mischievous grin. "Your husband is flirting with me."

Uno smiled. "Can you blame him? You're like an angel."

"Right!" I shouted.

"You both are too much." Golden laughed as they came over with a fine powder and a brush. "I'm glad this team seems back together."

"Really?" Uno and I said together.

Golden shrugged. "It's not easy being an angel, as you put it. All of you are also *angelic*, and miraculously you're all out, popular, and interacting with the public. I can't even begin to imagine how many people it's helping. It makes *me* feel safe enough to come to a skatepark, makeup bag in hand. That's not nothing."

Uno smiled, and I tried not to blush.

"I'm glad," Uno said.

Uno had pretty much taken control of the conversation, and he and Golden chatted together around me. Uno's arm was around the back of my chair, and he was softly stroking the hair at the back of my neck. Since we had gotten home from Arizona, his touches came even more freely. He had asked me what I thought about telling people we were dating. The only thing I could tell him was that we would do it when the time was right. He agreed even though we both knew we had different ideas about when that would be.

I thought about what they said as Golden finished brushing the powder on my skin. I wasn't much of an activist, at least not outside one of Uno's plans. I would donate when I could and had only marched once. The politics surrounding my marriage had become both wildly simple and drastically complicated. It was simple to love him and let myself be seen loving him so that other people might feel freer to express their love. Then again, it was complicated because being seen came with unknowable danger.

Uno's campaign had made national news, and he was starting to get as many threats as compliments. It didn't look like it fazed him. And I still didn't know how to support and protect him. Some days, I wanted him to quit it all just because hiding him was the only way I knew how to keep him completely safe. Uno would never stand for that, of course. And now Golden and others were saying their lives were different from having seen us—not just Uno and me, but also Flip, The Major, and Rocky—made it worth the risk.

"Pirate."

I blinked. "Yeah?"

"We're up next," Uno said.

"Question time."

He laughed, and we said goodbye to Golden. We walked side by side along the curtains that kept the public from seeing behind the main stage.

"Ready?" The Major and Chandler said, stepping up behind us.

"Yeah," I said. "Where's Nads?"

"I'm here," he grumbled, fumbling with his tie.

According to the schedule, the next thing happening onstage was a one-on-one between Chandler and Uno. Then the rest of us would come out and be interviewed. The one-on-one was mostly to give Rocky and Flip time to cool down from their performance and change clothes. The sponsor thought it would be nice to see us dressed up a little more. Apparently, that meant wildly different things for each of us. I was wearing all black, Uno had on a black shirt with a red tie and red jacket, The Major was wearing a blue shirt with a green tie, Flip was wearing a maroon jumpsuit and a pink tie, and Rocky and Nads looked like they worked at Olive Garden. We would have looked better in our regular clothes—at least it would have been cohesive.

"I don't know how to tie this," Nads whined.

The Major sighed and crossed to him. We waved at Chandler when he came around the barrier.

"Hey, y'all look great. They're giving us a minute to move the crowd, then I'll cue you, Uno," Chandler said. He went back on the stage, and we could see him step up to the DJ. The skating part of the event had been for the public and live on YouTube. The interviews were supposed to be available only to subscription holders of *Contend* for a small fee. I had no doubt that people would have paid to watch, but because Uno can't leave well enough alone, he leaked a promo code that would discount the sign-up price for the first thousand or so people who used it.

"Good evening," Chandler said, using a handheld mic instead of a concealed one like we all were wearing. Rocky and Flip came around the curtain sweating but grinning. Two techs descended on them to get them microphoned. Chandler's voice boomed enough to echo off the glass and metal faces of the skyscrapers and apartments.

"Tonight, we are sitting with the semi-pro skateboarding team The Major Leaguers."

Chandler had to hold for a full minute for the applause to die down.

"Get your questions ready because there will be an ongoing fan question-and-answer. Just text them to—"

"I could get used to this," Uno said, putting a hand on my shoulder.

"An adoring public?"

"No. Well, sure, but I meant setting up these kinds of events."

I laughed. I knew what he meant. After we got back, Uno had gotten a call from Chandler. He explained that the magazine was desperately trying to figure out how Uno had pulled off the miracle that was the team social media as well as the Un-Mister Campaign. I told Uno to tell them to give him a job. He did, of course. He had an interview at the end of next week. Uno told his bosses at the ballpark to fuck off. I would put money down that in his infinite optimism, Uno fully believed he had the magazine job in the bag. I wondered vaguely what that would mean for the team, but I didn't ask. Since coming home, there had been several team hangouts. I had also had a few lunches with just Flip and me. For the first time in my life, I was trusting the friendships.

"Now," Chandler said, working the crowd, "his name has been on people's lips for weeks, his hashtag is trending, and all of you demanded the chance to talk to him. *Uno*."

Uno winked at me before climbing the stairs.

"If you know, you Uno," the crowd screamed.

I wished I could have seen his face. His heaven sounded just like that.

"I'm nervous," Nads said, coming to stand with me.

"Where'd The Major go?" I asked.

He shrugged. "To help the others."

"We got this, man." That was all the comfort I could offer.

I looked at him. He really did look nervous. We didn't say anything to each other. Chandler let us know he planned on talking about the fights and everyone's relationship with Nads. I was ready to talk about it. I think he was too. I could tell he was willing to put in the work to rebuild, just like he said when he came to the apartment. The others had just barely finished getting ready when Chandler called for the rest of the team ten minutes later.

We filed onstage one by one. For the most part, the crowd was screaming, happy to see us. Some of them did boo as Nads crossed to his seat. He kept his eyes down and his mouth shut, dropping tiredly onto the chair in front of Rocky. Rocky, Flip, and I were on stools in the back while the rest sat in front of us. Chandler stood by his own chair off to the left, and there was a final empty chair opposite him on the right.

"Okay, okay. We held a contest online last week to find the person who took the sickest candid photo of the team captured during the contest. The winner was determined by judges from our event sponsors

Bored Skateboards and DropCloth Clothes. That person's going to come up here and ask the team the fan-submitted questions. Are you ready to find out who the winner is?"

The force of the crowd's screaming was almost destructive.

"Sarah Yargee," Chandler shouted into his mic before pointing it at the audience.

There was a high scream from somewhere in the crowd, and a short, curvy woman came up onstage. She cheered and pumped her fists.

"Sarah?"

"Yes, I'm so excited."

She came over to us and started offering hugs and handshakes. We obliged happily. There was a small do-si-do as Chandler tried to get her in her chair and the DJ tried to get her a mic. Rocky wasn't helping because she seemed to want to hug him the most, and he wasn't about to let go of her. Nads helped get them separated. When everyone was ready, Chandler addressed the crowd again.

"Let's start by meeting the team. First up, the team leader," Chandler said.

"Hey, I'm The Major," they said, waving. There was a cheer.

"*I'm Rocky!*" he screamed, leaning over The Major and waving his beanie around.

"Hi, they call me Flip," Flip said.

"Pirate." Instead of just screaming and clapping, the crowd shouted "Yo Ho" together and only once. It was terrifying, but cool.

"I'm Uno," Uno said.

They chanted, "If you know, you Uno."

Nads looked slightly nervous. I watched him brace for whatever the crowd might shout as he introduced himself. Before he said his name, however, Uno patted him on the shoulder and nodded. Looking surprised at Uno, Nads said, "Nads."

The crowd, getting the hint from Uno, clapped lightly.

"Fantastic. So, it's been a few weeks since you won the Colorado Amateur Street Sports Tour. What have you been doing since?" Chandler asked.

The question was handed right to The Major. "We've been trying to remember how to live a normal life. Last weekend, I loaded all my stuff in the van just because it felt weird not to. We all have jobs and families. Uno went home to Arizona for a while, and Rocky and Nads had a family reunion last week. We're just living and waiting around for our next opportunity to get to a skatepark."

Chandler nodded. "Sounds like you all are as normal as we suspected. Let's get one from the fans. Sarah?"

"Okay. Um…" She fumbled for a minute with the cards she had been handed. Someone backstage was writing down questions from the text link. She looked at each team member quickly. "What did you do with your prize money?"

"Saved it," Flip said.

At the same time, Nads said, "Bought a house."

I don't think he meant for everyone to hear him, but they did because he was miked. He looked at Chandler and waved him off.

"So, none of you spent it on anything?" Sarah asked, going off card.

"I got some sick new ink," Rocky said. He clambered up on his stool and ripped open the buttons of his shirt. The crowd oohed and cheered for the spaceship tattooed on his ribs.

"Here's a question I know everyone has. We know there was some internal conflict with the team at the end of the season. Can you tell us all a little about what happened?" Chandler asked.

"I…" Nads leaned forward in his chair and looked at Chandler instead of the audience. I was surprised. We had originally picked The Major to answer the questions about the issues, but Nads was volunteering.

"I made a bad call without my team's consent—without Uno's consent. I was blinded by some stress I was going through, and I got desperate. I'm…I guess I've always known Uno was a good guy, and while I might have taken that for granted before, I sure as hell appreciate it now. I realize how much I would've lost—*should* have lost because of my actions. I'm just going to do what I can to make up for it."

"Why did Pirate punch you, then? If this was about Uno?" Sarah asked.

They all looked at me. I felt panic rise in my throat. I had been told a lot of the questions beforehand, but again Sarah was off card, so this one wasn't planned. I didn't have a practiced answer. I said the first thing that came to mind. "Someone had to do it."

The crowd laughed.

"Uno? Any thoughts?" Chandler added.

Uno shrugged. "We aren't friends or teammates because we're perfect. We have incompatibilities and disagreements just like any other family. While Nads isn't off the hook, I want to repair our relationship as much as he does. He's been my friend for over a year, and to learn he was going through something hard, well, I don't take that lightly, either. I feel like he was trying to tell us in subtle ways for a while. Sometimes, I don't think before I act. That's why they call me the wild card."

The crowd chanted "Aces Wild" back, right on cue.

"But I know my actions have impacts. We're working on understanding the influences we have on each other even when we don't realize we are doing it. In short, we're working on getting him un-canceled."

For emphasis, Uno put his hand back on Nads's shoulder. Nads looked genuinely moved by Uno's words. I still kind of wanted to punch him.

Chandler said, "All right. Well, I know I speak for a lot of the fans when I say I'm glad to see you all working it out. Let's take another fan question."

Sarah grinned devilishly. "Uno and Pirate—when are you going to divorce?"

"We hadn't planned on it, actually," Uno said.

I nodded and watched the crowd. They murmured, and some people screamed, others clapped. It seemed though there was an air of suspense.

"Why not?" Sarah asked.

"We don't have a reason to," I said. Uno looked at me and I winked at him.

"Aren't you worried about what happens when one of you falls in love?" Sarah was a ruthless interrogator. A dreamy whisper passed around the park. I looked at the floor of the stage.

"I already fell in love—with Pirate," Uno said.

I smiled despite myself. I wasn't surprised. The heads of the rest of the team turned in unison, and the crowd drew in a breath.

"Are you serious?" Sarah asked, on the verge of bursting.

Uno got out of his chair, turned, and kissed me on the mouth.

The crowd lost it. I knew that the thousands of people who claimed to be fans of mine did so while knowing I was gay. And I knew Uno's fans were fans because he was Uno, and to them, he could do no wrong. The cheering from the crowd, though, surpassed any reaction I could have imagined. There were cheers and whistles and screams of congratulations. All of it was deafening.

The kiss wasn't long, and when Uno stepped away, we looked at the rest of the team. Rocky was hopping around the stage screaming "I knew it!" The Major was practically shaking Nads, saying, "I told you so," and Flip, who knew all along, looked nearly bored. It took Chandler four minutes to get the crowd and the team back in order.

"Well," Chandler said, grinning at us.

"Well?" Uno and I said at the same time.

"Can we get some details? You just gonna do all that and then expect us to move on?"

The other four looked at Uno and me. They wanted details too. I looked at Uno, shrugging. It was his show. He was the sun of my universe, so I didn't know what he was looking at me for.

"You know what?" Uno said standing again. "Fuck that. Who wants to see me skate?"

Everyone cheered—even I cheered.

"Wait, there are more questions," Chandler tried.

Uno ignored him. "Here's how it's gonna go," he said, crossing the stage and pulling off his mic. "Who's got a board from Bored brand?"

Several boards shot into the air.

"Good, uh, you. Here's the plan. Y'all are gonna crowd surf me to the bowl, that guy is gonna toss the board, and y'all are gonna toss me, and I'm going to drop in."

The fans loved it, waves of them surging forward to catch Uno. He turned his back to the crowd, his heels just barely over the edge of the stage. He made eye contact with me, dropped the mic and battery pack, and spread his arms like Jesus on the cross. Winking, he fell back into the waiting fans.

"Wait for me," Rocky shouted, ripping off his shirt the rest of the way and diving into the crowd. I watched as Uno and Rocky were carried away to the bowl. Two boards rose into the air.

"On 'uno.' Cinco…cuatro…" Uno started to count down.

With each number, the volume of the chant rose. On "uno," Uno, Rocky, and the boards were tossed. The silence after all the cheering was almost more raucous. I watched Uno flail, catch the board, barely get it under his feet, and disappear into the void behind the crowd. I didn't even see Rocky. Time froze, and everyone held their breath.

The sonic blast from the sudden cheering let me know that at least one—but probably both—had landed the stunt. I watched the bowl, waiting for them to roll up the other side. A moment later, Uno rolled into view, waving lazily at the crowd as if he had done nothing more than just stroll in. Rocky came through faster, racing up the far side of the bowl. He bailed out of the vert, though, rolling on the ground before popping up and screaming with two arms raised in the air. I looked back at Uno, and he was looking right at me. I smiled at him. He pointed at me and blew me a kiss. I gave him the middle finger.

"I'm thinking of calling this whole series *Extreme Hearts: Finding Love at the Skatepark*," Chandler said, coming to where I sat. The DJ must have killed our mics and was setting up to get the music going again.

I made a gagging sound. "Why not just call it *Chump Got Lucky: Thomas 'Pirate' Jefferson Doesn't Get His Stupid Heart Broken.*"

"Call it *Head over Heelflip: The Major Leaguers Story*," Flip said, coming over to put her arms around me.

"What? That makes it sound like we're all in love," I said.

Flip giggled. "You never asked if I had other ships on this team."

I gawked at her. She cackled. "Never look up your names on fanfiction sites."

Chandler howled with laughter. I laughed too. The cheering crowd drew all of our attention back to the bowl. Rocky and Uno were really skating now.

"He's gonna break his neck someday," The Major said, coming over.

"Yeah," the rest of us agreed.

After a few minutes, Uno and Rocky gave back the boards they had been using, and The Major and Nads took over the bowl. Uno came to stand by me, his expression wild and happy. I smiled back. We stood side by side at the edge of the stage watching and listening to the others talk.

"Crazy how it all turned out," Chandler said. He came to stand with us after he finished talking to the DJ.

Uno waved off the comment. "My plans always do."

I rolled my eyes. He laughed and his hand brushed mine, sending warmth flowing up my arm. I looked at him. He, of course, was looking ahead.

About the Author

Sander completed his master of science from Purdue University in 2017, has been published in scientific journals and a speaker for Ignite Talks, and is a published poet. Wanting to see more of himself in fiction, his works feature LGBT characters and characters of color. He lives in South Florida with his partner, his best friend, and their many pets. As a Colorado native, he spends too much time telling Floridians how great the mountains are.

Books Available From Bold Strokes Books

Head Over Heelflip by Sander Santiago. To secure the biggest prizes at the Colorado Amateur Street Sports Tour, Thomas Jefferson will do almost anything, even marrying his best friend and crush—Arturo "Uno" Ortiz. (978-1-63679-489-1)

Mississippi River Mischief by Greg Herren. When a politician turns up dead and Scotty's client is the most obvious suspect, Scotty and his friends set out to prove his client's innocence. (978-1-63679-353-5)

Murder at the Oasis by David S. Pederson. Palm trees, sunshine, and murder await Mason Adler and his friend Walter as they travel from Phoenix to Palm Springs for what was supposed to be a relaxing vacation but ends up being a trip of mystery and intrigue. (978-1-63679-416-7)

The Speed of Slow Changes by Sander Santiago. As Al and Lucas navigate the ups and downs of their polyamorous relationship, only one thing is certain: romance has never been so crowded. (978-1-63679-329-0)

Felix Navidad by Nathan Burgoine. After the wedding of a good friend, instead of Felix's Hawaii Christmas treat to himself, ice rain strands him in Ontario with fellow wedding guest and handsome ex of said friend—Kevin in a small cabin for the holiday Felix definitely didn't plan on. (978-1-63679-411-2)

Manny Porter and The Yuletide Murder by D.C. Robeline. Manny only has the holiday season to discover who killed prominent research scientist Phillip Nikolaidis before the judicial system condemns an innocent man to lethal injection. (978-1-63679-313-9)

Corpus Calvin by David Swatling. Cloverkist Inn may be haunted, but a ghost materializes from Jason Dekker's past and Calvin's canine instinct kicks in to protect a young boy from mortal danger. (978-1-62639-428-5)

Murder at Union Station by David S. Pederson. Private Detective Mason Adler struggles to determine who killed a woman found in a trunk without getting himself killed in the process. (978-1-63679-269-9)

A Champion for Tinker Creek by D.C. Robeline. Lyle James has rescued his dad's auto repair business, but when city hall condemns his neighborhood, Lyle learns only trusting will save his life and help him find love. (978-1-63679-213-2)

Heckin' Lewd: Trans and Nonbinary Erotica, edited by Mx. Nillin Lore. If you want smutty, fearless, gender diverse erotica written by affirming own-voices folks who get it, then this is the book you've been looking for! (978-1-63679-240-8)

Inherit the Lightning by Bud Gundy. Darcy O'Brien and his sisters learn they are about to inherit an immense fortune, but a family mystery about to unravel after seventy years threatens to destroy everything. (978-1-63679-199-9)

Pursued: Lillian's Story by Felice Picano. Fleeing a disastrous marriage to the Lord Exchequer of England, Lillian of Ravenglass reveals an incident-filled, often bizarre, tale of great wealth and power, perfidy, and betrayal. (978-1-63679-197-5)

Murder on Monte Vista by David S. Pederson. Private Detective Mason Adler's angst at turning fifty is forgotten when his "birthday present," the handsome, young Henry Bowtrickle, turns up dead, and it's up to Mason to figure out who did it, and why. (978-1-63679-124-1)

Three Left Turns to Nowhere by Jeffrey Ricker, J. Marshall Freeman & 'Nathan Burgoine. Three strangers heading to a convention in Toronto are stranded in rural Ontario, where a small town with a subtle kind of magic leads each to discover what he's been searching for. (978-1-63679-050-3)

One Verse Multi by Sander Santiago. Life was good: promotion, friends, falling in love, discovering that the multi-verse is on a fast track to collision—wait, what? Good thing Martin King works for a company that can fix the problem, right…um…right? (978-1-63679-069-5)

Fresh Grave in Grand Canyon by Lee Patton. The age-old Grand Canyon becomes more and more ominous as a group of volunteers fight to survive alone in nature and uncover a murderer among them. (978-1-63679-047-3)

A Different Man by Andrew L. Huerta. This diverse collection of stories chronicling the challenges of gay life at various ages shines a light on the progress made and the progress still to come. (978-1-63555-977-4)

Loyalty, Love & Vermouth by Eric Peterson. A comic valentine to a gay man's family of choice, including the ones with cold noses and four paws. (978-1-63555-997-2)

Bury Me in Shadows by Greg Herren. College student Jake Chapman is forced to spend the summer at his dying grandmother's home and soon finds danger from long-buried family secrets. (978-1-63555-993-4)

Best of the Wrong Reasons by Sander Santiago. For Fin Ness and Orion Starr, it takes a funeral to remind them that love is worth living for. (978-1-63555-867-8)

Death's Prelude by David S. Pederson. In this prequel to the Detective Heath Barrington Mystery series, Heath discovers that first love changes you forever and drives you to become the person you're destined to be. (978-1-63555-786-2)

Death Overdue by David S. Pederson. Did Heath turn to murder in an alcohol-induced haze to solve the problem of his blackmailer, or was it someone else who brought about a death overdue? (978-1-63555-711-4)

Death Takes a Bow by David S. Pederson. Alan Keys takes part in a local stage production, but when the leading man is murdered, his partner Detective Heath Barrington is thrust into the limelight to find the killer. (978-1-63555-472-4)

Death Checks In by David S. Pederson. Despite Heath's promises to Alan to not get involved, Heath can't resist investigating a shopkeeper's murder in Chicago, which dashes their plans for a romantic weekend getaway. (978-1-163555-329-1)

Death Goes Overboard by David S. Pederson. Heath Barrington and Alan Keyes are two sides of a steamy love triangle as they encounter gangsters, con men, murder, and more aboard an old lake steamer. (978-1-62639-907-5)

Death Comes Darkly by David S. Pederson. Can dashing detective Heath Barrington solve the murder of an eccentric millionaire and find love with policeman Alan Keyes, who, despite his lust, harbors feelings of guilt and shame? (978-1-62639-625-8)